Lifelines

Books by JAMES MOSSMAN

BEGGARS ON HORSEBACK
LIFELINES

Lifelines

A Novel

by James Mossman

An Atlantic Monthly Press Book

LITTLE, BROWN AND COMPANY · BOSTON · TORONTO

LIBRARY OF CONGRESS CATALOG CARD NO. 76–154950

FIRST AMERICAN EDITION

T08/71

To Louis Hanssen

ATLANTIC–LITTLE, BROWN BOOKS
ARE PUBLISHED BY
LITTLE, BROWN AND COMPANY
IN ASSOCIATION WITH
THE ATLANTIC MONTHLY PRESS

PRINTED IN THE UNITED STATES OF AMERICA

I

The storm sprang without warning. Black clouds ran up the sky with the speed of spiders and began to spin back down towards the steamers and winged junks. The light in the harbour became unnaturally clear.

From the stern of the car ferry Dan Fenwick could distinguish the names of other ships and the names of the places to which they claimed allegiance. He could see their peeling skins and the stitched scars on their discoloured sails. Barechested sailors stared at the sky, humble, obstinate. Nothing moved in the narrowing space between the clouds and the sea except a small rowing-boat that two Chinese were lowering jerkily down the side of a keeled-over junk. Grey mist rolled across the surface of the water and in silence the concourse of vessels readied themselves for the wind.

When it came it smelt like flying garbage, a carrion bird that lunged and doubled blindly in the web of mist. The ferry noised in its innards and dropped chains. From the bridge a searchlight went on, illuminating a yard or two of greasy, heaving liquid.

The object that rode into the circle of light might have been one of the kites he had seen some boys flying when the ferry left Kowloon had he not known from experience that no combination of wood and cloth could have confronted the conflicting forces around it with such certitude as this thing did, the same certitude with which he had seen the dead confront the living a few weeks ago in Vietnam and which had

5

stirred in him the same mixture of outrage and expectation, the same wrench of panic as he began to feel now. It was as if his own body was trying to drop out of his grip. He had to take hold of the ship's rail to prevent himself from falling.

He had seen plenty of dead during his work in Asia. As a newspaperman war and famine were his stock in trade and although the women saddened him the sight of the men would quicken the life inside his own gut. The vigorous, descriptive style of his reports had prompted a former editor to remark more than once that he could think of few men in Fleet Street with fresher metaphors of death than Dan Fenwick, drunk or sober.

Then without warning the metaphors refused to come any more. It had happened three weeks before in Vietnam on the morning of his forty-third birthday. He had walked into a glade in the jungle and found three American soldiers lying there on their backs. Or perhaps they had found him. Their bodies had been stripped of their equipment and that the men lay with their feet touching and their bare heads forming the three points of a star. It seemed to him that they were unmarked by wounds, although in retrospect he became uncertain on this point, having been half blinded by the power of the sun, which forced him onto his knees. Trying to piece the experience together later, he thought that it was when he was unbuckling his belt and easing the pack off his shoulders that he had noticed how still everything was, that instead of the usual insect chatter, a close silence occupied the glade, as if nature was holding its breath. The feeling had come to him that he was being watched, had grown so strong that his skin had begun to crawl. He had wanted to look round but had found that he dared not do so, but had blundered forward on his knees into the triangle formed by two of the dead soldiers and stared into the face of one of them, but he learned no more from it than if he had read

6

the man's dog-tags. The open eyes and the lips half parted like those of an exhausted lover had seemed to conceal something vital to his own continued being. That was all. To avoid the consequences of a discovery which self-preservation warned him might be irrevocable, he had turned from the face, on whose burned chin dribble had been falling, his own, and had tried to concentrate on those sort of details with which he had been used to enlivening his reports, the cheap watches, still ticking, a brass and glass graduation ring, an eagle feathering a bicep, but such trifles had been submerged in the privacy of the three soldiers, which had been so calamitous in its huge indifference to himself that he had taken the graduation ring from its owner's finger and put it on his own, as if trying to join the fraternity.

During a week's leave in Bangkok at his newspaper's expense he had tried to explain his experience as the product of strain, but a sense of expectancy and a fear of disappointment persisted to remind him of the panic that was still inside him waiting for the next time, which was now.

He could see that the body was lashed loosely to a raft and that a rope led from the raft to a rowing-boat. The rope was looped under the arms and had rucked up the blouse, exposing the girl's flesh. Her skin seemed to be glowing in the dark sea. Dan heared a sigh and looked behind him, but there was no one to be seen. The deck and bridgehouse of the ferry were invisible. He sighed again.

The faces of two Chinese in the rowing-boat were orange blurs. The oarsman, judging from the feebleness of his strokes, was old, but a huskier figure was crouching over the stern, playing the body like a fish. When he saw Dan he waved both arms and tried to shout something, at which the body dived away from him. The man half rose to his feet and made a flinging motion with his arms while the oarsman began pulling away.

7

'I can't hear you!' Dan shouted. Perhaps the younger man had been telling him her name. Perhaps one of them was her husband. Perhaps she had been his wife. The words had fallen short, and they were leaving him without a second try.

The body rose so close to him that he could see its fingernails and the pattern of its clothes. The light streamed over it. The girl was wearing a dark-coloured bracelet, coral perhaps, or painted bone. Her hands unfolded in the water. She lay on her back on the raft so that, even if the neck were broken, as Dan thought it might be, he should have been able to see the face had it not been for that gently averted head.

'Look!' he shouted.

Gobs of bread and vegetables span where she had been. Dan held his breath, as he had done in childhood for the little black diver ducks on the pond near his home.

When he saw it again his escaping breath formed the word 'now'.

Without taking his eyes off the girl he unhooked a lifebelt with the word 'Star' printed on it from its shackle on the ship's rail and would have thrown it over the side had not the body forestalled him by rising rapidly towards him, legs first, as if it would leap onto the deck.

The heave of nature was like clotted hair in his mouth. He lost grip of the rail and slid along the deck, the lifebelt clutched to his chest. He was halted by a piece of tackle, which jammed into his shoulder, but by this time the body had disappeared.

Don't let her leave me. The water beneath him was immeasurable and meaningless. There was nothing in it, yet he was sure he had seen her. The soles of her feet had been pale pink. He sobbed and put his face against the lifebelt, tasting the sour rain on his lips.

'Seasick?' Dan recognised the first mate of the ferry,

8

with whom he had drunk once in a bar in Hong Kong.

'There was a dead body in the water.'

'No use wasting a lifebelt on it, then. I have to account for those.'

Dan hauled himself off his knees and hung the lifebelt back on its hook.

'There were two Chinese in a boat. They had a body strapped to a raft.'

'Sure they did. There'll be plenty more after this lot an' all. They load those junks with everything bar the kitchen sink. Serves 'em bloody right.'

'It was a Chinese girl.'

'Well, there's seven hundred million more where she came from.' The mate unhooked the lifebelt and readjusted it. 'That'll fix 'er,' he said.

Aware that the man was studying his face, Dan looked at his watch, whose dial told him that it was shockproof, waterproof and altogether reliable.

'Some tart they was gettin' out of the way.' The mate managed to imply that the distinction between a Chinese girl on a dance-floor or face up in the harbour was negligible.

Rain streamed down their faces, down their collars and out again through their sleeves. Sailors and passengers tramped past them and Dan wondered why he had seen none of them during the storm. According to his watch hardly twenty minutes had passed since they had put out from Kowloon. Now the mist was being blown away and ships all over the harbour were hooting to one another to mark the return of an order whose reality had seemed briefly in doubt.

'Where you been this time?' the mate asked.

'Vietnam.'

'Sooner you than me.'

'Oh well.' Dan took his hands off the rail.

9

'See you in the old Pagoda,' the mate said. 'That Lily's been tellin' me things about you.'

Dan went down to the car-deck and edged between vehicles until he reached his own. He got in and took a long swig from the flask in the glove compartment. He was watched by a Chinese woman through the window of a neighbouring car. When he caught her eye she turned away and he wondered what was happening to him, or if anything was happening at all.

He had a proper drink at his flat, a large brandy and soda which his houseboy brought to him without having to be asked.

'You wanna eat tonight?'

'No thanks.'

'I got, aah, frozen steak from the cold store and I got, aah, apple pie.' The houseboy, whose name was Lim, had been taught English cooking by Dan's wife, Jean, during her brief stay in the flat. Sometimes, to please the boy, Dan would sit through four-course dinners served with two kinds of wine.

'I'll have another drink.'

With the brandy came his mail. There was a cable from the editor asking why he had filed so little from Vietnam and a reminder from the features editor to say that a colour piece about a new American device for smelling out the body odours of concealed enemy troops was overdue. A circular, overtaken by the event, invited him to a memorial service for a colleague called Monks, who had died on the pavement outside his newspaper's premises after a heavy lunch. There was also a letter from Jean, which he opened last.

'I tried to call you the other day. I knew from the paper where you were, and not seeing your byline for over a week I got worried. It's childish to say be careful, what's it to do with me? You always liked those dangerous places. Getting up early to go to Saigon was the only time you looked really pleased with yourself.

'I went to Henry Monks' memorial service. I was the only woman in black. Imagine! Most people treated me as if I was Lazarus except Edie Harrison – in case you're out of touch, she's running the Woman's Page – who asked me if I'd start a regular column again at the old rates. I suppose she needs allies now that she's so exposed. It'll be female frills but beggars can't be choosers. She wanted something on life in the hospital for a starter, but I couldn't face doing an 'I was there' bit. Not for public consumption.

'Oh, the publisher sent me at long last a copy of your book. Were you afraid I wouldn't like it? They said you hadn't authorised a copy to be sent! Still, it was nice to see something of yours in print at last. Have you done any more with the play? I haven't touched your 'work in progress' so it's still tucked away in that basket in the sideboard.

'Summer has come and the birds make a terrible racket in the roof (which needs mending and will cost about three hundred) and I think of what you used to say, that summer made you choked up because it was the best nature could offer and just wasn't good enough. I love it unashamedly. The old dears in Lacking are all out in their best hats and the antique dealer down the road has got himself up in the most unsuitable rural drag. I wish you could see.

'I got the cheque. When the paper begins paying me I won't need any more. I wonder how you are, Dan? Tell me, to satisfy my curiosity, did you dedicate the book to me because you thought you ought to? I'd really like to know. We should be able to have a proper conversation by now. After all . . .'

He stopped reading. The tone would get increasingly reproachful. It always did. He could see her with a cigarette dangling from her lips, bending over her portable typewriter and looking up now and again at what he always assumed to be some vision of herself in the creative realms, then banging away again at the keys with her strong fingers.

He placed Jean's letter and his editor's cable in a tray marked 'pending' which occupied a prominent position in the middle of his desk.

They had had their first row outside England about that desk. Dan had returned from a trip somewhere and found that she had moved his 'office', as she called it, into the spare bedroom. It made the place look less like a no-man's land, she had said. She had announced this with the mixture of timidity and obstinacy that had become habitual with her. Dan had been drinking on the aircraft and told her that no-man's land was where he felt most in place. He had elbowed a vase off the mantelpiece and they had stood there eyeing one another, their feet among the flowers.

Compared with later fights it had been a mere skirmish from which they had retired and made love, she with the passion that had never failed to surprise him. It was in the weeks when they had ceased to touch one another that their daytime quarrels got so vicious.

On the day Jean went back to England Dan had returned his desk to the sitting-room and pinned a cheap map of Asia over the mantelpiece with green thumb-tacks. Except for Lim's room, to which a gaudy paper shrine gave a landscape of its own, the flat became as blank as a corridor.

After he had bathed and changed his clothes Dan set out for the Press Club, seen off by Lim, who was pleased with his boss, preferring the distance between them to the hollow familiarity of the Australian who had employed him when he first arrived from communist China. He had never had to haul the Australian onto his bed and take his clothes off, as he had sometimes with Dan, but then Dan never grilled him about the grocery bills, nor did he have a wife any more who sat around telling him how to do everything except the real work. One unforgettable day the Australian's wife had seen fit to show herself to Lim, opening the front of her kimono as he stood before her to receive his orders. Next day he had spat in her soup and watched her drink it.

Dan liked the resilience and sense of spectacle of the Chinese and in order to be near them he had chosen to live beside a turbulent housing estate from which at this time of evening everyone who could walk came out onto the streets to catch the slight breeze. Rain, still falling, rose in steam from their shoulders and mingled with their breath as they talked into each other's mouths. Jean had hated the noise they made and despised their lack of privacy. She had shrunk from the thin, half naked men and the women with faces like walnuts, old before their time, but when she found a pretty bungalow on the coveted heights of the island, whose windows looked down on the inner harbour through a thicket of sweet shrubs, Dan had refused to budge.

He found himself driving behind a dripping truck piled with cages of live ducks. The birds in the lower cages were being fouled by the ones above them and those sharing the same prisons were pecking at each other's necks as they were driven to their execution. It was a ready-made metaphor of the kind he used to record in the notebook which he always carried, but now his only reaction was to think how Jean would have hated it.

A house-high poster of Mao Tse-Tung outside a cinema stared down benevolently on a street market where Dan had made Jean walk one evening after a quarrel about his never taking her anywhere. He had made her watch a man slitting open live water-snakes with a soft zipping noise before throwing them into a tub of bloody water. Women had been standing at the neighbouring stall lighting joss-sticks and having their fortunes told. Seeing that Jean was upset, Dan had deliberately let the crowd separate them from one another. He had heard her call out to him with quiet desperation but he had ignored her and it was she who fought her way back to his side.

That night he had refused her for the first time and she had said 'not to worry', but he had heard her crying in the dark.

A month later she had returned to their cottage in Berkshire. Not long after that his editor had telephoned to say that Jean had had an accident with some sleeping pills and was in hospital. Dan had flown home and found her in a mental ward. She had been sitting with other women in a long room whose locked windows looked out over a busy suburban street. She had stared at him without blinking as he approached across linoleum between whose worn flowers a young woman was edging as through a mine-field.

They were all helping each other, the psychiatrist had told him.

On the way out of the hospital he had looked through a grille and seen a little padded room as bright as a jewel in which a naked woman was standing, as if staring at her own death. The woman had been covered with bruises the colour of the dark juice that Chinese vendors toted round the streets of Hong Kong on carts hung with bells.

At a traffic light a man on a bicycle rested his hand on the side of Dan's car to retain his balance. It had stopped raining and the streets were busier than ever. Among the families and single strollers certain men and women were pushing their way, half running, under loads slung on yokes across their shoulders. These people looked neither to right nor left as they went but directed their eyes to the piece of ground immediately in front of them.

'What we try to do,' the psychiatrist had said, 'is make the patient accept responsibility for his own life.' Dan must not be surprised if his wife blamed him for what had befallen her.

She would see things in proper perspective when she had learned to cope again. At present one might say she had dropped out of the race and it was the job of the hospital to tune her up for the next lap.

Driving faster than he should have done, he entered a street which looked as if it was being racked on its own spiked gateways. This was the street of the banks, under which ran rivers of gold and uncut gems. Since the communist riots of the previous month the banks had come to resemble gun emplacements. A wire-masked police jeep rolled slowly past. Dan reduced speed and made a sharp turn to the right. Tincan refuse glinted at him from a mess of straw huts. He reversed savagely. Nothing was where it belonged any more.

At the hotel which housed the Press Club, American tourists drifting through the lobby restored some of his confidence. At least these blue-rinsed widows were nothing if not themselves as they pressed into the elevator with armfuls of trash, ready for the next experience offered by the hairy Greek tour leader.

'See you downstairs,' he told them, making it sound improper. They gave him grateful backward glances. Not for them the resignation of widowhood in a small town back home. Their husbands dead and buried and their children gone, self-pity was a word apparently unknown to them.

'They gonna kill me,' the Greek said to Dan. 'I'm the travelling stud, that's for sure.'

He did not expect to be believed. If he had gone to any of their rooms they would never have dared to receive him, although his lie invited Dan into the male conspiracy and Dan smiled at him and began humming to himself.

It was only when he felt the chewing gum under the rim of the Press Club bar that his fears returned.

The feel of the gum sent a shiver up the length of his back and he placed his hands flat on the black shiny counter. He had what his mother would have called good hands, to whose shaping generations of middle-class Englishmen had imparted both delicacy and the appearance of vigour. Dan angled his finger until he caught the thin pencil of light from the ceiling in the coloured glass of the dead American's ring.

'Old graduation ring?'

'No.' Dan recognised the nasal Brooklyn accent of Joe Koltz, the Combined Press man.

'It sure looks like one to me. The booty of war, maybe.'

'What the hell does that mean?'

'I thought maybe you'd traded it with some poor slob. You know.' Koltz giggled.

'Some slob stuck gum under the bar,' Dan said.

'Some cad,' Koltz mimicked. His skin looked several sizes too small for him and stretched his mouth into a permanent half-smile. Dan had shared a room with Koltz in Indonesia and the smile persisted even in sleep.

'I just got back from Vietnam,' he said, twisting the ring round so that the collegiate inscription was hidden.

'Big deal. Is that why your hands are trembling?' The American held out a brimming martini. 'I bet we couldn't balance that on our knuckles tonight,' he said. It was a game some of them played when they met in distant bars, as if to affirm their detachment from whatever scene they happened to be converting into pictures or print.

'You're chicken,' Koltz said, easing himself off his bar stool, neat feet probing for the floor. I guess I'll go take another look at the fair Miss Maine.'

'The who?' Dan was reluctant to be left, even by Koltz.

'Sally Maine. Don't say you haven't heard of her. You should have, she's a fellow limey, I believe. Also she's a budding movie star, and I mean budding! Boy, she's got boobies that could put your eyes out and she's sitting in the annexe on her cute little butt displaying a quite remarkable

16

cool to a bunch of lecherous pressmen. Just listen to those guys!'

The dim bar was empty again. The wind, trapped by the air-conditioning plant, was being forced into the room with a defeated sigh. The television set flickered soundlessly in a dark corner. Dan pulled his stool closer to the bar, grinding his teeth in anger against himself. Fear was what you felt when you were shot at or saw a shadow pointing the wrong way. It was something that could be described. It had a beginning, a middle and an end. When you write a story, his first editor had told him, be sure that it has a beginning, a middle and an end and that the essence of the whole is in the first paragraph so that if the subs have to slash all the others to make space, the story will still be there.

He looked round at the corners of the bar, whose walls were papered with blown-up stills of Chinese bar-girls struggling out of tight dresses or framing diminutive sailors in the triangles of their muscular legs as they stepped out past the ferry quays. He felt as if some animal had stirred momentarily in its sleep and when he saw something move in the mirror behind the bar he spilled his drink and had to tell the man who looked back at him to pull himself together. The man's face was long with somewhat hollow cheeks, the hair fair and thick, running to grey at the temples. The mouth was large and sensual, the nose short and delicately carved, the upper lip long, like an Irishman's. The whole was carried on a pair of broad shoulders, with a practised coolness which was belied by a certain heat behind the green eyes. Something in the contrast between the man's delicate neck and stubborn, even cruel-looking lower lip, denoted a propensity for violence which, judging from the irony of his smile, might just as easily be turned against himself as others. The eyes looked into the mirror forthrightly, although anyone who knew Dan Fenwick at all well knew that under the appearance of a proud candour he was a man who shunned confidences.

He had been drinking methodically all evening, but not more than he could handle. He knew that his colleagues talked about his knack with liquor, saying that however big a load Dan Fenwick had taken on he could always be relied on to file respectable copy, and that was the test.

Better get on the road again. The cliché floated to the surface of his mind like a Portugese man o' war, paralysing all other thoughts.

'Dan! Long time no see.' The man who hoisted himself onto the next stool was one of those rare people whose looks can be called imposing. He was tall and bony and his whole body from the head downwards looked like a pot that had shifted slightly while it was being fired, producing a rather lopsided impression. The man's indifference to this, his easy control over the space he occupied, modified now by an evident inner tension, his careless clothes, which showed too much bony wrist and ankle, created the effect of strength without arrogance.

He looked like a man who would neither give or take trouble. He had a slow, rather crooked smile and big farmer's hands. He came from Kansas and his name was Andy Burns. He was a freelance journalist who worked for two papers at once, one American, the other British.

The two men were often on the same stories together and because they were both tall and fair, other correspondents called them the heavenly twins, although their natures were hardly alike in any way. Andy's reactions to the world appeared to be of a childlike spontaneity. He could say what he liked about things more easily than what he disliked. He looked on the bright side. He would climb out of his sleeping sack at some jungle camp in Vietnam and scratch and stretch like a wise, warm animal, and immediately look around for something to be thankful for. Dan, meanwhile, would have stayed where he was, sparing himself from the day for as long as he could. If Dan despised Andy's *joie de vivre*, which he believed to be forced, if not dishonest, he was impressed by the other man's effortless maleness, and if Andy disapproved of Dan's coolness, which he, too, believed to be forced, if not dishonest, he was in awe of his education.

Both men were glad to see one another.

'Jesus, it's dark in here,' Andy said. 'Are they saving on electricity?'

'They must be.'

'It's like the inside of a sock. When you get back?'

'This morning. I was in D Zone with the Marines after they shipped you out. Are you better now?'

'Sure.'

'What was it, did the doctors tell you?'

'Some bug or other, nothing really.'

'It didn't look like nothing at the time"

'Yeah, well. Did you get any action?'

'Yes I did. Too much. Yet I want to go back, isn't it odd? I have to, anyway, or the paper will start squawking. Will you be coming along?'

'I hope so.'

'Why hope?'

'I mean my English clients are pressing for more coverage of the demonstrations here in Hong Kong while the *Chicago Messenger* wants more Indo-China material. I feel like sending them both a cable saying "I can't dance with you all!" '

The two men relapsed into a thoughtful silence, then both began speaking at the same time.

'Sorry.'

'No, go ahead.'

'I was just wondering if you'd ever got scared about something for no reason, I mean, not for no reason exactly, but because you couldn't see how the damn thing was going to end?'

'No one gets scared for no reason,' Dan said. They fell silent again.

'I didn't mean that,' Andy began, then stopped. 'How's Jean?'

'Seems to be better. She's gone back to the cottage and she's working for the paper again, women's stuff.'

'That's great, hey, good old Jean! Picking up the threads.'

'She asked after you in her last letter, last letter but one, the last one came today. I forgot to tell you. She may have asked after you in this one as well, for all I know.'

He looked at Andy, but the American was examining his nails.

'She's better, then?'

'She's better.'

'You must remind me of her address, your address. I've some pictures of her I promised to send on.'

'I didn't know you'd taken any pictures of her.'

'Oh, some happy snaps once here on the beach. I guess you were away. I wrote her at the hospital but they sent the letter back. I assumed she'd left.' Andy wiped his face with his hand, moulding his chin between fingers and thumb.

'She likes you,' Dan said. 'Used to say she liked the way you do that with your hand on your face. She likes shy men.'

'She once told me the best kind of Americans lived abroad and the worst kind of Englishmen, something like that.'

'I thought it was the other way round.'

'She's a fine girl,' Andy said, as if to himself.

'A nice stockbroker, that's what she needs, but she will hanker after the arts.'

'Hm.'

'She hated being a housewife.'

20

'She seemed so joyful to me.'

'She was a dry and angry lover.'

Andy was shocked by the unaccustomed intimacy. He looked at Dan's face in the mirror and felt indignant. Dan did not know when he was lucky. He did not know what trouble was about.

'Dan, I really do wonder sometimes what the hell goes on inside your head. Wait till you need some help one day.'

'I don't know what you're talking about. What kind of help?'

'I'm speaking hypothetically.'

'Well, I'm more interested in facts.'

Andy offered his crooked smile and said nothing, but studied his reflection in the shine on the counter. His hands looked strong and brown. Their deception appalled him.

'Well, I guess I'll be off,' Dan said.

'Don't forget that address.'

'Which one?'

'Jean's.' Andy had his pencil and notebook out and ready. He would send her the pictures and maybe tell her at the same time. He had to tell someone. 'I guess I'll go home,' he said.

'Come with me to the Pagoda.'

'Thanks a lot but whores turn me off.'

'Please yourself. I think I'll take a look at Miss Thing next door, then.'

After Andy Burns had checked the tapes in the lobby of the Press Club he drove back to his flat, which was larger than Dan's, but so cluttered with possessions that it looked a good deal smaller. Andy was a collector of oddments of a mechanical nature. He would spend much spare time making intercommunicating telephone systems to enable him to speak to his houseboy in the kitchen or a magic box in which colours would turn and fold in dreamlike sequence behind frosted glass. He read little, preferring to use his hands.

Stripping to his underpants, he rolled a sheet of paper into his typewriter and began to type.

'Jean, honey, I have a disease of the blood. I hate to look at my skin any more, can't you help me . . .'

He ripped out the paper and crumpled it up. Then he sat for a while, stroking and kneading his face, before beginning again.

'Jean, honey, I saw Dan tonight. He looks great, a bit tired, but who isn't after D Zone? I guess things got tough up there, but he's in good shape. So stop worrying! Well, I promised to keep you up to date when you left but you promised to do the same for me, remember? So how about your end of the bargain, eh? Enclosed are the pictures we took. Don't I look great? My doctor says I'm not supposed to travel so much, but I asked him how the hell he thought I could be a reporter if I didn't travel and he said that was my business. But I don't have to tell you about doctors. It's something wrong with my white corpuscles, or else I have too many, I forget which. That's why I've been losing weight. Believe it or not, I'm even thinner than when you were out here. It seems a long time ago and you have been very far away since, Jeanie. I'm not about to pry into that unless you want to write about it. Dan told me some. I can guess the rest. Please write, honey, even just to say you remember who I am! Once I can be sure you receive me loud and clear I'll write a real letter. Serving a highclass Chicago daily and a Brittish gutter tabloid has played hell with my style. (Ha, ha. As if I ever had one.) But honestly, I want to send you some pearls I got in Tokyo so confirm your address. God bless you. Andy.'

He sorted through the pictures before putting them in the envelope. Jean was standing in front of a lemonade and noodle stall at the crappy end of the beach, holding hands with two little Chinese children. She was smiling self-consciously. There was another of her sitting on Andy's sofa and this time she was letting herself go, laughing at some joke and tilting her chin at the camera. She had taken two of him, forgetting to wind the film on, so that one of him was squatting on a rock holding up a dead fish by its tail and the other was floating in the sky above, arms akimbo. Both looked serious because in the small town where Andy came from being photographed was still no laughing matter.

He sealed the envelope with a lick and a thump and put a stamp on meticulously. He disliked receiving letters with crooked stamps on them, he liked things to be right. After this he climbed out of his underpants, carried them to a dirty clothes basket, then switched out the light and lay on his bed smoking and watching the neon signs going on and off outside the window. They threw watery patterns across the ceiling, crazy, proliferating corpuscles of light. He felt his heart beating inside his body, pumping the rotten blood around.

'Wow,' he sighed aloud, remembering the way his former wife, whom he had married on furlough in the Korean war and lived with for a year after being demobilised, would place her ear to his chest and listen to his heartbeats. They were irregular, she had said. Her hair had been blonde and dry-looking. He had massaged her scalp, wondering what was on her mind.

It had turned out that she was planning how to escape from the dullness of their two-roomed apartment in Newark, New Jersey, where he had found a job in a local news agency, from the traffic noise and the unpaid-for furniture, the television snacks and, indeed, the television itself, at which they would stare of an evening, being too hard up to go out much. She was ashamed, he remembered, hurt pride stored up over the intervening years offering him its sudden sharp bouquet, of the second-hand car he had bought for their honeymoon spent at Niagara Falls in a motel which housed a dozen other newly-weds. A photographer had asked all the couples to look out of the bedroom windows one morning. He had said it would make a nice shot.

She had had very large breasts, which he could now see had embarrassed her. He had liked to bury his face in them, believing then that there was nothing more he wanted.

To his genuine surprise she had begun to ration her favours, until one night he had forced her to receive him and she had said he was no better than an animal. He rubbed his stomach with pleasure at the memory, until his fingers encountered the glands in his groin which the doctor had shaken his head over that same morning. It hurt to touch them.

He had never blamed her for getting out. He had come home one evening and she had gone. A note told him that she had left him a telesnack in the icebox and gave a forwarding address in New York City. This time he was not so surprised. Andy was a modest man with a strong sense of survival.

Since then, the best times he had ever had were with women whom he thought he was talking to, though mostly they had only pretended to conversation. In the end his total trust seemed to depress them and he could see now, as he lay in the never quite dark of the bedroom, the collective gleam of ennui in the eyes of all the women who had ever appealed to him at the moment they were deciding to quit. Until they did so he believed everything they said. All they had to do was cry a little and there was Andy, suffering alongside them.

He sighed again, not wanting the parade of memories to

end. At least he had a past, however incomplete, to think about, which was better than Dan Fenwick and his whores and his brandy.

When Andy had collapsed in Vietnam it was Dan who had known what to do. He was a cool son of a bitch. Andy had never seen him make a fool of himself. He could not help resenting him for it. Dan was so lucky. He had his health and he could have Jean. If only Andy had met Jean first, but to do that he would have had to be English and he could not imagine not being American, or even from the Midwest.

A Chinese love-song came through the thin concrete of the bedroom wall as if played by an orchestra of mice. Andy had always been a pushover for torch singers. When he was a kid, physically advanced for his years, he would sit in the Italian drug-store in the main street of his home town, which was called Milton, population 637, and listen to the music, not in those far-off days the crash of electronically shattered souls, but songs about lost lovers out in the city and Lena Horne telling them there would always be a place for them if ever they came home.

Without in the least wanting to be a woman Andy would sometimes see himself in those days as someone in waiting, sitting drumming his fingers on the plastic table-top in the Italian drug-store, lost to his companions.

In a wind-licked, never to be finished housing project outside Milton, their car radios playing gravelly hill-billy music punctuated by the 'phoned-in homilies of insomniacs, Andy and his buddies would do their best to find relief, though despising the girls who accommodated them, while the girls, anxious, inexpert, tried their brave best to enact a passion they could not imagine, let alone enjoy. Andy would emerge from these sessions longing for something he seemed to have lost before thought began at all. Women, he told

25

himself, or rather, the woman, would enable him to find it again.

That was twenty odd years ago and here he was now, as many years and as many women later, rotting to death, still hoping.

The ticking of his watch scratched at the softer sounds floating through the window, cries, the crash of objects falling, the clatter of them being retrieved, whistles. He had not had time to be afraid of what the doctor had told him. It was something other than fear that turned now like a rusty key in the region of his chest. He wondered if Dan had meant it about wishing she would fix herself up with another man. Even if he had, so what? Jean might like him but, incomprehensibly, she loved Dan. Anyway, when she knew what the doctor had told him that morning it would be too late to think seriously about women. No one could foist that responsibility on someone.

Poor Mother, what were those little red pills you used to take to make you get through the pain, little red eggs in a glass nest by your bed? I have never needed such things, never known too much about them, why should I have? I never even knew too much about my body, never really looked much at it once I had done with showing bits of it to other kids and established that I had the regulation number of everything.

His mother had died of a malignant tumour which had crouched behind her stomach for years before seizing her and shaking her to pieces. Perhaps his doctor was being too dramatic. These things sometimes stop all by themselves. Doctors know so little. He would have more tests. Perhaps he should go home and have them.

When his mother died he went into her room and found that the doctor had covered her head with the sheets. She had got so small that she made no shape in the bed and for a moment he thought that they had taken her away, leaving rumpled bedclothes only. But she was there, on her side, like a little girl. The eye uppermost was shut, but the other one had been forced open by the pillow and stared crookedly at the white linen. His father had come in and begun to cry. His father had kissed his mother's forehead and cried without shame.

Andy turned on the light beside his bed and looked around his room with incredulity. He had never been to college but he surprised people with the things he knew about engines, clocks and viniculture, things like that. If he knew how things worked he cared little about why. He should have been a construction engineer, was what he told his girl friends. His walls were hung with gadgets to measure humidity, altitude, temperature and time. He had collected them over the years, but looking at them now in their shiny cases he seemed unable to recall what they were doing there.

With his right-hand index finger he traced down the side of his stomach the white course of a wound inflicted by shrapnel in the Korean war. His body felt slack to the touch, a lump of flesh with no future.

When they buried his mother, on a bitter February day, they had stood round the open grave while a fat priest with a blue raincoat over his cassock intoned the committal and scattered bits of dirt on the top of the coffin. He had patted Andy on the shoulder and said, 'Well, son, you had her a long time'. It had been one o'clock and the priest was hungry. 'She's all right now,' he had said and had rubbed his red hands.

Andy went to the mirror and looked at his face. A girl had told him once after making love, 'My, you're ugly!' He laughed now at the recollection, wondering how his face could hide the anguish inside him. He yawned and went back to his bed. Ten minutes later the body which was now so important to him had betrayed him into sleep.

*　　*　　*

The first thing Dan thought when he saw the girl in the annexe was that if he could get near enough to her she might burn the dark fears out of his skull for him. He had never seen anyone so physically alive in his life. It was as if her body inside its gold trouser-suit was kindling a fire at which the men who enclosed her against the bar were warming themselves.

They were showing off to her with a mixture of elation and cruelty. Dan was stirred by the contained violence she was stirring up and pushed into the hot throng, absorbing sweat.

'They can't do that,' she was saying. He was aware of her appraisal. 'They can't ban feelings.'

'They have in Red China, honest to God they have.' The speaker was oldish with a greying crew cut and a tightly belted paunch. 'They're not even allowed to hold hands.'

'In Egypt I saw a guy arrested on the railway station for kissing his girl goodbye on the lips.'

'In Red China it is absolutely forbidden to have sex out of wedlock any more. No one is allowed to marry until he or she is thirty years old. That leaves a lot of frustrated Chinamen.'

'They have to take Chairman Mao's Red Book to bed with them,' Koltz said. He was standing at the girl's side. He put his hand on his heart.

'Golly, you people have interesting lives,' she said. She spoke breathlessly with a trace of a lisp, her breasts rising and falling dramatically at each intake of air. 'I tried to get a really good book about Asia before I came here, it's so much easier to read about things than ask people questions, but now I'm glad I didn't, you all know so much! My director says I'm not observant enough, but how can you be if you don't know what you're supposed to be looking at? It's as simple as that.' Dan noticed that she never looked at anyone for very long.

'Well, try looking at zat.' A German cameraman, scarred from older wars, held out a photograph to her with a quick, furtive gesture. She opened her lips and looked away.

'You can see zat one's head under ze tree, but ze ozzer one I never found.' He offered the picture to Koltz, who ignored him.

'We get used to that kind'a thing,' Koltz said to her.

'I admire objectivity,' she replied.

Koltz grinned and tried to put his hand on her knee. She crossed her legs and Dan was thinking what a pretentious little teaser she was when he surprised a look in the deeps of her blue eyes which startled him by its amusement and contempt.

'You haven't got a drink,' he said, looking closely at her.

'I was hoping someone would notice.'

When he turned back from the bar she had put on a pair of dark glasses with mirrors on the outsides.

'You've withdrawn, I see.'

She shook her head, running her fingers through her hair with a habitual gesture. He saw that her front teeth were set somewhat apart, leaving a little wet gap between.

'I could listen to them all night,' she said.

'This is your scene, is it?'

'One of them. I want all the experience I can get.'

'You have to pay for experience,' the German said.

'You sure do,' Koltz put in. 'I've been paying alimony for mine ever since, but then I'm not a beautiful blonde.' He reached towards the girl's glasses. 'Hey, honey, let's see who you're looking at.' He would have removed them had Dan not taken his wrist and forced him to withdraw his arm. As he did so both men looked at the girl, only to find themselves staring at their own distorted reflections in her glasses.

'O.K. Joke over. Can I have my arm back, please?'

'We seem fresh out of manners here.'

'I say, old chap,' Koltz mimicked. The girl smiled and Dan felt a prig.

'Have you been in the Vietnam war as well?' she asked him.

'It's not a war, it's a die-in,' Koltz said.

'Next time I wish you'd take me. I'd like to see if death is really as scary as it sounds. Is that terrible?'

'Dangerous, I should think,' Dan said.

'Well, yes. That'd be the point.'

'I mean death might not be prepared to sit there and be stared at as if it was a toothless old lion in a zoo.'

'Or a parrot,' Koltz said.

'That sounds very subjective,' the girl replied.

'It sure does,' Koltz said, determined to keep the initiative.

'I was asking him,' she said.

'I meant . . .' Dan regretted that he had begun. 'I meant that you might be forced to recognise the real situation you were in, as if someone had you by the scruff of the neck. That's very dangerous. All that reality could kill you.'

'I can be in a scene with friends and pull out of it as I choose,' she said. 'I can pull out, take a look at the scene and go right back into it again. It's as simple as that.'

Perhaps she was a fool, after all. He imagined what it would be like to undress her.

'All you need,' she was going on, 'is to keep a lifeline out to your real "you" and you're safe.'

'Spoken like an intellectual,' Dan said.

'I admire the mind, why not? It's all we have over the animals.' She smoothed her hip.

'This baby's an intellectual.' Koltz yawned.

30

'You make yourself sound like a pearl in an oyster,' Dan said. 'You lie in the world becoming more and more a thing of value as the oyster becomes more and more irritated.'

'You're very aggressive.'

'You trapped me into being serious and now you put me down,' Dan said.

'Why not be cool as well? Say, will you show me that dance you were talking about?' This was issued to Koltz as a command. She offered Dan her jacket and he held the shimmering stuff, warm from her, as she raised her arms and faced the American. Koltz was standing on the balls of his feet in an effort to look down on her, aware that she was somewhat less than in his arms. Rather sooner than she decently should, she broke off the dance to retrieve her jacket. Her arms were bare to the shoulder and Dan saw a band of sunburned skin where the bolero ended and the trousers failed to begin.

'I have to go,' she said.

'Come out on the town. Show you places.' Koltz winked.

'I've an early call. My director's a tyrant if anyone's late.' She moved away, drawing the men after her. She was carrying a black sling bag which showed hard and shiny against the soft gold of her trousers. Dan stayed at the bar and waited for her to look back. When she did she had taken off the glasses and her expression seemed to be one of complicity.

Yet she sounded surprised when she found him standing beside her outside the hotel.

'I wondered if you'd like a drink?'

'No thanks. I meant what I said about that early call.'

'It's only half eleven.'

'Don't you sleep?'

'Not alone, if I can help it.'

She took it better than he deserved. 'It's waking up that's the worst.'

'I'll run you back.'

'I'm just across the square at the rival establishment. I'd rather walk. Really.' She stepped into the night as if it belonged to her.

2

When she heard him calling after her she made no reply. She was so used to men trying to detain her that their voices at such times had become one of the background noises of her life. To have answered would have been as superfluous as saying thank you to the woman who told you the time on the telephone.

She strolled, mulling over the night's events. She had enjoyed all that talk of facts because it intimated that man's world into which she wanted admission. She had been raised by an Irish father who, when not writing gushy Celtic verses, had entertained her from the dawn of her consciousness to the day when he had delivered her to a surburban convent school in Dublin with enough well intentioned emotional drivel to last her a lifetime. In the convent she had found that emotion was not always so benign and by the time she emerged at the age of seventeen she thought she knew all there was to know about how nasty the female half of the species could be.

She had not come out of the evening too badly. Most of the men had been sweet and informative and had taken her seriously, although one or two had been too subjective to fit her requirements; but she had managed well enough. She breathed deeply, inhaling new smells with a sense of well-being. Even the undeniably rotten smells were right for the torpid sky full of its half-melted stars. Men, she thought, prefer women to keep them at arm's length if it's done tactfully. They are relieved, even though they deny it. Her theatrical agent, Maslyn Martin, had told her that, saying that men only visited what she called the women's department when their stock of manliness needed replenishing, at which times they would come like cocksure shoplifters. Sally often wondered if Maslyn knew anything about men, after all. She felt warm inside, not because she was conceited, which she was not, but because she was young and admired. She put out her hand and ran her fingers through the darkness, her darkness, for as long as she wanted it.

The stars reminded her of an impossible dress she had worn in her first movie three years before, and of her dresser who had suddenly confessed to being illegitimate as she picked at the awful dress with finger and grey thumb. She would never forget to her dying day, she had said, how a boy at school had told her she was a bastard right out in front of all the others and how she had run home to ask her auntie if it was true and the auntie, who turned out not to be related to her at all, had told her that it was.

The dresser, with grown-up children of her own, had threatened to become tearful and Sally had had to put her arms round her and kiss her powdered cheek, thinking what a feeble creature she was.

Everywhere has room for me, she told herself now, and even the thought of Gaston waiting for her at the hotel could not spoil her pleasure. With luck he would be asleep. She thought she had been at her cool best tonight, both truly concerned with what they were saying and at the same time conscious of that exquisite detachment which was as steady as a pulse-beat.

She paused beside the noise of an invisible fountain. It was too dark to read her watch, but she guessed that in London it would be afternoon; she might be leaving a restaurant after lunch, or going to have a sauna with Maslyn. In New York it would be morning; she would be percolating coffee and listening to the passenger aircraft flying in and out like bees, while on the Coast she might still be dancing or, more likely, asleep.

The desire to be everywhere at once took hold of her like a lust. What time was it in Egypt? She wanted to send cables to people and make telephone calls. 'I am fire and air. My other elements I give to baser life.' When the nuns had caught her in bra and panties rendering the immortal death scene for the rest of the dormitory the mother superior had told her that she was rotten to the core. She decided that before going to bed she would ring Maslyn in England.

'Stop it!' She was not a nervous girl and the discovery that there was a human being squatting in the fountain, scooping up water and throwing it at her, only annoyed her. 'Don't be silly.' The figure bent over in the water, hissing through its teeth. More drops wet her face.

'It's not your fountain, is it?' she said, a hint of Irish in her voice. The figure retreated, splashing vigorously. A bicycle hung with shorts and singlet told her that she had intruded on someone's ablutions. This quaint person was naked and outraged. She tried not to laugh. It was the first time a Chinese had stepped out of the Hong Kong backdrop and she wanted to show him that she regarded him as human, but all she could see was a shadow as the being crouched and wallowed.

'I'm sorry,' she said.

'Long nose,' he called after her in Cantonese, and spat.

There was a tray of half-eaten food outside Gaston's door. She stole a strawberry and crept into her own suite like a thief. Before going out she had locked their communicating door. In a low voice, so as not to disturb him, she booked a call to England, then she undressed, wandering about, dropping garments. She was sitting in a flimsy pyjama top taking her make-up off when Gaston Gaillard opened the

35

communicating door without knocking. She wished she had not been in such a hurry to take her clothes off.

He stood behind her watching her in her dressing table mirror, his head cocked to one side. As a young man his smile had made moviegoers miss heartbeats in a dozen languages, but the years and a tendency to deafness had made it less shy than quizzical and the flamboyant virility that had taken him from his mother's pastry shop in Orléans to a Spanish-colonial-style mansion in Beverly Hills, was more restrained though no less persistent. Grey hairs gave his sexuality the appearance of a fatherly authority, although the hand with which he tried to fondle her shoulder was hesitant. It probed her mood.

'They locked the door by mistake.' He had a carefully preserved accent. 'I made them open it.' Sally scraped at her face savagely. 'I worried about you.'

'You needn't have.'

'Franco told me he thought you were looking tired, sweetie.' He was not above malice.

'If the director has anything to say about my work he can say it to me, or send me a note.'

'He has. It's on your writing table. Shall I get it?'

'No.'

'It says my little girl should go to bed earlier.'

'Some chance with you next door.'

'I thought those wolves had eaten you up tonight.'

'We were discussing politics.'

'It wouldn't be your mind they were after.'

'Don't leer, Gaston.'

'Anyway my little politician has come back where she belongs and that's all that matters.' He picked up her hand-mirror and examined a spot on his chin which he had noticed on an earlier inspection. He had the unhappy knack of treating other people's remarks as if he had not heard them,

36

returning to his own theme as if there had been no interruption. He knew this irritated her, but he was unable to behave differently. Moreover, the locked door had hurt him.

'I suppose you don't care if the Chinese drop an H-bomb, just so long as you are not around. Some people are so selfish!'

'It doesn't cost much to worry about the H-bomb, sweetie.'

His dressing-gown had opened to the waist, revealing a chest full of hair in which St Anthony dangled at the end of a gold chain. Sally sighed audibly. He was like an old nanny who treated her thoughts as if they were toys to be swept off the nursery floor and put away for the night, except that nannies did not usually follow their charges into bed. The idea amused her: she would tell it to Maslyn.

'All people think about is me, me, me,' she said.

'You, you, you,' he echoed unhappily. She was saved from hurting him further by the ringing of the telephone.

She flopped onto her bed and picked up the receiver. What was it she had wanted to talk about? She could no longer remember and there was Maslyn's voice rasping down the line all the way from her mill-house in Lacking, Berkshire, England.

'Darling,' Sally said. 'Did I wake you up?' She cuddled into her pillow, feeling babyish.

'No, certainly not,' said Maslyn. 'I'm having a lovely smoke with a friend who's scored some very good stuff, Cambodian.'

'That's practically where I am,' Sally said, giggling.

If she wanted younger men from time to time, Gaston was thinking, let her have them. She would come back, as she had in Dublin that time, having got over her 'crush', as she termed it, for a hollow-eyed, unwashed youth who posed as some sort of writer and whose pyjamas he, Gaston, had had the pleasure of posting on to him. He had put a card in the parcel with

'Don't catch cold' written on it. He was fond of a joke. He stared at the backs of her legs, where the flesh made soft shadings behind the knees.

'Yes, he is,' she was saying. She gave him a cross look. 'Oh, you know, the usual. One might just as well be a dress in a sale, all the pawing that goes on.'

'All you have to do, darling, is grope them first. Imagine going up to a man in a crowded room and before he can pinch your bottom or squeeze your arm for you, you just feel him up. He'd be devastated!' Sally heard Maslyn coughing and knew she had lit one of her Navy Cut cigarettes.

'Franco is being beastly. Sometimes I almost hate him.'

'You don't have to love him, just learn from him. He's one of the best directors in the business and between you and me it wasn't all that easy to get him on our side.'

'Now you tell me.'

'All I meant was that Panni had visualised an older person in the part. You knew that, so don't get neurotic about it. It's a compliment to both of us that he changed his mind.'

'He's so vague, Mas. I can't understand what he wants. And he won't explain.'

'Then keep after him.'

'I'm not a mind-reader.'

'Ask him. You're a serious actress. Ask him. Listen, there's only one way to be a success and that's to think about nothing else and let nothing get in the way. Right? Have your fun, but never let it interfere at the deep level.' Maslyn was off on one of her two hobby-horses. The other was women's rights. 'At the deep level there is only room for one thought, how to perfect your talent. Otherwise you might as well give it up. And there's no room for grumbling, because that is self-indulgent and frivolous. Right?'

'What time is it there?'

'What's that got to do with anything?'

'I wish I was coming to lunch with you.'

'Lunch is over, dear. I had to do some straight talking. It's unpleasant to tell someone they're all washed up.'

'Who, Maslyn? Do tell.'

'My lips are sealed.'

'Was it Marcia?'

'You'll read all about it. Someone with more talent in her toe than most people have in their entire bodies and she won't get herself together. So she pays for it. It's a gruesome lesson.'

'It is Marcia. That Greek, what's his name?'

'I'm not saying yes and I'm not saying no. Now let me have a word with that Frenchman.'

'What's the matter?' she asked when Gaston came on the line.

'Our baby is overtired,' Gaston said. 'Too many goodies all at once.'

'What do you mean by goodies?' Maslyn despised Gaston but thought him suitable for Sally.

'Not what you mean, sweetie.'

'Then why did she call? There must have been some reason.'

Gaston put his hand over the mouthpiece. 'Sally dear, Maslyn can't believe you just rang her to say hello. What shall I tell her?'

'Whatever you like.' Sally was beginning to think that she would have to sleep with Gaston after all.

'I must go now, Maslyn dear. Sally wants to say bye-bye.' He held out the receiver but Sally shook her head. He leaned over her to replace the receiver.

'Good old Maslyn,' he said.

'I want to go over my lines, Sally said. 'Will you hear me?'

'Of course, my love, but wouldn't it be better to have a

session with Franco in the morning, so he can explain for you?'

'There won't be time. It's a six o'clock call; anyway, he always tells me I don't understand.'

'He never tells me that.'

'Your part's more obvious. It's mine that's the hard one. I never know from one scene to the next what my relationship to you is meant to be. If Franco is so vague why doesn't he check with the author?'

'You are meant to be a lost child. You love and need me and sometimes you are afraid, like tomorrow, when you can't decide whether to get out of the taxi when you see me. That's because suddenly you dare not face me. That's my interpretation.'

'You mean that's what Franco said. Can you get the script please?'

'Here it is,' he said. 'You are in the taxi, you express confused emotion. Well, that's not difficult. You are wondering how to be worthy of my love when suddenly you look up and there I am standing on the pavement.'

'Confused emotion doesn't have to mean a feeling of unworthiness. I could be feeling guilty because I was going to leave you.'

'For someone else? It's too early.'

'Of course for someone else. What about the scene on the ferry when I meet Leo? Unless I foreshadow my general disillusionment tomorrow, people are going to think when I run away with Leo that I'm a nympho or something. Well, aren't they?'

'They will think you are a lost child, that's what they're meant to think.' He spoke seriously now and she listened with respect.

'I can't agree. I am a kind of, of female Christ figure, going down to the gutter before I can rise again. I am supposed to be guilty about my whole life, not just you. Otherwise why the scene in the elevator, or the night scene?'

'A lost child can be all those things.'

'You may be right. I'd better ask Franco at breakfast.'

'Of course.'

'I must get some sleep,' she said in a feeble effort to dislodge him.

'So must I.' He took off his dressing-gown, climbed into her bed and pulled up the sheets. He felt confident and at home.

'It's you are the lost child,' she said. 'You've lost the way to your own bed.'

He put out the light and turned her to his familiar body. 'Sally,' he said. He was kissing her hair when the girl on the switchboard rang to ask if they had finished the call. In his annoyance Gaston missed the cradle and had to fish the receiver out of the dark, after which he began making love to her with his usual dexterity. She made her body respond but let her mind slip away from under him back to the Press Club, the photograph of the severed head, the little man in the fountain. Gaston began to mutter in French which meant he was coming into the home stretch. The tall man had almost unnerved her, treating her with neither condescension nor gallantry. He had been out of place until he followed her down to the street and she had been able not to want him. 'Not want it, what's come over the girl?' Poor Father, he had been so surprised when I told him I did not want any sugar in my coffee. 'But you always have it, darling.' 'Yes, but not any more.' She had suddenly discovered that she had never wanted it and this was the first time she had made a decision on her own. Or had she only thought that? Gaston was indulging in a last-minute go-slow, his tongue darting from her mouth to her ears and back like a hen that had lost its chicks. My life has been a journey from the back of my head to the front, where my eyes look out on the here and now, which is all you've got, so make the most of it. Maslyn had taught her that, yet Maslyn encouraged her to put up with Gaston and surely that was not the best use of the here and now? She took his wiry grey hair in her hands and dug her nails into his scalp. There. He fell gratefully, triumphantly from her and was soon asleep, his bottom pressed against her side.

She tried to trace their relationship to see whether it had grown in its two years, but all she did was to lose herself in a country without shape or colour. She had been nineteen when he had taken her up. He had been kind and considerate but he had never really roused her. She discovered that when the Irish boy came on the scene.

Poor Gaston, he had been terribly upset. He had bought a revolver, even bullets. The episode had become compressed in her memory into a single rainy afternoon, the wind rattling the windows of a Dublin hotel bedroom and Gaston striding about the city hunting for her. When they had heard footsteps in her private sitting-room next door the boy had leapt out of bed and instead of getting his clothes on had stood naked behind the door, in full gallantry, brandishing a stick. The sight of the two weapons at a parallel angle to each other had made her laugh until the tears came. The footsteps had departed and so had the boy and it was only when she realised that he would never come back that she began to think she might have loved him.

If Maslyn got to hear that she had tried to lock Gaston out she would tell her she was being unwise, one of her favourite adjectives. Poor Maslyn, she felt sorry for her, sitting astride her icy mill-stream making telephone calls and smoking pot.

She wondered whether to get up and clean herself. At the convent the nuns had smelt of urine when you walked behind them. If only Panni would explain the part better. If only he would come and put his arm round her in front of all the others and say how good she was. She was leaning on the fountain and Panni was kissing her hand and the convent wall was covered with thick ivy, hard as wire. 'I didn't know they made them like you any more,' Panni was saying. They were in the fountain together and the little Chinese was swimming past, spouting water.

'Action!' Panni kept saying, as if he was drunk. The Chinese bobbed up beside her. He opened his lips and a hard, spiky insect began forcing its way out, splitting the corners of his mouth.

'No!' She woke herself with her cry of rejection and was comforted to see the dial of the telephone glowing in the dark. She got out of bed and stood on her balcony looking at the sky, from which a star detached itself and fell gracefully into the harbour. She exclaimed aloud and Gaston's breathing stopped for a moment, then resumed greedily.

3

In the absence of its male commuters the village of Lacking was like a rabbit skin pegged to a barn door. It wanted guts.

Such a thought would have been entirely alien to Maslyn Martin, whose mill-house lay several fields away from the last of Lacking's celebrated Tudor cottages, but it occurred forcefully to Jean Fenwick as she stood in the middle of her sitting-room and told herself to stop being hysterical.

The bluebottle had disappeared. Perhaps it had had enough. Now that its mindless whining was stilled, Jean felt perplexed that it should have upset her.

Sun streamed through the cottage window and lit up her reflection in the Regency mirror. On the other side of the street a young labourer on a yellow bulldozer was demolishing a building with insolent strength. His easy movements made her feel old and dried-up.

Two sparrows out of the roof were hovering in the sunshine, beak to beak, wings whirring, fighting or flirting. She had been wrong to say in her letter to Dan that she enjoyed the summer. It was like a steamroller out of control. She drew her curtains half across the window, smiling wryly at her image in the glass.

She thought how depressing she would have looked to anyone at the window, a woman of forty, her hair falling over her disgruntled face, striking at the air with a rolled-up *Daily Mail*, alone in her house, hunting a bluebottle.

Yet most men would have thought here was a real woman,

and might have offered to help. Jean smoothed her hair with the palm of her hand and dabbed at it with her fingers. Most men would have liked the shape of her body: a fine, straight back, a long neck balanced by good breasts, large hips and a waist so slim, despite her height, that it seemed made to be caught in two hands and shaken a little. Her legs were long and the calves rather thick, the buttocks generous but not yet profligate.

Most men would have tried to attract her attention in order to see what her eyes had to say to them. They would have found that the eyes, which had tracings of lines under them, were large and made to shine, but that they were not shining now. They would have said that Jean Fenwick's eyes were dark blue, humorous, tender, but that down inside them was something alarming, under the dark blue a darker demand, which might have caused some of the men to take off like the bluebottle.

Someone rapped quietly on the front door. A young man in a brown tweed suit was standing outside. He was holding a paper in his hand.

'I'm a member of a group called Unity,' he said. 'We're a nationwide movement for the young, a sort of club. I wondered if I could put you down to give us a chat on one of our evenings.'

'What about?'

'Your work and life.'

'But I've nothing to say.'

Jean backed into the open doorway of her sitting-room and the young man followed, looking at her with unshy blue eyes.

'I was visiting a client here, I'm in insurance, and she told me about you, so I called.'

'Thanks, but I'd be no good.'

'Everyone has something to say.'

'But not worth while.'

'We try to make the young people see that everyone has something to do and that it ought to be respected and that one of the finest things in this country is that everyone is different.'

'But they're so much alike, I always thought.'

'Then we organise charitable work, digging up old people's gardens for them, that sort of thing.'

The telephone began ringing. Jean had installed a new lightweight instrument whose birdlike shrill was less disturbing to her than the old menacing summons. 'You just throw it a handful of canary seed,' she said to the po-faced young man. The joke fell flat.

'Is that you, Jean?'

It was an alcoholic called Nancy whom she had met in Lacking's prim little tea-shop. They had shared a table and Nancy had touched her by telling her straight off how in winter she wore two pairs of knickers and was always forgetting to pull both pairs down when she went to the loo in a hurry. She had made a scene in the tea-shop because the manageress had forbidden her to drink from a half bottle of British port she had produced from her enormous handbag. The wine had run down her chin and she had broken a plate and been thrown out. Jean had found her later propped in a doorway, and because she had made friends with an alcoholic in the mental home she had asked Nancy back.

Alcoholics had been safe at the mental home. They had seemed appropriate and there had been the common bond of disliking the staff, but when Nancy made Jean's little cottage into a regular port of call, Jean got scared and began to dread her ring at the bell and the sight of her empty half bottles like droppings on the doorstep.

One afternoon she refused to answer the bell, but Nancy saw her moving behind the curtain and began shouting through the flap of the letter-box. In the end Jean had

46

shouted back, telling her in a hot fury to go away and never come back.

'Can I come round and see you?' Nancy asked now.

'I'm afraid not.'

'Don't be afraid, dear.'

'I have work to do and people are coming.'

'I'm people. I won't be in the way.'

'No.'

'I'll sit as quiet as a whatsit.'

The slow voice had the cunning of declared desperation. It was the shamelessness of Nancy's unhappiness that Jean found obscene.

'You must find somewhere else to go.'

'Don't be unkind. There's nowhere.' Jean could hear pop music in the background. Its connotations of drift deepened her alarm. She grimaced at the young man.

'I mean it.'

'You can't stop me.'

'I can't help you.'

'I just want a chat.'

'No!'

'You're cruel.'

'I've told you to see a doctor.'

'Just half an hour.'

'You're not the only one with problems. Just try to pull yourself together. You just don't want to be helped.'

'I'll come in the middle of the night and I'll . . .'

Jean rang off.

'An alcoholic,' she explained.

'Give them an inch,' said the young man. 'Where was I? Ah yes, I'm particularly light on personalities this year and I have to fill in evenings till June. They told me you were a journalist, so I thought you could talk about that and the places you've been to.'

47

'Latterly I've been in a loony bin.'

'Yes, well, we're organising a visit to one of those.' The young man's voice was like well-spread butter.

'Ask them to show you the kitchens. Oh, listen, there's the cuckoo.' She suppressed a giggle.

'My uncle was an alco,' the young man said. 'He used to drink everything he could lay his hands on, hair-oil, fire-extinguisher fluid, every mortal thing.'

'If you leave a number I'll see what I can think of and let you know.'

'A lot of people say they're shy and then they go on for ages.'

She climbed the narrow stairs to her bedroom and washed her hands. On the windowsill was a one-eyed teddy bear which she had had since she was a child. She hated throwing things away. 'Poor teddy,' she said aloud.

Beside the bear was a framed photograph of Dan's head and shoulders. He was laughing so that his nose was stretched and you could see the pores on the end of it. His eyes followed her as she moved from the basin to the bed and back again. She picked up the photograph and put it down again, aware that she had been about to kiss it.

Loneliness, touching in the young, seemed contemptible to her in the not so young. Even eating alone, she had discovered, made one act like an animal. Not that she was sluttish, she was meticulous, but at meal-times she could not help feeling like some creature in its lair. It was something to do with the way one's head went forward when one sat alone at a table, in front of the single mat, glass, knife and fork. Her hand, cutting a slice of brown bread, seemed to claw somewhat, yet when she opened the casserole dish, in which she had stewed half a pound of steak, a small turnip, three carrots and a large chopped onion, she did so indifferently. She ladled herself a helping, and ate rapidly, directing her eyes towards some small, fixed object whose identity she did not register.

'Oh, don't be so tiresome,' she said to the fork, which had fallen out of her hand. She had always talked to herself aloud, though in the hospital she had controlled herself because she had been afraid they might have misunderstood.

The central heating hummed and rumbled. The cottage was warm and clean. Chintz curtains and oak beams and rough whitewashed walls. Lamps, built for oil but wired for electricity by merchants on the King's Road, stood on an assortment of early Victorian tables, none good but all tasteful, cared for. It was all there, as she often reminded herself, sitting-room, kitchen, eighteenth-century tiles found when they tore down the bake-house, witty prints on the walls and in the downstairs lavatory a large stoneware dish with 'Thou, God, Seest Me' written on it. Upstairs the bedrooms, one double, one single. It was a small cottage, worth twice now what Dan had paid for it ten years ago, a nest of rooms where ten generations of countryfolk had coupled and bred and died. It seemed to be waiting for a switch to be thrown which would fill it as the heart fills the arteries.

She washed up the lunch things as soon as she had finished eating. We need a new stove. She still thought in the plural though they had lived apart for three years now. She put away the knuckle of cheddar cheese in a greaseproof bag and the half loaf into its plastic bin. She knew the price you paid for letting outward routine slide. She had seen too much o that in the asylum – she declined to use a less shocking or accurate name for it – their hair like last year's bird's nests and their dirty dehumanised faces.

'Jean! We just dropped in to bring you a present. Isn't he a perfect pet? He's called Nimby.' It was her new friend Ginger Steadmanton, filling the kitchen doorway, a marmalade and white kitten struggling in her arms. 'Some company for you in the evenings. A little person.'

'Oh Ginger!' She wished Lacking people would knock before entering each other's houses.

'It was Monty's idea, actually. He's just gone on to the shops.'

'It's not fair to leave them alone too much and I'm in London a lot now for the paper.'

'Monty thinks you need a mate. He's right, you know. Think of all those women who live alone with a sacred memory. I knew one who had a lock of someone's hair in a brooch. Said he'd been killed in an air-raid. Of course, no one could disprove it. Someone who'd got away, I used to think. And you become a positive target for all the spinsters and divorcees within range to pot at.'

It was already true. Jean had become a Lady with the Lamp for a number of women who offered to share her sorrow with her by unburdening themselves of their own. The Steadmantons were in their late fifties. Ginger was bulky, genial, and consciously frank, her husband, who farmed a thousand acres outside Lacking, spare and stretched, an army man put out to grass. They were the only people she knew whose marriage was in good working order. They radiated pleasure in one another.

'A mate is a great consolation as you grow older,' Ginger said.

'You make it sound like gorillas,' Jean said.

'Gorillas are very good family people, I'm told.'

In the ward in which Jean had recovered consciousness she had got friendly with a woman called Queenie, who had told her that there was a tiger in her tank. The tiger came down from her brain, she said, and prowled about in her womb to see if there was anything there to eat. One day the woman's husband and two sons came to visit her and made a sort of encampment round her in the big sitting-room. Queenie refused to speak to them, and lay back with a handkerchief over her face. They offered her legs of chicken and buns, but she was not to be tempted. Once they had gone she perked up and offered some of the delicacies to Jean.

'They think I'm made of glass,' she said. 'But I'm not. I told them I wasn't. Have you ever been so smothered with love that you wanted to scream?'

'No,' Jean said.

Queenie had stuff in the corners of her eyes and smelt high but she was a compelling talker, unless the tiger was about, prowling inside her tank, when she would run up and down the ward crying obscenities and removing her clothes. Jean had thought that the difference between herself and Queenie was that at the very centre, where her life had its being, Jean was whole, whereas Queenie was shattered, which was what most of the patients secretly thought about one another.

They had brought her to the hospital by ambulance and there they had pumped her out and put her to bed and the first thing she had seen on waking up was the face of Queenie covered with sticking plaster, which she put on, she said, to stop herself laughing. A couple of weeks later they had moved her a few cold corridors away to join a mixed bag of depressives, who kept themselves to themselves, unlike Queenie, whose terror had sent her rocketing from one person to another, talking and talking. Jean had missed Queenie, but not enough to go back to that awful first ward to find her.

'The trouble with despair,' the doctor told her, treating her as an equal, 'is it can drive people completely nuts'. He was bold with the vernacular. 'In the end patients sometimes prefer to shelter inside a nice warm psychosis than to try to find out why it is they can no longer hold their two lives in balance.'

51

'What two lives?'

'The private one and the one in the world. We all have them, you, me, all of us.'

'Can I go home?'

'I'd rather you didn't. You're a bit bruised, you see. What we have to do, you have to do, is to restore your motor control mechanism. Are you with me? So that you can cope with these two lives as you were doing before. No one else can live them for you and neither can happen at all unless they are lived in a workable relation to each other.'

The doctor's pipe had ashen teeth-marks on the stem and his hair, she could not help observing, was filled with dandruff.

When Dan arrived his shoes made explosions as he walked towards her across the linoleum in the sitting-room. Instinctively she turned to the other patients in the face of this fresh assault.

'Is there anything you want?' he had asked, his eyes roving the big room where male and female inmates were receiving their uncomprehending families.

'Do you make your trips to London by train or car?' Ginger was asking.

'By train, but the best ones don't seem to stop here any more.'

'I know.'

'Don't you hate it when a train rushes through and you're standing on the platform?'

'I'm just thankful I'm not on board,' Ginger said.

It took two to make a mistake, Jean was thinking. She had not been ready for babies. Her own mother had had her first child when she was only twenty, a year after her marriage, then Jean had come and then a second brother, one after another. With the house full of steaming nappies and mess from morning to night for years her mother could never have had the time to be a person at all. She had been too busy being a good wife.

'I always envy the people in the dining-car. They look so safe,' Jean said.

It was she who had persuaded Dan to buy the cottage and together they had decorated it, room by room. She remembered that when they were doing the lounge they both painted from the centre of the room to its periphery and afterwards admired it through the window. The room had looked so splendid and sparkling that they had just stood there and admired it from the outside. The same evening Dan had told her that he was going to apply for a job as correspondent in Asia.

She had stood there with paint on her cheek and it was as if she was seeing him for the first time, or as if he was someone else. She had felt snubbed and bewildered and a panic had squeezed her heart, yet she bit her lip to prevent herself asking him if he no longer loved her.

'What about the play?' she had said at last.

He was a whole act into it and he had told her that it was more important to him than any kind of journalistic career. She had believed him. He was more than a journalist. He was creative. He was one of the rare ones and she was helping to quicken his genius. That was how she had seen it.

'I'll do it out there,' he had said. 'We can let this place now we've cleaned it up and I'll do it out there.'

He was strong when it suited him. Yet when she had wanted the abortion he had been passive.

'It's as if you'd been slapped in the soul.'

'What is?' inquired Ginger.

'When a train goes through a station and you're standing on the platform.'

A car pulled up in the street opposite the low kitchen window, but it was only someone asking the way. As Ginger

53

gave directions through the window, the kitten escaped from her arms and broke a cream-jug.

'Not to worry,' Jean said. 'It was cracked anyway.' She threw the pieces into the waste-bin.

'I like your turn of phrase,' Ginger said. 'You should write a book.'

'I always wanted to be a writer,' Jean said. 'Ever since I was a little girl. I used to say to my mother that I'd never marry because I would be a famous journalist and become a Dame of the British Empire, imagine it! And have lots of books written by me on a shelf. And I'd get into tubes and buses and watch people reading the things I had written. I used to say that.'

'Well, back to work with you then.'

'My mother made fun, too.'

'I'm not making fun.'

'She used to say women writers were "funny". She used to read my diary if she could find it, so one day I put something about her, something terrible, and she read it and she cried or pretended to. I felt dreadful, but I wanted to show her how powerful words could be, written down.'

'And to try to hurt her?'

'Not really, just be free.'

'You can't be free and be married as well, dear.'

'Oh, but that's where everyone is so wrong. You should be able to be, at least as much as in any other situation, because until you are the relationship is so immature.'

'I don't know about relationships. I thought that was out of date, that sort of word. All I do know is that I love Monty, warts and all.'

'But why should the woman make all the sacrifices?'

'Because a woman can more easily afford to swallow her pride than a man can. And a house is not a home, never was and never will be.'

With which Ginger took herself off with her unwanted kitten.

Even in England Dan had disliked sitting at home, and had insisted on taking her with him to pubs and staying until closing time. He would drink pints of bitter and talk to the locals while she nursed a light ale. To her, the conversation had been repetitive and dull, a kind of hollow ritual. Dan's play was less in evidence and by the time the transfer to Hong Kong came through it was stashed away in an old basket along with some poems and stories and a half-finished novel, unmentioned between them.

Sitting in front of her typewriter, she stared at the piece of paper she had rolled into it before lunch. Women like Ginger made her feel that she hardly existed. The paper was blank. She had as much right to her ideas as any man had, yet for all the good that had done her she might just as well have followed her mother's example and had babies to start with.

What was she? A kind of hybrid. She even bored her friends, she knew that, because she could seldom talk for long without getting onto the subject of her marriage. Though her sense of outrage might be sterile, it was all she had. It flourished like a churchyard yew.

The editor of the woman's page had asked for a thousand words about the vogue for country cottages among young marrieds. 'I know you have one,' she had said. But Jean could think of nothing to say except that she watched a lot of television in the evenings, too shy to enter the local pub, and liked to stand in the middle of the house and look at things, the lustre jugs, the Sèvres plate with its gold cherubs. Writing seemed even harder since her treatment, though while she was inside she had never stopped scribbling in notebooks in a pencilled hand she now found almost impossible to decipher.

What had she been trying to say in all those pages, whole chapters about the tables and chairs in the ward and the faces of the other patients, fragments of poetry? What had she been getting at? She could no longer remember. There had been women in there with nothing in the world except a cardboard suitcase, had that been it? Or was it to do with the invisible forces that made the occupants of the beds on either side of her walk sideways with the greatest stealth, rigid and smiling? Perhaps she could stick the cream-jug together again. After all, they had had it a long time. She got up and retrieved it from the waste-bin. They had bought it on one of their excursions to a London market. It had cost four and six because it was cracked.

4

'Try that again and I'll clip yer!' The sailor might have risen but for the girl on his knee, who declined to slide off when he straightened his legs in front of him. Dan, who had slopped the man's drink, was grateful for his anger, but did not look round. When he reached the bar he gasped like an athlete breasting the tape. The barman served him a large brandy and wiped beer from the counter to make a place for him. His usual stool was occupied. He stood close beside it, waiting to recognise himself.

He was still frightened, but it was useless to try to exorcise his fear by giving it a name because what he had experienced in the street had been too new for his vocabulary. How could terror and embarrassment be companions?

Once the girl had taken herself off there had been nothing for it but to go to the Pagoda. He had followed her a few yards out of habit, until the gold of her jacket had been extinguished in the dark, then he had turned, hunching his head forwards on his shoulders, and set off like a man making a dash through a rainstorm from one doorway to another.

To reach the warmth of the Pagoda he had to cross narrow streets where in the daytime women and girls crouched on their haunches in gloomy sweat-shops and made sprays of artificial flowers for export. Dan tried to keep his mind on the young actress, but already her smile and the little tuck of flesh between her front teeth were blurring and eluding him.

He tried to think of the Pagoda with its gold wallpaper and welcoming red lights. He quickened his pace, the sooner to leave the sour vacancy of the street he was in. He had been there before, but had never noticed how hard it was to see into the shops. He glanced at them now with reluctance and a certain foreboding. Their façades were visored with steel grilles and their doorways stacked with the discarded rubbish of the day's commerce. Sagging first-floor balconies shadowed the glass, making it impossible to identify the shapes inside.

He found himself pausing outside one of the shops and pressing his nose against the pane.

There was no one to be seen in any direction and the noise of the city had ceased to be even an echo over the black roof-tops. Dan took out his lighter and held the shrinking little flame to the window, but all he saw was his own reflection. He was studying this when it happened. The stillness began to come alive for him.

He extinguished the flame of the lighter by the simple act of removing the pressure of his thumb and stood with his back to the window and looked at the sky. He shut his eyes and opened them. It was still there, patient and cruel. The stillness which the street had become was watching him; an eye should be in its socket, lidded and fringed, but this was a whole, enormous ball of an eye, trailing nerves of primal silence.

The sensation, if such it could be called, was gone before he could try to define it. He stepped over an open culvert running along the gutter and searched for a name. His hand had reached unconsciously for his notebook, filled with jottings about Vietnam. He began to copy some Chinese characters which he could see on a board above some double doors, but they were so blurred that he gave up, tearing out the page and folding it into a boat which he lit with his lighter and

58

launched carefully along the culvert. When the little flame vanished under a grating he could think of nothing else to do to distract his mind from the silence, which he knew was moving again. He could hear his own feet along the pavement as if they were someone else's. He personally seemed to be making no progress. Terror began to gain on him.

His feet stopped. The whole physical context was about to fall apart. He dared not look round. Embarrassment at being himself in the face of this catastrophe flooded up in him. He tried to think about the girl's golden trousers, but all he could see was himself, zigzagging over the veined eyeball of silence, a fly with a dribbling baby's face.

The cry could have been his. Indeed, he thought it must have been until he realised that it had come from some animal fighting in an alley. He straightened his body and followed the noise to where the back of a locked restaurant was spilling out its guts through a waste chute a few feet above the gutter. Red rinds and loops the colour of a whale's belly were unwinding from the chute and hanging over the alley just out of reach of some fierce cats who were leaping like dancers to try to hook them down, slashing at one another whenever their bodies touched. They backed off, mewing and straining forward on their haunches as Dan tried to ease the offal out of the hole for them. He worked slowly, as if drugged, murmuring 'yes, yes, yes' to the impatient cats in an absorbed voice.

The guts came free with a rush, all over his shoes. The cats darted in, snarling and tearing. Sometimes as they ate they looked up at him with misty eyes. He watched them for a while before walking on down the alley.

The wall on his right side was covered with crudely painted Chinese characters, a communist homily, perhaps, or an advertisement for a patent medicine. He ran his finger along the wall and found that the characters were still wet. He began to wonder if he was ill. He felt heavy, yet unreal.

It was with relief that he found he was being followed. His pursuers, as he thought of them, paused whenever he did. The alley had petered out and he was skirting the side of an open building site, from whose concrete apron columns of intricate wires reached into the air, waiting for floors. Dan waited under a light slung on top of a barbed wire fence. Nothing happened. Impatient for the encounter, he walked back into the mouth of the alley but he could see no one.

'What are you waiting for ?' He felt like telling them to play the game, allow him their hatred.

When they faltered out of the alley they were not what he had hoped for, but three schoolboys, one with a pot of red paint, much of which had gone on his face and blue shorts. They were not even sure whether it was illegal to smear walls with political slogans, but they thought the white man swaying about in their path might be some kind of policeman, so when he spoke to them they scurried past.

All Dan had asked them was whether they knew how he could get to the Pagoda. He was feeling more lost than if he had been in the closest jungle, and even when he raised his eyes and saw, floating in green gas behind the girders of the building site, the name of the bar he sought, he still felt displaced.

It was the same inside the Pagoda itself. Smells and noises were parodying themselves. Faces exploded like runaway balloons. It was as if the real bar had gone away without the clients noticing.

Most of the customers were sailors, who sat at round wooden tables with their legs stuck straight out in front of them, or folded themselves into the booths lining the walls. Chinese and Eurasian girls trafficked to and fro between the booths, wheedling for drink tokens. Girls who had not been given the eye sat quietly on a bench near the door, their hands resting in their laps, waiting to be beckoned forward for inspection by the madame.

She liked Dan. He came in the afternoons when business was slack and sat in his favourite corner writing in a book or gossiping with them. Often he did both at once. The thump of the jukebox and other people's half-heard remarks prevented his getting lost in his own image-making, and usually he could align the twin pillars of his existence, work and drink.

But tonight voices surged around him so that he could no longer tell the difference between anger and mirth.

An American stoker was going down the line of women, feeling them up and sniggering. At the end of his inspection he shook his head, and the women sauntered back to their bench yawning and fanning away the clouds of tobacco smoke, their faces like tired moons. Dan searched for one he knew, but without success.

'It's no go, mate. She left, I saw her leave. With a bloody great Kraut. Havin' it off by now I shouldn't wonder.' It was the first mate off the ferry.

'I wasn't looking for anyone.' Dan felt relieved to be able to talk.

'Don't apologise, old boy. We always agreed she was the goods, didn't we?' He made it sound as if they were resuming a favourite dialogue. He had changed from officer's uniform and there were dried soap-suds around his ears. 'Trouble is they get booked up when they're new and you have to join the line and I don't fancy sloppy seconds.' His accent see-sawed between the ward-room and the lower deck.

The madame approached them enquiringly.

'He wants Lily,' the first mate said.

'All my girl same good like Lily.'

'Not enough meat on 'em.'

'Plenty strong,' she demurred, indicating the bench of girls with her fan.

'We like 'em with teeth, we're funny that way. Have a drink,' he said to Dan.

'I have one.'

'Have I got bad breath or something?'

'Well, have you?'

'I found out about that bird you said you saw in the drink this afternoon. She was there all right.' He spoke with a kind of anxious condescension.

'Of course she was.'

'Well, any road, she was trying to sling her hook from Red China and swam for it and drowned herself in the cross-current. That boat was trying to tow her to the police mortuary when the storm came up. They pay so much per object over a certain size.'

'Where is she now?'

'Still out there, I expect. If she's washed in no one'll get the money. How about that drink?'

'Large brandy, then.'

'You're not doing me a favour, you know.'

Dan was seeing her walk down the long beach, her black hair coiled on her shoulder.

'You can't have what I'd call a real conversation with any of 'em in this place,' the first mate was saying. 'They swill like pigs and they screw in places I wouldn't put my umbrella, if I had an umbrella.'

As she went deeper over the shelving pebbles her clothes rose about her and began to float on the surface of the sea. She lifted her arms and touched the water with her fingers as bathers do.

'Hey, I don't know your name.'

'Daniel.'

'Daniel what?'

'Fenwick.'

'Mine's Jack Bell. At school they used to call me Tinker. It's funny about names, isn't it? I'd have stayed longer at school only our dad died so I had to get a job. I studied for my navigation and that in the evenings. I believe in education.'

'You decided to leave school?'

'You've had a few jars, haven't you?'

'A few.'

'What are you sighing about?' Bell's eyes were almost round, and gave his face the look of a worried monkey. 'Whenever I get depressed, which I do, I always know how to snap out of it. Do you know what I do?'

Dan shook his head.

'I go to a blue movie.' He dropped his voice. 'Course you got to see a good one. The bad ones are worse than not going at all, but the good ones – know what I mean?' Dan said nothing. 'Well, what do you like then?'

'What do you mean?'

'Everyone gets a kick out of something, don't they? I was reading the other day that Hitler was impotent. Am I boring you? Hitler was impotent and he worked off his frustrations kind of thing by killing people. Have you heard that before?'

'It's a common enough theory.'

'I'm a common enough man, thank you very much. I don't care who knows its. There isn't anyone, I don't care how la-di-da they are, who doesn't behave like a bloody animal on the job, there now!'

These people, Dan thought, are refusing to admit that something terrible has happened, or else it has only happened to me, in which case why can't they let me concentrate, for how else can I get that eyeball back where it belongs?

'I'm a complicated chap, really.'

Something would surely have snapped but for the pressure

of Bell's hand on his arm. He disliked being touched by other men.

'Where are you off to?' Bell asked.

'Take a leak.'

It pleased the first mate to see this public-school type lurching against the tables as he made his way to the men's room. His eyes glistened with anticipation.

In the foetid cubbyhole an Irish sailor was berating the Chinese attendant, who was pressing his thin shoulder-blades against the tiled wall.

'Communist bastards, all of youse,' the sailor was bellowing as Dan walked in. The Chinese tried to retrieve the small red-covered book which the sailor had knocked from his hand, but the sailor kicked it into the trough of the urinal.

'Piss on it, matey,' he enjoined Dan. 'Ain't I right, though? They oughter drop the bleedin' atom bomb on the lot of 'em, yellow apes.'

Dan's urine bubbled over the *Thoughts* of Chairman Mao.

'I'm talkin' to youse,' the sailor said, prodding Dan's back.

'Well, don't. You talk like a fool.'

To Dan's surprise, the sailor withdrew, but not for long. Dan was still finishing when the door opened and he returned, with friends.

'Is that him?' one said.

'Aye.'

'My mate says you've insulted him. He thinks you'd better come outside and apologise.'

'He was big wid the words before,' the first sailor said. 'Siding up wid dis animal here.'

'Make 'im lick the bloody book,' the third sailor suggested.

'He's coming outside.'

When Dan tried to push past them two of them butted him back towards the urinal with their chests while the third trod carefully on his feet.

64

'Nice and polite,' the first man said. He had taken a flick-knife from his hip pocket and opened and shut it with a flourish. The attendant showed a gleam of enthusiasm at the prospect of the long noses damaging one another.

Smiling, as if to excuse a friend for being the worse for drink, they escorted Dan from the men's room, their fingers digging into his arms. He made no effort to resist.

'What's up then?' Bell intercepted them at the street door.

'Nothing for you, mate,' one of the men murmured.

'He's a friend of mine.' Bell put a hand against the sailor's chest and the sailor kicked him in the shins, at which Bell gave the man a blow in the face with his right fist.

It was as if a starter's pistol had gone off. Bottles began exploding against the walls and glass sprayed the bar. Tables went over as men freed their legs from their women in order to hit one another. The madame made for her office to telephone the police while her girls scrambled behind the bar, where they waved their fans and yelped. The jukebox continued to pound out its music, like a band on a sinking ship and the eyes of the sailors became murderous.

Two Americans, clawing at one another's faces and ears, rolled under a bench on which some of the women were standing. The bench went over and the women came down in a heap of heels and stocking tops. One of them lay with her head on Dan's shoe. He stood perfectly still, waiting for her to go away, until a man began to rip the gold paper off the wall against which he was leaning. The paper was loose and already a panel of it hung down like skin, revealing rotten plaster full of pellet-shaped insects. Dan toed the woman's head off his foot and put his hand on the man's arm.

'I wish someone could say something that would change my life,' he said, to which the man responded by punching him on the mouth.

'Let's blow.' Dan recognised the voice of Bell and was

following it through the door to the street when the man who had hit him on the mouth grabbed his right arm and began to pull him back. Dan's remark had clearly enraged him. There was a tug-of-war until the sleeve of his jacket came away and he tumbled onto the pavement and tripped over a dustbin. Bell pulled him to his feet.

'Did you see that character helping himself to the bottles?' Bell's arm encircled Dan's body. 'Whenever you get a good scrap some crafty bugger goes for the full bottles while everyone else is havin' 'is 'ead bashed in.' Bell was laughing wildly. Lights sang in Dan's eyes. Someone was spluttering and coughing and he could hear the gusty whine of a police siren.

'There was this bird havin' a shower, see, soaping 'erself all over, when through the shower curtains comes this bloody great doberman pinscher and shoves 'is nose up 'er you know what.' Bell was crushed up beside him as they were bowling along behind undulating buttocks.

'Well, afterwards, when she'd dried herself . . .'

'I want to get off.' He could not remember entering the pedicab in the first place.

'Not on your nelly!'

'I don't want to see your dirty pictures.'

'Who said *pictures*! Christ, you never listen. It's a new place, I've told you. New girls, new decorations, the lot. We're going to fix you up tonight, mate. Look at the mess you're in! You're lucky to have any teeth left. Are they your own?'

'I have things to do.'

'Are they your own?'

'Yes.' Dan retched into the road, which was dividing before their wheels like a split stick.

'Cough it up in Mother's hand.'

He could hear the driver gasping as he pedalled them along. 'There isn't time,' he murmured.

'Course there's time.'

'No time.'

'A man can make bloody time.'

The driver turned into a passage between two darkened buildings and stopped outside a garage. His pedicab trembled on its spidery wheels. Bell waited until Dan had lowered himself to the ground, then led the way up an open staircase to a veranda which ran along the first floor of the building. He knocked at a door in which a panel opened, exposing a nose and an eye, at which he directed some remarks, after which the panel was shut and the whole door opened by a fat Chinese woman wearing glossy black pyjamas. She smiled at Dan coldly, her tongue moving behind her long teeth like a captive at the bars of a cell.

'She can fix us up in the outhouse,' Bell said. 'Rather tatty but not to worry. First things first; she's taking us to see the girls.'

The woman led them into a long windowless room decorated in majestic reds and yellows around whose walls half a dozen Chinese and Eurasian girls were lolling on worn sofas drinking tea.

'Now then,' Bell said, rubbing his hands. The girls evidently knew him. They stared indifferently at Dan's bruised features.

'If you haven't any definite preference, I'll choose,' Bell said. 'I know them all. Let's see, now. What about you? Come out of there, I can't see you. That's better. Just what the doctor ordered.'

Only a doctor with a blighted passion for the incongruous would have ordered such a partner for Dan, who was six feet four inches tall, whereas the girl, when she slid her feet into her rubber sandals and came to stand before them, was almost a dwarf, although well enough proportioned. Her skin was tanned like a peasant's and her broad cheeks were

67

covered with shallow white pocks. Bell gave her a little shove.

'A pocket Venus,' he said.

'Pay now please,' said the madame.

'He'll pay,' Bell said. 'It's sixteen dollars a throw, old man. That won't worry a big shot like you.' He winked at the girls and patted the pockets of Dan's mutilated jacket until he found bank notes, from which he took sufficient for both of them.

The madame counted the money under the lamp, licking her fingers, while the girl stood tiptoe at the wall cupboard and reached down a towel and a paper cup of lubricant.

'I don't understand,' Dan said. He was staring at a Buddha's head, a massive fragment on the floor between two busy tables. It had been hacked from some temple wall, and now nothing could be learned from its broken eye, the perfectly damaged circle on the brow, the appalling sockets and the stone mouth, cold as a dead star.

The girl came towards him and took his shirt-sleeve between her finger and thumb and led him out of the room.'

She tried one of the doors which opened onto the dark veranda, but a woman's voice uttered a hoarse monosyllable. Dan paused, taking hold of the rail of the balcony, but the girl went on tugging at him.

'What's the hurry?' She made no reply. 'Do you have a name?' He took her shoulders and tried to turn her towards him, but she twisted her head away, making small gasping noises as she did so. When she found she could not budge him she pressed her face against his chest and explored his body with her free hand. He pushed her away and let her lead him again. She rattled another doorknob. This time the door was opened by a large, naked man whose hands and belly shone white against the darkened room behind him. He vanished inside again and there was a moist slap, followed by a laugh. Dan could see the faint rectangle of a window from which a pale cobweb floated into the centre of the room, undulating as if in a wind, and some vague rigging-like shapes and others more massive. There was a reassuring human smell and it occurred to him with relief that there might be several couples concealed in the dark. He extended a foot, half expecting to feel a body, and put his arm round the girl's shoulders to regain his balance.

She protested when he lit his lighter, but he held it beyond her reach for long enough to make out a row of cubicles divided from one another by ragged curtains and inside one of them two figures. The man who had admitted them was lying on his back on a cot too small for him, while a woman crouched above him, her hair touching his belly. They looked like wax apparitions, frozen in the act of devouring one another.

The girl led Dan to another cot and began pulling at his belt. Her breath on his face smelt of cloves. He let her undress him, as Jean had done on the night they had come back from their honeymoon. There was the same damp smell here as there had been in their cottage. The electricity had been cut off and the bed had not been delivered. They had left everything in the car and had lit matches long enough to open a bottle of wine and a tin of pâté and then they had feasted in the dark and lain all night on damp coats. Dan had never been so happy before or since. He remembered the smell of the coats and light filled his mind.

He drew off the girl's panties, remembering as he did so the provocative breasts of the young actress in the Press Club. His foot touched something which made a metallic noise on the stone floor. There was wet under his bare feet.

Jean had always stroked his hair after they made love, her bracelet, which she always wore, touching his forehead. It had had an opal in it, but it fell out. Jean said that it was just as well, since opals were meant to bring bad luck. She had been happiest when she was lying nursing his head like that. She would lie there and stroke away, admiring what she could see of their home as she did so. Jean was always rooting in antique shops for bargains, an old door to be used as a headboard for their extra large bed, a ship's lantern to match the rope mat in the lavatory.

The room stirred. There was a rustle and a gasp, as if rats were sporting in an attic. The girl's fingers brushed his eyes. 'Boys don't cry,' his mother had said, as so many others must have done. Tears were lodged inside you like dried acorns. He had looked in a drawer at his mother's flat and found all his letters, articles and despatches, neatly clipped and dated in black ink. The paper had sent someone to visit her when he was reported missing in Iraq. Dan's mother had shown the man her husband's medals and he had said, 'Well, it's easy to see where your son gets his guts from'. The medals had been pressed into a plaque of liver-coloured wax and framed with velvet.

'I'm going to be . . .' He reached for the chamber-pot, but the girl took it from him and pushed him towards a dark hole in the wall. He felt about until his fingers touched a basin.

'Jesus!' He gripped the edges of the basin and waited for the next spasm. Vomit dribbled down his lower lip and over his chin.

'What?' He was sure that there was someone else in the black room with him. He was sick again and when he raised his head whoever it was had gone.

Back in the dormitory he found that he had lost his bearings. He blundered towards what he gauged to be his cot, crummy things under his feet, but when he reached it he found that it was empty and without sheets. He sat on the edge of the bed and began to rock to and fro, his hands on his bare knees, his movements becoming more and more limited as his sense of exposure grew, until he was sitting rigidly, his mind grinding on emptiness, with not a stitch or a sentence between the room and himself. Ridiculousness took possession of him. He was like a shell-less crab on a beach where the birds gather, carrion birds, dead women, their arms floating like stems of flowers, cobwebs of light from the window, draped curtains between the cots, dust in the nostrils. There was the stillness again. It menaced with its terrible indifference, there being more menace in the smooth bulk of a table than in the complex folds of the nearest curtain, and yet more in the stillness of his own hand as it lay on his knee. There was no end to it.

He was rescued by the girl, who came to find him and took him back to his own cot. Using the sheet, she wiped the vomit off his mouth and would have dabbed his eyes had he not prevented her. He pressed his face to her hair and allowed his tears to ooze onto her cheek. Jean, her arms full of white flowers, wearing her red plastic raincoat, was coming into the flat where he was sitting typing and telling him that she was pregnant. He had knelt by her and kissed her belly while she stroked his hair and told him how it would be all right.

'You bet it will.'

'I mean,' she had said, sitting on the edge of the sofa and looking into his eyes, 'that I don't have to have it. It's hardly eight weeks old yet.'

He had not understood until she had reminded him of their agreement not to have a child until they were ready for one.

'We're ready now.'

'You know that's not true, Dan. We've no money to start with. Do you want him dragged up?'

'We aren't starving exactly, are we? And anyway that's a ridiculous argument.'

'I want him to come when I can do right by him.'

'But he *has* come. He's decided for himself.'

'Eight weeks, Dan, that's hardly a person, is it?'

'Anyway, what can he be given by us more important than life?'

'He can be given a chance – and so can we.'

'You mean *you*, don't you? I'm ready and the baby's evidently ready. It's you you're on about. You don't want a child.'

He kissed the girl's mouth, holding her neck.

'I want us to be mature people together before a child comes into it. I want us to get more constructive and marvellous for one another before something so tremendous happens.'

He had given way to her, had known all along that he would. Lying in delirium after the abortion, which had gone wrong, she had cried out that he had killed the white fish. He could see the doctor's nervous face. There had been so much blood.

'Now,' he said aloud. He straddled the girl. 'Whoever you are.'

He spoke low but with sufficient force to rouse another. Bell had followed them along the veranda and had stood behind him while he sicked into the basin, had then sat gingerly on a nearby cot, awaiting the action, but had dozed off. Now he eased himself onto the floor and squatted as near to Dan's cubicle as he dared.

But Dan coupled silently, offering himself tenderly to the girl beneath him, who lay quietly with arms beside her until he took her wrists and placed her hands behind his neck.

When he had done she would have replaced her underclothes within reach on the floor, but he remained over her, unmoving, even when a mosquito gorged on his shoulder. The girl took his behaviour for a customer's quirk and waited.

Inside his head, on prairies of grey light, white circles

expanded, touched, retracted. A bowed figure toiled up an intricate scaffold carrying a sealed box. He opened his eyes with a start and the darkness rolled over his face. Just before losing consciousness again he saw the face of the young actress he had met at the Press Club: perplexed and contemptuous eyes, upturned lip, young breasts rising and falling as she spoke. The mouse scratch of a cigarette-lighter must have roused him again. He focussed on its spark, watched it become a little pool of flame into which there floated the face of Bell. The light went out.

After that Dan slept like a sentry who cannot stay awake, though knowing that the enemy is every unmoving tree.

The Chinese girl waited until he was breathing evenly before she wormed her way from under his body. She replaced her panties, searched the pockets of his trousers and selected a bank note, then lay beside him again. She wondered if he was ill. She hoped it was nothing infectious.

From Tinker Bell's point of view the performance had been a failure. He should have stuck to his usual GIs, yet they were seldom much fun. They grunted and slobbered about like pigs. There was no artistry or cruelty about them, such as he had hoped for in Dan. Had Bell lived in the French Revolution he would assuredly have applied for the job of gaoler to the young Dauphin. He would have enjoyed showing the little toffee-nose a thing or two. But who wanted to watch a pig rutting? Quality was the kick.

He waited like the girl until he was sure that Dan was asleep before getting up and creeping away.

5

When Dan woke he was lying on his back with his arms hanging down either side of the cot. He was alone. There was a slight ringing in his ears and, knowing that it would hurt him to move his head, he tried to locate his clothes by looking out of the corners of his eyes, but all he could see was the ridge of his nose and the hairs on his cheekbones. An irregular shape shimmered on the dirty ceiling above him. It took him some time to grasp that it was a reflection of water and further that the sounds coming through the window were of someone slopping about on the veranda with a bucket and mop.

The floor of the room was covered with a debris of empty beer-cans and cigarette-ends. In the midst of the mess a piebald cat was stretched out on her side suckling some kittens. She ignored Dan as he left.

The clouds had blown away during the night and a clear sky was being slowly filled by the day, which shone down the ends of the narrow streets with the colour of pearls. A few Chinese were already on their way to work and small shop-keepers were scratching themselves and removing their shutters. The water in the harbour was opaque. It concealed spiny wrecks and gave Dan the illusion that the ships on its surface belonged to the same natural order as itself. At this hour, before the sun had watered the world's eyes, it seemed to his exhausted mind that he could see underlying unities that would later be concealed: a hand on a chrome handlebar, a foot in a sandal, a sandal on a stone, a gap narrowing between a ship and its berth, a mouth opening before a shout, a woman's shoulders reflected on a jeweller's window. He felt a sharp nostalgia for each arriving moment and a longing to merge with the place he was in, to vanish painlessly.

It was in this dreamlike state that the events of the night before returned as memories, passing across his mind like harmless pictures as he wandered between the stares of the passers by.

So absorbed did he become in his recollections of the body in the harbour and of Tinker Bell's face floating in the darkened bedroom of the brothel that he remarked without surprise that the street along which he was passing, and which he had reached through a small passage between two high buildings, was filled with unnaturally bright light. He must have been walking in the road because a taxi passed so close to him that some part of it nudged his arm. He was about to hail it when he saw that it was occupied by a girl who raised her hand and ran her fingers through her hair. The taxi stopped a few yards ahead of him and he hurried towards it, realising as he did so that the right sleeve of his jacket was missing. Without stopping, he took the jacket off and folded it over his arm. From the air above him a voice amplified by a loudspeaker shouted to him to 'clear the set' and then said 'cut' several times.

The door of the taxi opened and Sally Maine stepped onto the pavement. She stood there, her breasts thrust out and her hands on her hips, and having glanced at Dan without appearing to know him, gave her attention to a man who was standing on a small balcony suspended a few feet above the street.

'I come down,' the man said, leaping onto the pavement like a cat. He was a short, massive person with a brownish bald head and a large mouth full of strong white teeth. His eyes were like shiny black stones.

'Gaston, that was fine, really quite fine.' He was addressing a second man whom Dan now noticed lounging in a doorway beside the balcony. 'Now, Sally,' he said, turning to the girl. 'Tell me something. Don't you like this scene?'

'I would if I knew more clearly what it was supposed to be about.'

'Well. The point now is that he,' indicating Gaston, 'has a premonition that his affair with you is about to end and he believes it is the last time he will even make it with someone like you, someone young and beautiful. It is his last time, you see?'

'Yes, but . . .'

'Thus in a way he is seeing you for the first time, and so he sees himself for the first time.'

'What is he seeing when he does that?'

The bald man clenched his fists in front of his chest as if he would tear open his rib-cage. 'It is indefinable. He simply sees. It makes him very sad.'

'But he has to see something otherwise nothing will add up. That's what I meant earlier by there being a lack of definition.'

She spoke, Dan noticed, with a tone of challenge laced with a kind of wheedling appeal.

'You must look more confused.' The bald man gave a demonstration. 'And more business with your hands, that was nice.'

'I saw it as hope rather than confusion. I mean I am looking forward whereas he is looking . . . nowhere.'

'Don't complicate it. Try to get one level right for now. The rest comes later.'

'How later, if we're doing short takes all the time?'

'Comes later.'

'When ?'

'Sally, you must be kind to your audience. Take them by the hand and lead them, step by step, through your experience, which is changing, yes ? Changing from scene to scene. So, one step, bewilderment, two steps, awakening relief, third step, hope, fourth step, disillusion, fifth step, pain and hurt, sixth step, resurrection of the spirit in you and so forth. Scene by scene.' The bald man smiled coldly at her. 'Don't worry so much about the why of it all. I will care about that.'

The girl looked dubious and the bald man shrugged rudely, showing his dangerous teeth. 'Play it young. Surely that should not be too . . . be too much ?'

'You wanted an older person for the part.' Why, Dan wondered, was she so unsure of herself in this, her world ?

A new figure wearing a back-to-front baseball cap emerged from the doorway behind Gaston. He consulted a light metre which he wore round his neck on a silver chain. 'I'll have to reset the lighting in a minute.' He seemed pleased at his discovery.

'All right, I'll look confused,' Sally said.

'It sounds safe enough,' Dan said to her.

'Who are you ?' the bald man asked.

'I mean how else would anyone look when someone sees them for the first time instead of using them as a mirror for themselves ?' Dan smiled at Sally, ignoring the others. Needing an ally, she smiled back.

'Talking of mirrors,' she said, 'you could use one yourself. What hit you ?'

'Oh, in a bar, after you went home.'

'I knew we'd met,' she said. 'You *are* a bit different looking, you know. Let me introduce my director, Franco Panni, and this is Gaston Gaillard. I'm afraid I've forgotten your last name.'

'Fenwick, Daniel.'

'Break for coffee. Ten minutes,' Panni said.

'It's last names I forget. We met at the Press Club. Mr Fenwick's a journalist.'

'You should not come on the set,' Panni said.

'I told you we should have got the police to block both ends of the street.' This was from Gaston.

'Let me show you what you look like,' Sally said in a social voice. She took Dan's sleeve and walked him to the taxi, from which she produced a little silver hand-mirror. There,' she said. 'We hold mirrors to one another.'

'Is this whole street a film set?' Dan asked.

'Panni drives about and when he likes the look of a place he just stops and that's the set. Except he forgets to tell the police sometimes and you get strange people walking on.

'Like me.'

'I was glad to see you. They were really getting me down this morning. Panni just won't treat me seriously. Why can't people say what they mean?'

'It would only hurt if he said what you say he is thinking. Anyway you don't really believe it, do you? You just want him to deny it to make you feel good.'

'Perhaps you can tell me how to play my part, since you're so knowing.'

'Well, why not? Let's see. The old man, whatsisname, Gaston, sees you in the taxi as you really are and because, to you, he is already half dead, that is how he will see himself.'

'That sounds great,' she said. 'I must tell Gaston.'

'It's what your Mr Panni was saying earlier, only shorter.'

'You are beaten up,' she said. 'You need a rest.'

'I need a nice dry martini, followed by a good dinner in a bright, but not too bright, restaurant, from which you can see the lights of China across a darkened sea. Of course, I'll want you to be there as well. How about it?'

'When?' Gaston was looking at her dolefully.

'Tonight.'

'He should clear the set. We are not on vacation,' Gaston said.

'Take your places,' Panni called. 'One more rehearsal and then a take.'

'That sounds good,' she said.

'Clear the set, please,' Panni shouted at him. 'Right back. We have little time.'

'I'll call for you at your hotel, eight o'clock. Why don't you wear that gold thing?'

'Do you like it?'

'Very much.'

He saw now that the road and pavement were covered with chalked crosses and lines marking the limits within which the actors were supposed to move and stand. Gaston was already on his mark and a make-up girl was dabbing at his face. He wished he could think of things to say to shake or amuse his Sally, but perhaps, after all, the best was to keep one's mouth shut. He stroked his coat over his stomach with both hands. He was of an age when he had rediscovered his body and felt affection for every crease. She would come round. The young could usually be worn down in the end.

Shadows were dissecting the pavement as the sun rose higher. They were cutting across the cracks in the concrete, imposing over the chalk marks a pattern of their own. Already the delicate uncertainties of the dawn hours were being dispelled. In other streets than Panni's the vendors were trotting along, one foot after another, balancing little steaming kitchens on their heads or shoulders. The pedicab drivers were hauling to work petty Chinese officials whose children were parading in thousands in the yards of schools. Nearer the centre of the city a centipede of communist students was making its way towards Government House to vent yet another grievance against the British authorities. Every so often, at a word from its leader, the centipede's right arms would shoot up in a clenched salute, a unanimity only briefly marred when one of the limbs fell off to become a worried-looking youth tying up his shoelace.

A riot truck roved past the end of Panni's set taking tear-gas from one police station to another. Looking back down the street, Dan could see two men stretching a tape measure between Sally Maine's taxi and Gaston Gaillard's doorway.

He looked at the taxi hungrily. When she had shown him his bruised face in her little carved mirror she had seemed interested. He had seen it kindle in her eyes. He had at once become embarrassed by his uncouth appearance and had resolved to go home, clean himself up and get in touch with his Chinese stringer to give him his orders for the day.

6

Andy Burns was woken by the familiar kitchen noises of his houseboy. For as long as fifteen seconds they delayed recall, then back it came like an axe hitting a chopping block. He shaped the word in his mind. The letters were white and woolly at the edges, as if an aircraft had spelt them out in the vacant sky over the prairies where he had been raised. They used little one-engined planes to spray the crops against disease. Leukemia. He wanted to pull the sheet over his head then and there.

But his fear was too frightening to accept and a stronger impulse of self-preservation got him out of bed and made him check his clocks and tap his barometers as he always did, though doing so today was like trying to remember a drill from another time.

Outside his bedroom window people were getting on with their lives. They made Andy feel better. Self-pity receded. He stared down at a man who was crossing the broad, sunny court which separated his apartment block from the one next door. The man looked British. He was striding along, indifferent to the windows all around. He was all right. If he had glanced up, Andy would have saluted him. I am like you, the wave would have said, a fellow human struggling along with a load of problems, taking the rough with the smooth. In half an hour or so I shall be out there, too, joining in. I am not dying like my ma, yellow as tallow, because I am a man with problems, and problems belong to life.

In the cold shower he thought his body looked perfectly healthy and the blood tingled inside it with its usual enthusiasm. His father and mother were both gone and there were no more of his Burnses left in America. Andy had never given much thought to raising a family, assuming that he would do so when the right woman came along, as he had never doubted that she one day would. But now it was different.

He soaped his torso, probing under his arms as the doctor had done and feeling with his fingertip the little scar where they had taken a sampling of his breastbone. The swelling under his arms had gone and so had the palpitations and bleeding gums. Perhaps there had been a mistake after all.

When Dan Fenwick had found Andy in a tent in a marine camp at Da Nang, Vietnam, two months before, he had been so ill that for several days Dan had had to file his copy for him. Dan had looked after him in ways Andy disliked reflecting on and had arranged with the Marine doctors to have him flown to Saigon and thence to Tokyo, where he had been hospitalised for his tests before returning to Hong Kong.

As he soaped and scrubbed all there was to remind him of the state he had been in when they hauled him onto the helicopter, jack-knifed with stomach pains, was a mild fever which dried out his eyes and made swallowing uncomfortable.

Shaving made him feel more than ever in control. There were some odd-looking spots round his adam's apple, but as he examined his face in the mirror, which magnified every pore, his fear became no more than an imprint on a damp pillow. There was nothing you could not come to terms with. When he saw that German doctor again at noon he would tell him so. He would insist on frankness.

The houseboy came in with chilled orange juice, his young face as reserved as ever. Andy could never imagine what Lee was thinking about, nor had tried to find out.

'Have you ever been ill, Lee?' The boy looked alert.

'Number two brother was ill.' Lee had had a fierce bout of tuberculosis once but he had no intention of telling his employer this in case he got the sack. Lee was the breadwinner.

'How many brothers and sisters have you?'

'Five brothers, two sisters.'

'Your dad's a busy man.'

'My father is dead.'

His parents had had a neighbour in Milton called Ranger who had fathered eight daughters. Andy could never remember Mrs Ranger being thin. Just an old battery hen, his father used to say. Andy was an only child. His father used to say it took a man to make boys. He remembered an Italian farm-hand telling the attentive kids one harvest time that it wasn't the size but the squirt that counted.

'He must've been a great guy,' he said to Lee, who gave him an unexpected smile.

A cable arrived from New York while he was drinking his coffee asking whether China would use force to support the communist demonstrators who had been marching about Hong Kong for over a week. Andy's paper was always requesting impossible predictions and once, in Taiwan, he had cabled back 'My balls are not made of crystal', which had provoked a letter from the editor reminding him that women as well as men handled the copy and would he please watch his language.

He put the cable on top of a heap of others on his desk, noticing as he did so that the nail of his right index finger was chewed to the quick. Babies, he thought, have perfect nails from the day they are born. He picked up the letter he had written to Jean the night before. Babies, he thought, tapping his cheek with the letter, they said you could buy them on the open market down in Singapore. People bought them who wanted to have someone look after them in their old age. The parents sat on the sidewalk of some special street and peddled their kids and people bought them and took them home like peaches.

7

The clinic was in an old, damp stained villa whose garden had been filled with asbestos huts. Blue ceramic dragons guarded the entrance gates, but on the flattened grass between the huts groups of Chinese squatted and made litter. From time to time a nurse came out of the main building and went from one group to another calling out names from a register.

As Andy walked through the lobby, which was full of patients who were coughing and spitting, he wondered if he should trust a man who kept such a run-down-looking clinic, though everyone said that Dr Schreiber had given up a great practice somewhere in Germany to become a medical missionary. At least he could get someone to clean the spit off the floor. Andy winked at a child which was sitting in his path. The sick depressed him. He did not mind being with men who had been wounded, but the sick he avoided. He told himself that all he had to get from this man were a few basic facts and a decision on treatment and then he could get back to work on the Hong Kong demonstrations. Yet when he was shown into the doctor's consulting-room he felt nervous and apprehensive.

The doctor was a pale man with almost transparent ears which stuck out of his head like clam-shells. Across his desk stretched an uneven double line of pill-boxes and specimen jars, labelled and dated in red ink.

'How are *you*?' he said. His voice was slow and deliberate.

'I'm fine. I really feel pretty good. It's hard to believe, you

85

know, that . . .' As he spoke he had the wild idea that he might really be better and that this doctor was about to change his diagnosis.

The telephone rang and the doctor told someone that he would not be long.

'Urm, I don't really have much to add to what I told you yesterday, yes? But I assumed that you would wish me to clarify some points now that you have had the time to digest the diagnosis. Excuse me.' The telephone was ringing again.

'Tell her ten minutes, say, fifteen, *ja*.' Not enough time, Andy thought.

'How is your throat today?'

'A bit sore, nothing much. Maybe I should have some lozenges.'

'Why not? Mr Burns, the chronic form of leukemia is somewhat erratic. You may expect to feel fine from time to time.'

'And then?'

'Then you will feel not so fine.'

'Is it bound to get worse?'

'It can be arrested for long periods. It can arrest itself even.'

'Did you mean it literally when you told me yesterday that no one knows what it's caused by?'

'Just one of the many things we don't know. But we will one day. One day, I have no doubt, we will be able to reverse the corpuscular insanity which is the main characteristic of leukemia.'

'Insanity?'

'In many ways it resembles a form of malignant disease, I tell you frankly, a disease characterised by uncontrolled over-production of white blood corpuscles.'

'Why should that be so . . . debilitating?' Andy had nearly said 'fatal'. Following the collapse of his brief hopes of a

86

reversal of the verdict, he was beginning to feel a perverse satisfaction in establishing one devastating fact after the other. He did not want Schreiber to stop talking and as he listened to the slow, unaccented voice he told himself that there was still time.

'In your case, the lymphatic form of leukemia, there is a vast increase, often up to sixty-fold, of the corpuscles which resemble what we call the lymphocytes, which in healthy blood are present in only small numbers, you see?'

'What does lymph do?' Just keep talking and something manageable will emerge. Andy noticed that the top button of the doctor's white jacket had been sown on with black thread.

'Oh, several things. For example, some of the lymph vessels in which it circulates help to digest fat after meals, others nourish the tissues and some fulfil the function of drains, you might say. They have many uses all over the body so when the lymph glands become infected and swell, the ramifications are widespread. Look here.' Schreiber held out a large book which he had flipped open at a marker and showed Andy a coloured picture of lymph capillaries, delicate, flat cells, joined edge to edge in perfect discipline, like dancers touching fingertips.

'It's beautiful,' Andy said.

The doctor flipped to the next page and Andy saw a picture in which the cells had lost both formation and individual shape and were heaped like fungus.

'Is that my thing?'

'No. That is a form of cancer. I was simply illustrating my use of the word insanity. Life gone mad.'

The greed of the diseased organisms filled Andy with abhorrence. 'Is there nothing?' His voice was petulant.

'Nothing. Perhaps, however, you would prefer to check with your doctors in America.'

'That won't be necessary.'

'I find that people often want to go back to their own place at times like this.'

'It's just there's so much to absorb in ten minutes, that's all. I suppose it's only another case to you.'

'It depends what you mean by "just another". There may be a hundred people outside that door and half of them are dying. In that sense, yes. Do I answer your question?'

'How long does it go on?'

'It is hard to say. Your best option is to start treatment as soon as possible. Much will then depend on how you react to it.'

'But how long have I got?'

'It is not possible for me to say just now.'

'There must be something more to say.'

'Mr Burns, I suspect you are not really asking me for information of a medical nature.'

'It doesn't make sense.'

'Do you want me to preach to you? You don't strike me as being that kind of man.'

'Can I be treated here?'

'If you wish. The main treatment is chemotherapeutic, that is to say, with drugs. There have been advances up to a point. I can treat you as a paying patient. The Chinese are usually treated free or pay what they can. I'll work out a schedule for you and we'll discuss money then. Mostly we will use a drug called chlorambucil.'

'Do you – I won't keep you – but do you always just tell people when they have things like this?'

'It depends. Some not. They would receive the information badly and this would perhaps exacerbate their condition as well as causing them much distress. Others seem to accept, yes, but in reality they are refusing to believe. Then there are those who both believe and understand the process of the illness, whatever it may be, and learn to live with the implications. For them it is a challenge. I concluded that you were in that category.'

'Can't we start treatment today?'

'I have to work out a regime for you and get drugs and various things. You must be patient, Mr Burns. Now I must go, there have been people waiting for me all morning for treatment.'

'All right, I'll wait, but don't forget I work for a living. I have to go to Vietnam again in three weeks. That'll be O.K. I guess?'

'Tell me, when you are in Vietnam writing all those things,' said Schreiber, ignoring the question, 'do *you* find it acceptable to make individuals the sole basis of your reporting or do you paint with a wider brush?'

'A wider brush, I guess.'

'There are so many, many individuals.'

'A report only makes sense if you try to put them all in a wider context.'

'Exactly. My people are starving and poor and ill. Seventy per cent of the people on this earth don't get enough to eat, the rest have too much. That is the picture, Mr Burns. There is no room for individual sympathies in a situation of such mass injustice. No room at all!'

'Do you have any children?'

'A man's life should not be measured by his children only but by his general usefulness to society.'

'You didn't answer my question.'

'My son died of typhoid in Sumatra.'

'I'm sorry.'

'Be sorry for the world, Mr Burns, because then you will become really angry. You will rage.'

' I only meant I was sorry I asked about your children in the first place.'

'Ach, then we are not talking about the same things. I thought we were having a conversation.'

With a regal nod Schreiber left the room to begin a kind of progress through his waiting-room, pausing from time to time to hear someone's story. The patients were galvanised by his presence, relapsing into torpor again as soon as he left them. Playing God, Andy thought. Yet he had been ready to be impressed by this cool German with the not so cool eyes. He decided that from now on he would try to see him after his Chinese patients had gone home, if they ever went home. Schreiber was said to be an active communist. Andy would not have been surprised. He seemed to despise journalism all right. Andy felt prepared to agree with him. He had done many odd jobs in his life and it was his wife who had urged him into his present calling, thinking it superior. To Andy it was strictly a meal ticket.

He set off for the police headquarters with an idea of trying to find out more about Schreiber, on whom he must now depend for so much, but changed his mind and went instead to a large book-store. He sidled between the rows of shelves until he found the medical section. He took down a fat black book and held it for a moment as if trying to guess its weight, then he opened it with a crack of glue and began leafing through the pages towards the letter L.

On his way out of the shop, the medical dictionary wrapped and paid for, he spotted the conspicuous cover of Dan Fenwick's book on Indonesia. Dan's face stared up from the back of the dust-cover. 'Born 1926,' it said. 'Educated Westminster School and Cambridge.' The dedication inside was brief: 'To Jean'. It reminded him of his unposted letter to her and, feeling in his pocket, he touched it with his fingers.

8

'I'm disturbing you.' It was a statement, made unregretfully, which gave the woman time to look Jean over without appearing to take her eyes off her face.

'Not at all.' Jean did not hide her curiosity. The woman's clothes asked to be stared at. They were bizarre rather than trendy. Her huge-brimmed black hat sagged over her ears, from which hung brass rings of Chinese puzzle complexity. A fringed Buffalo Bill coat covered a homely sweater which reached to her knees. Bellbottomed trousers of fragile black velvet flapped over mud-caked gumboots. Over her shoulder was slung a leather pouch and round her neck were half a dozen strings of bright plastic beads and a gold talisman the size of a tea-cake.

When Jean opened the door the woman was wearing massive, circular sun-glasses, which were spotted with rain, but she removed them as she spoke, revealing a small oval face, cream-white in colour, in which were set a pair of green eyes which were large and shiny.

Jean's first thought was that her visitor was one of the gipsies who were camped in a local wood to the indignation of her neighbours, but the throaty, commanding voice dispelled any idea that the pouch might contain wooden clothes-pegs or the props for fortune-telling.

'My name is Maslyn Martin. I live just outside the village. I got a letter this morning from the *Daily Message*, I think it was, to say they wanted to interview me about my younger actresses, I'm an agent, you see, and saying that someone actually living in Lacking here would do the interview. It seemed rather odd, but judging from the address they gave me, someone is you.'

'How like them to tell you and not me. Come in.'

Together in Jean's tiny entrance hall the two women nearly touched. Jean had never seen anyone stand so still in her life. With her arms hanging loosely at her sides this Maslyn seemed to her enviably at ease.

'I was writing a piece just now, as a matter of fact. About living in the country.'

'I don't want to be interviewed now,' Maslyn said. 'I was coming in and was curious to see who it was.'

'Well, you might as well come and sit down for a bit. Have a drink?'

'No thanks. I'll have a fag, if I may.'

'It's tiring, walking.'

'Is it? It's tiring coming into Lacking, that's for sure. I feel worn out just looking at the place. All those terrible little gardens and beams and roses. Oh, how I loathe roses. And copper kettles.'

'Why do you hate roses? I didn't think anyone could.'

'And all those dreary public relations men who slip into a little corduroy number the moment they come off their train.'

'You seem to wear what you like.'

'I wear what I think is expressive of my personality, which is a mixture of different things, all of which I've come to recognise and accept. I don't change for town.'

'Are you sure you won't have a drink?' Jean was enjoying herself.

'Well, just a small bloody mary, perhaps.'

'I've no tomato juice. I could nip out and get some.'

'No, no. Nothing then. Perhaps a vodka and tonic.'

'Gin, you can have. That's about all. Or sherry.'

'No.' She managed, by a half laugh, to make her refusal sound inevitable and the very question absurd.

'I rather like gin,' Jean said.

'So many women do. Personally I think it's shit.'

The coarseness was intentional, experimental, even. Jean was unmoved.

'It warms me up,' she said.

'Does it help you to cry watching the television?'

'I beg your pardon?' As a matter of fact it did.

'I once walked round this so called village at night. I just wanted to see how my neighbours lived. I thought I already knew and I was right. A lot of battery hens. I've a mill up the road, I didn't come here for the community, I don't suppose you did either. At first they tried to get their claws on me for their terrible societies for the preservation of the amenities, and there's one that paints watercolours, and one that decorates bottles. I told them I was opening a home for illegitimate West Indian babies and that got rid of them. Anyway, this night. Everyone was sitting in his or her country gear watching the telly. And I thought, when they turn off they'll go to the kitchen and make themselves the final nightcap and then they'll go to bed and sleep, some with the aid of pills and some without. We won't even talk about their sex life. I just don't want to know.'

'Don't you ever watch TV?' Jean was unashamed about the grey-faced saviour in the corner, and some nights when the last picture had faded and the light inside the tube had contracted to a hot pinpoint, she would wish she could squeeze through into its teleworld, like a modern Alice, and spend the rest of the night in a bright room full of microphones, commentators and snatches of old Hollywood films.

'I only watch plays, really,' Maslyn was saying. 'I have to keep pace with things like that. It's my job. I've about ten young actresses on my books, in my life, I should say. I can't let them down, though they feel free to let me down, so I watch the Wednesday Play and the Play of the Month and Armchair Theatre, the lot!'

She inhaled and gave Jean a long look of calculated intimacy which ended in a spontaneous mischievous smile.

'I'm not a dike, don't worry.'

'How on earth. . . . You must be a gipsy after all. You can read thoughts.' Jean was charmed.

Why she was putting herself out to impress, Maslyn could not have said. She had knocked on this woman's door because she believed in being nice to the press and Jean's subdued directness had intrigued her and got her going. She declined a proffered cork-tip cigarette and took out a half-finished, hand-rolled object which she lit and inhaled with almost reverential care. A smell of herbs drifted across the room.'

'Are you married?'

'What did they call me in the letter about me?'

'Of course. I'd forgotten. Only I didn't detect a male influence about the place, that's all.'

'My husband's a journalist, too. He's working in Hong Kong.'

'Ah, they showed the demonstrations on TV last night. Horrible, screaming faces. Does he go away a lot, then?'

So she does watch TV, Jean thought. 'He lives there. He's stationed there.'

'And you are stationed here?'

'I had to come back to look after things for a while.'

'Oh.' Maslyn sat forward, knees apart, hands in lap, a male gesture which in no way unsexed her.

'You had to see the children into school, I suppose.'

'We haven't any. I just came, that's all. I didn't like it.'

'Didn't like coming home?'

'Didn't like out there, though I didn't like coming home

either, really. It's possible not to like everything sometimes.'

'Not for long.'

'You sound very confident.'

'I've worked at it. No thanks to men, I might say. My husband sapped my confidence. Men usually do. They need it all for themselves. It takes it out of them, you know, playing that bull hero bit year in year out.'

'Is your husband . . .'

'Gone with the wind, my dear. I walked out on him. That's how he would put it, I expect. We'd been married for twelve years. He was a producer, Ronald Namier, you probably know him, most people seem to, and I'd been the faithful housewife, gave him two sons, ran his home, sat through his dinner parties listening to his stories, of which he had an incredibly limited number, week after bloody week, and watching my life running down the sink with the washing up water. Then, one day, I met a boy. He was twenty-three and young enough to be my son, nearly. Actually I was thirty-four at the time, and he had a motor-bike and he was in with some gang, burn-ups and the Great North Road, all that, and he was creative and desperate and hated his father and he had been to Borstal because he once blew up an old folks' home with explosives he had made in his parents' garage, not really blew it up, just a wall, I think, and he had this motor-bike and we met, and he was so full of life and he was interested in the theatre and had started to write and we met, as I say, and one morning I just got on the pillion of his bike and we went off, and never went back.'

Drawing one leg up beneath her on Jean's sofa, Maslyn gave a gurgling laugh, puckering up her nose.

'What happened then?'

'Well, then we went off to Cornwall and after that to Morocco, and we lived there for a while and I wrote to my husband and said I wanted a divorce and he said we should

95

talk about it. He was shattered. His whole male posture was shattered. So I went back and Randy, that's the young man, had a flat, so I went there to live and I saw my husband and we talked and talked and he was very hurt, he said, and what about the children, you know, they always use that moral sanction to try to get their claws on you again, and I said the children would be perfectly all right. The older one stayed with him and the younger one came to me and moved over to his father later and then both of them went to boarding school and now they are very relaxed, sweet kids.'

'And your husband?'

'Oh, he married a girl so dumb that there was no danger of his ever damaging his *amour propre* again. He's so vain. He also thinks he's an intellectual: in reality if he lived down here he'd be changing into his corduroys with the rest of them and preserving Celtic barrows. Tell me, why are you such a good listener?'

'Because you're such a good talker.'

'I see.' Maslyn contrived to look snubbed.

'My husband,' Jean said hastily. 'It was my idea to live down here, not his.'

'Why did you want to?'

'I thought it would give us a base and roots.'

'But it didn't.'

'It could have done if he hadn't been so set on a scorched earth policy.'

'Can you blame anyone wanting to set Lacking on fire?'

'He set out to be destructive.'

'While you were flying in and out of the nest with your little twigs of Chippendale, by the look of it.'

'Men don't like to see women as people, don't you think?'

'Of course not. They give them special qualities in the way they give names to Negroes. They say Negroes are specially rhythmic or specially potent and by giving them names they rob them of the one thing we all have in common, which is our being human on this earth. But you won't make them admit that if you go on acting like a cowering little homemaker. You have to spit in their eye.'

'What became of your friend? Randy?'

'Oh, he went off in the end. We weren't what is laughingly known as well suited. He wanted a mother to show off to and I realised that I was beginning to enjoy the role, so I turned in my cards.'

'You mean you left him?'

'Well, yes.' Not true, Jean thought.

'So now you live alone?'

'On and off. I do what I like. I'm not one of those people who have to find a man beside them all the time, though I have to admit that to have something nice pointing at one in the mornings can be more agreeable than otherwise.'

'What do you do?' She wondered how much this talkative woman knew about the menace of early mornings, of the unlived day.

'I work like hell for my girls. They don't appreciate it. There's one in Hong Kong now, that's why I was so interested about your mentioning it. I expect you've seen her on TV. She's really talented, but what makes her so special for me is that she could be a really free person. The trouble is she's too blasé and if there's one thing I hate it's people being blasé. It's just an excuse for not looking inside yourself.'

When the body shivered and the heart broke, all between the lights going on and the nurses coming round to check the beds, did she know about that?

'Do they need you, these girls?'

'Yes, they do.'

'That's the thing.'

'But I never thought my life should revolve round a man,' Maslyn said. 'Ever since I was a child I wanted to do something with my own life. My father was a bully. He bullied my mother into the grave, then he went to pieces and took to drink. He was weak and cruel. I loved my mother and I ended up nursing him and I thought, when she died, this will never, never happen to me. It very nearly did, but I slipped through the net.'

'I always wanted to live my own life, too,' Jean said, thinking how thin she made it sound.'

'Then do it. Go ahead.'

'I am. That's why I'm supposed to be interviewing you.'

'Yes, but not just because there's no man to make the centre of your universe. You mustn't be a bloody moon goddess. I can sense that that's what you're longing to be. Circling round some hairy great sun. The age of phallus worship is over! Look, the computer has cut the balls off the men after thousands of years in which they've caught the food and fought the wars and gone off on ships and had a great old phony male time of it. It's over, darling. Astarte is back. But you have to decide where you stand. The more you try to be wanted the more impossible freedom is.'

'But that's equally true for men. And what's the point of being free if no one cares?'

'Look, I must go now. When shall we have this interview? Why don't you come for lunch next Thursday? I'll look out stills of my girls, you may need them. See you then. Bye.' She was gone, declining to be cornered or crossed. Jean envied her determination and admired her glamour. She had an aura of authenticity rare, she found herself thinking, in a woman.

The trouble with her, Maslyn thought, is that she's trying to run with the hare and hunt with the hounds. Like most people. And what a frantic little house!

Her own place had been a warren of small side chambers round a central grain store until she had removed all but the

98

supporting walls. Now she had one main room the size of a squash court, a gallery and open staircase painted bright blue, and two bedrooms off. Her furniture blended medieval monastic with contemporary plastic. Strobe lights on aluminium stalks winked blue and red in the evening and music fell from the air at the flip of a switch.

She had come to Lacking in days when you could still see rabbits nibbling in the steep lanes off the High Street and when the roads around the village were clotted with clay from the tracks of the farm vehicles. She had come, unlike the interior decorators and the well-known television moralist who had followed her example, to try to find herself. Instead of running after other people, it was they who came to see her. At the centre of her cultivated wilderness of rhododendrons and mouldering willows and giant rose-bushes she had had the courage to sit it out alone. She had mastered the art of the telephone and by the time she was forty-eight she had built up her much talked of agency for the discovery and promotion of young starlets.

Some said she was a wicked woman and her former husband, describing her to friends as if she had been a hunting tigress he had just got up the tree ahead of, used to say that she had no feelings at all. In this he was mistaken.

Men were right to treat women like slaves, she told herself. Most women liked it that way. They had never known anything else. Maslyn's husband had wanted sons, ah, how he had wanted sons! Well, she had provided him with a couple and had to admit that she felt more complete for having done so.

What did Jean Fenwick know about freedom? She had never even had a child. Her words were empty. No doubt like all the other women journalists she had met she too was a betrayer of her sex, meekly accepting a special role which confined her to articles about food and clothes or, worse still, about men of affairs as seen from the woman's angle: 'I married a genius,' 'A harem window on the world,' 'The hand that rocks the cradle drops the bomb'. Deliberately she tramped through a puddle which stretched from one side of Lacking High Street to the other. Yet there was something there. The woman had a sense of deprivation worth working on.

She was aware of being stared at through a window hung with lumps of raw meat. Slick, slick, the burly butcher was sharpening his knife and his women customers were showing their appreciation of his remarks. Let them laugh, the poor bitches. But she never felt conspicuous nowadays, as she had when she was married and went out shopping as they did. Most of them lapped up the rubbish women journalists served them. 'When the Beast returns from his labours the golden rule is never to let him catch you with your hair down. Always try to leave that last fifteen minutes for a fresh-up and a long cool look at yourself. If pressed for time, and even the best organised housewife has those kind of days, save just five minutes to give yourself an inspection and a whiff of something "candlelit", though never too much, by the by. Also how few of us realise that the back of the head is as important as the front! Remember HE sees you in the round!'

She had read that once while waiting to have her hair done, in the days before she had cut it off.

There were those who said that, alone, she would go mad, that she needed her London friends as a fly needs garbage. That had been after Randy had found a younger mother figure to ride pillion with him. She had begun to act like every other woman she had ever despised, slopping gin, buttonholing strangers, telephoning her friends and finally gravitating to a well-known, trendy psychiatrist who explained that the first thing she had to do was to get rid of her hang-ups about women's rights because these were the product of her own deficiencies and fantasies, or words to that effect. This had made her so angry that she had resolved there and then to leave London and face her situation alone. So she had taken that awesome one-way train ride into the dark tunnel and she had come out into the light with her self-respect newborn.

Men have their problems, too, her husband had told her (or had it been Randy?), a fact she was well aware of, having gone into a men's lavatory once and seen the wild claims and piteous appeals scrawled there. She had felt sorry, she had told Randy (or had it been her husband?), but really she had no more time to cut sandwiches and bandage heads in the causes of men. She had no more time. She had to find out who and what she was and that would take her the rest of her life.

At the chemists she collected a three-guinea pot of cream guaranteed to stave off wrinkles, then drove back to her house, shutting and locking the drive gates behind her. The drive was a tunnel through trees whose branches closed over it, letting in shafts of filtered light. She would have a bath and perhaps a tiny smoke. She was basking in the anticipated delight of a solitary evening when she saw the battered Mini standing before her door.

'Ghose! Honestly! You promised never to feed that foul thing in the house. Get it out of here! What are you back for, anyway? I thought you had to get to London.'

The young Indian, who was trying to feed a small alligator which was spreadeagled on her kitchen table, ignored her.

'I won't have it near the food!'

'I think he is sick.'

'Filthy they are. Why aren't you in London?'

'I got tired and I thought I would stay another day, so I came back.'

'Tired? Wow! No wonder India is in a state of collapse.'

'Don't be like that, Maslyn. You know I can get tired in the mind.'

'Look out, it's moving. Take it to the shed. It's quite capable of laying one of those beastly beer-coloured eggs in a minute.'

'It is a male.'

'You're so futile, Ghose.' She had visions of the alligator getting into the mill stream, which ran beside the house, making its way to Lacking and ending up in the butcher's or the pub. There would be a scandal and her privacy would be endangered because of this selfish boy's squalid affection for reptiles. The thought momentarily depressed her.

'Why do you never get dressed? That's another thing.'

'Because I am more comfortable like this. Why do you nag at me?'

'I don't nag.'

'I thought you were such a great scout for freedom.'

'Freedom isn't the same as filth and I don't dig that walking handbag there, so take it out of my kitchen.'

'*You* are an old bag,' said the boy complacently. He picked up the alligator and held it out to her. The creature twisted in his hands, but Maslyn held her ground.

'Bite her,' said the boy. The creature's eyes were like dead beech-leaves covered with spawn.

'This is ridiculous.' She was conscious of behaving as her husband might have done. 'You're such a slob, Ghose. You talk about writing and all you do is drink and waste time. I thought you'd be gone when I got back. I'm annoyed now. It's not funny any more.'

'Old bag.' He stuck out a pink tongue.

'Very crushing,' she said.

'It is I who am bored at this place,' he suddenly burst out. 'I have too many young friends, yes, boys and girls also, who are loving me. We have a good time because we love our youth and we do not worry about things as you do.'

'I worry only about . . . I don't worry, I just hate this mess and . . . and your insincerity. I was stupid enough to think you had something to say.'

The boy put the alligator back on the table, where it sat, flexing a muscle in its cheek.

'It is not what I say you like but having a boy in your bed to ruffle his hair and give you his thing.'

'Nonsense.'

'Keeping me here like this, are you not ashamed?'

'Keeping you here? I can't wait for you to leave!'

'Me, I am a little ashamed that I should go to your bed.'

'You're a liar.'

At this he came at her and, stretching out a long, black hand, he pinched her bottom as hard as he could. Maslyn slapped him hard across the face and the alligator fell off the table and lay threshing and hissing on the linoleum.

'You've overstayed your welcome.' The tremble in her voice was almost imperceptible.

'Have I not satisfied you, memsahib?'

'Oh God! Yes, you were splendid. Now will you please get your clothes on and take your racial hang-ups somewhere else.'

'When I am good and ready.'

'I have people coming from London. They wouldn't understand.'

'If there is a young woman coming I will please her.'

'To think I mistook you for a serious revolutionary!'

'Black Power is not inconsistent with sexual satisfaction.'

'Revolutionaries have to be objective, so I'm afraid you'll never make it. You will drift. I know it. I can feel your vibrations. They tell me you will drift and get soft and in the end become a pimp, either in London or back in whatever overpopulated slum in the Punjab you first came from. You might even get a job in a newspaper office.'

'You are bitter.' The boy was nonetheless nettled.

'Don't be feeble. You know I'm telling the truth.'

'I will leave now because I am ready to do so.'

'Thank God for that.'

'You are tough and insensitive.'

'You are a bore.'

'That is an evasion.'

'What is?'

'To say someone is a bore in this context is to evade the issue and you are not usually evasive.'

'Are you offended with me?' she asked.

'No, disappointed. You are the same as the others. Everything is just so fine and dandy, isn't it, with your lover who is the obligatory, black-is-beautiful hue, but as soon as I put my alligator on your table you become hysterical and dull.'

'You can't put me down. That's my job.'

'Can you lend me five pounds?' He was cradling the alligator in his arms and blowing down its nostrils, which it seemed to enjoy.

'Yes.'

After he had gone she scrubbed the kitchen table, sniffed it, and scrubbed again. The incident had been unpleasant but it was over. In any case, she told herself, dignity was for slaves.

9

'Bring out the dog's head of the Governor! Punish the criminal, fascist murderer!'

Pacing about inside Government House, which a reporter had described the day before as being 'alert behind its barbed wire', the Governor of Hong Kong heard but did not understand. In due course an interpreter would type out the insults of the demonstrators in English and place them on his desk.

The Governor paced not to induce thought but to compensate for exercise denied him by the emergency. His garden was planted now with coils of wire, booby traps and spikes.

The cry firecrackered down the line, leaping the gaps between the demonstrators, who were drawn up in uneven formations along one side of the street which ended at the Governor's residence, before whose unpromising, padlocked gates each group in turn presented itself to read out to the half-turned back of a sergeant of Marines, just visible behind the railings, grievances and selections from Mao Tse-Tung.

There were several thousand demonstrators, each waving Mao's *Thoughts* bound in red plastic, creating the effect from a distance of a field of poppies seething under a high wind.

The Governor called for tea and went to sit in a long room in which the furniture rode like a flotilla in a quiet harbour, a tired, unflustered man attended by a young captain from a good regiment, who brought him a summary of the London press coverage of the emergency.

Having satisfied himself that none of the reports contained

errors of fact too damaging to his administration, he laid them aside. Interpretations and opinions did not interest him at this stage. The situation required will-power and tactical imagination and he had a fair share of both. The key was the morale of his police force, which was high and had to be kept that way.

He began to pace again.

The demonstrators in the street beyond his grounds did not so much dispose of space as fill it and flow out of it, unlike the Chinese police who were lining the gutter three deep on the opposite kerb. The constables wore riot masks and carried clubs and shields, which gave them the appearance of characters out of a Chinese opera. Perhaps because they were defending property their faces were composed, whereas those of the demonstrators had a schizoid mobility.

While the demonstrators were waiting in their white shirts and cotton trousers to take their turn at the gates, which they seemed to be trying to puff down with their slogans, their faces were as cold as clay and when they raised their right arms to elevate the Red Book the movement seemed perfunctory, yet no sooner did their leaders give the order to move than their eyes began to flash and their mouths flowered into black blossoms and there was nothing simulated about their instant rage as they yelled out the dogmas of their mystical, earthly, soldierly, fatherly, ancestral leader, the Chairman, whose face shone like a mottled moon from the frontispiece of each of their plastic-covered bibles.

'These commies are like shy lovers the way they shuffle past the police kinda glancing at them sideways!' Since no one responded, Koltz repeated his analogy. 'Shy goddam lovers, the jerks!' Koltz was strung with cameras and his pockets were swollen with rolls of unborn film.

Like prompters to the principal actors, the press were strolling about in the no-man's land between the students and the police, accompanied by two television teams which crawled down the lines of demonstrators looking for telling close-ups.

'Andy Burns, for God's sake!'

'Well, I'll be damned.'

'You've lost weight.'

'I sure as hell have.'

'I hardly knew you.'

It shows, Andy thought. Of course it does. He felt feverish, as he usually did by noon. The optimism with which he had confronted his situation earlier on that day had gone. He was unable to take his mind off the pictures he had seen in the medical dictionary, now lodged on his bedside table. As the pressmen moved up and down, Andy moved with them, glad to belong.

'Gentlemen, not too near, if you please. We don't want anything unexpected to happen.' Ignoring this advice from a British police inspector, a cameraman crept closer, angling a face into his lens until its owner, a pigtailed girl student, broke ranks and hit the lens with her book. A boy joined her, trying to block the lens with the palm of his hand. The cameraman, whose equipment was supported on an aluminium brace round his shoulders, slapped the boy's hand away while continuing to film. At once twenty more demonstrators surrounded him, shaking their fists at him and jabbing him with their elbows. The sound man, who was attached to the cameraman by a wire, began pulling at it like a fish on a hook.

'Silly bugger, hasn't he been in a demo before?'

'German, I should think.'

'Looks like it.'

Police encircled the swaying group and the inspector coaxed the angry cameraman away. The demonstrators returned to their formation and a pattern was restored, both the students and the police accepting a self-denying ordinance by which neither crossed to the other's side of the street. Later on, some random act would precipitate the first trickle of blood down a student's scalp or a constable's cheek and the pattern would change.

Looking down at the scene from a mound of gravel and dirt from which wild palms drew meagre nourishment, Dan Fenwick could see from past experience that neither students nor police saw each other yet as individuals but rather as indivisible parts of a whole, a body of police, a mass of demonstrators. There were the police, identically masked, and there were the students, masked also in identical self-righteousness, and there were the gentlemen of the press, he permitted himself a sneer, and here on this mound was himself. No one, he thought, dared look into another's eyes and say, 'This is my enemy'. No one believed that eventually he could be cut off from his collective identity and that it would be his lips alone that would be opening to scream all by themselves.

On leaving Sally that morning he had thrust such thoughts to the bottom of his mind, slammed a manhole cover over them, ashamed of harbouring them at all. His nervous energy was immense and after a bath, a shave and a stiff drink he had made himself do a hard morning's work at the US Consulate sifting monitored translations of Chinese radio broadcasts. But by noon he could no longer keep up the pretence. His depression returned. It was as if Sally had given him a shot in the arm which, wearing off, had left him with an addict's craving to see her again before their evening appointment.

He had gone back to the street where she had been filming, but it was thronged with ordinary people and although the chalk marks were still on the pavement the balcony was empty and the doorway in which Gaston had lounged was shut. At her hotel they had told him that she was out watching the demonstration and it was in the hope of finding her and not from any professional consideration that he was scanning the crowd now. The demonstration, of which he had seen so many before, seemed far less real to him than the now persistent sense of that unseen something which he apprehended to be on the move. He could sense it between the shoulders and the banners and the insects whirling in the hot sky. It was like glue pouring out from between the joints of a table, like the cracks between buildings, yet unlike either of these things. It was as if his life was rushing noisily out of him, down the shafts of sunlight coming through the wild palms, and being eaten up in the dust above the banners.

His reporter's vocabulary was as dead as the stones under his feet. A sliver of mirror glass, embedded in the ground, beamed a hot white spot onto his arm. He wondered how he would have described that light if he had had to report on it. Would he have compared it with those flames now playing over the straw effigy the students had propped in front of the Governor's gates on a pyre of cardboard boxes? The flames were transparent, like burning air, sunlit flames, whereas the spot on his hand was dense and milky. Inertia weighed on him and he put out a hand to support himself against a tree.

Smoke was rising above the heads of the demonstrators and police. He heard cries and the sound of a gong.

The students watched the flames with expressions of nostalgia. If English farm labourers smile secretly before a bonfire because somewhere in the closed cells of their history they are relishing the burning of a great house, a mountain of portraits, a witch, so the demonstrators began to dream without knowing it about fragrant sacrificial fires to propitiate ancestors.

'Burning the Governor's effigy. Usual thing.'

109

'Did you know we're not allowed to go to the cable office after curfew?'

'Yes we are, they're issuing special passes.'

'No, but they still say we have to be in by eleven.'

'Who do?'

'The police, I guess.'

The student who had ignited the effigy had pinned a cardboard face to it with rouged cheeks and a pair of rather slit blue eyes. He now took a paper from his shirt pocket, smoothed it out and began to declaim from it in Mandarin.

Twenty-four hours before Andy would have worried because he could not follow what the man was saying and would have sought a Chinese colleague for a translation, but now, watching the young man's taut neck muscles and slightly protuberant teeth, all he could think was how healthy he looked.

He probed his own neck where it hurt him to swallow, but felt nothing unusual. When he touched what he thought to be the seat of the discomfort it seemed to have moved. It was not a big pain, only a kind of twitch like the sharp tick of a clock somewhere inside his neck. He made spittle and swallowed again, stroking the pain as it coursed, spread itself up the side of his neck to his earlobe. His notion of a gland was of something dark of uneven consistency, rather like a clam dipped in red sauce.

'Got a sore throat?' Koltz asked him. 'All the dust these monkeys are kicking up.'

'If I was their age I'd have better things to do than set fire to straw dummies,' Andy said.

'I'd be on the beach,' Koltz said.

Of course it was the dust. He had overlooked it, although it was whirling about everywhere. He felt warm towards Koltz for the explanation.

'I got a poisoned finger,' Koltz was telling him.

'That's dead white corpuscles,' Andy told him. 'That's what pus is.'

'How do you know that?'

With difficulty Andy restrained himself from explaining. He had formed a vivid picture from the turgid prose of the medical dictionary of the march of the red and white corpuscles, the red carrying oxygen to the tissues and the white warding off infections, of the factories in the marrow of the bones where more whites were produced to replace the dead ones, of the numerical inferiority of whites to reds and of the sudden outburst of the whites, which began to multiply faster and faster, never stopping, a noiseless, blind plethora.

Under the subheading 'Treatment' it had said, 'Unhappily there is no known cure,' adding that a new, experimental drug called by some initial or number had abated lymphosarcoma in an eleven-year-old boy who was now 'alive and well' and back at school. Andy intended to tell Schreiber about this discovery. He might just not have heard of it.

'If the US monopoly capitalists insist in pushing their policies of aggression and war, the day is bound to come when they will be hanged by the people of the whole world.' The student stretched his own neck as he said this and spittle flew from his lips. 'The same will apply to the running dogs who are their accomplices! Neo-colonialism and colonialism are the disease to be ruthlessly cut out.'

'What's he saying?' someone asked.

'Ask me another,' Andy replied.

'Look at that dog,' Koltz said.

The dog was lurching along the road looking for a way through the barrier of legs. Its fur had been eaten by mange, leaving blotches of crummy purple skin. A policeman thwacked it with his club and the dog yelped feebly and veered to the other side of the road, where a student kicked it in the rump.

'Get the dog,' one of the TV producers told his cameraman. 'Quick. It's symbolic. They're going to hit it again.'

Cameras followed the dog from blow to blow.

'Leave him alone!'

'Hey, it's the kid from last night. Cute!'

'Just leave him, he's harming no one!' Sally Maine, who had slung a camera over the shoulder of her denim suit in order to pass as a press woman, was upbraiding a grinning Chinese policeman. 'He wasn't harming anyone,' she said. 'I suppose that's what none of you can bear!' Unsure of what she had meant by this cryptic remark, she tried to reach out for the dog and would have touched it had Koltz not stopped her.

'Watch it, baby, you get rabies that way.'

'I don't see what he finds so amusing,' she said, glaring at the policeman.

'They smile when they're embarrassed,' Andy said. 'They're not like us.'

'You wouldn't want them to stick a six-inch needle in your unblemished midriff.' Koltz made it sound like an assault.

'You go mad and start biting people,' Andy said.

'Movie star bites policeman.'

'Can't someone do something?' She made a gesture of helpless frustration and it was then that Dan saw her.

He had stooped to pick up a stone which had resisted the pressure of his foot and was wondering what a piece of flint was doing so far from its natural formation when he saw the flash of her blonde hair. She appeared to be chatting to a policeman, creating a situation around her which seemed to Dan to be as distinctive as the one she had created the night before in the Press Club. She was giving meaning to the previously meaningless lines of students and police.

At first he thought she must be filming, that Panni had

subsumed the demonstration to his shooting script, but she was alone. He began to walk rapidly down the little hill.

'The poor thing,' she was saying. She thought she had attracted too much attention and was looking for a way of extricating herself. 'It's half dead already.'

'That's Dan Fenwick on that hill,' Andy said. He was thinking that if she put her hands on his forehead they would be excitingly cool.

'Moses comes down from the mountain,' Koltz sneered.

'Dan's a fine reporter,' Andy said.

'That guy over there, now that's a really great newspaperman.' Koltz indicated a portly man in a polo shirt who was making a place for himself in front of the police lines in order to perorate into his camera. 'Bill Smiley's a household word in the States.'

'Only on the east coast,' Andy said.

'Are *you* a household word on the east coast?'

'Like Persil,' Sally said.

'Can you get the cops in behind me?' Smiley was calling to his cameraman.

'Over to the left, Bill, no too far, back aways, O.K. O.K., stay there, I got you with a shield and a club, we're in business.'

'Are you a friend of Dan's?' she asked Andy. 'What's he like?'

'If you're on a story with him he's great.' Andy thought of Dan kneeling beside his sleeping bag on the greasy groundsheet in the Marine tent holding a basin and cloth.

'Here comes the wet blanket,' he had said, something funnier than that, actually.

Men are nice the way they are so reticent about each other, she thought. Women try to blab it all out at once.

'. . . aware that only a few miles away across the peninsula the troops of their sacred heartland stand in their legions

113

under a heaven they firmly believe to have handpicked China as the centre of true enlightenment. Yet the crux of the problem here is this teeming entrepot . . .' Smiley droned on while his sound man knelt over his tape recorder in an attitude of devotion until it was kicked out of reach by a demonstrator. The camera toppled and Smiley found himself talking into snarling, spitting Chinese faces before he was elbowed aside by the charging police.

Gratefully, students and police embraced. The police came in waves, but allowed themselves to be outflanked. Both sides broke into choppy little groups which met, fell apart, foamed elsewhere.

Side by side with the peaks of violence were troughs of inertia. It was in one of these that Sally found herself after losing her feet in the first rush. She had never been hit by a man before and she had found it stimulating as well as scaring to be shouldered aside by policemen whose faces grazed hers while their eyes stared past her. Buckles and belts dug into her knees jabbed her legs. She had seen the gold fillings in the mouth of one corporal and wondered how he could have afforded them. Half-winded, she watched a pack of men trying to free their elbows in order to strike at each other more effectively. Two students fell at her feet, to be followed by a policeman who had lost his helmet. The three of them knelt side by side, shoulders touching.

She saw a student tug a policeman's mask off and jam a broken bottle into his face with a noise between a snarl and a sigh. The policeman cringed, his eyes filling with blood. The student tried to get away, but another policeman clubbed him into a kneeling position, where he remained as the blows came down. Then suddenly the skirmish was over. The combatants broke from one another and swarmed into Sally's space. A girl who had seemed about to pass her turned without warning and tried to scratch her face. Sally had learned how to fight at her convent school and parried the attack with a back-handed movement of her right fist which happened to break the girl's glasses.

I know about you, Sally thought, looking into the short-sighted black eyes. She felt more at ease with the girl's malice than with the anger of the men, which seemed to her insatiable and finally hopeless.

The girl grabbed at the lapels of Sally's denim jacket and shrieked for help. Sally's arms were held from behind by several pairs of hands. They will mark me, she thought. She wants me to be as ugly as she is.

Bodies pressed against her, and by a reflex action she tried to shut her legs. Someone took hold of her neck from behind and began pushing her head forward. She realised with revulsion that they intended her to kneel. Beheadings in Japanese prison camps flickered through her mind as slowly they forced her face nearer and nearer to the ground. Did they want her to kiss the earth? She had heard of that, too. Inches from her mouth a score of rather small shoes were kicking up yellow dust. She was beginning to choke when they made her tilt her face upwards without allowing her to straighten her back. Above her stood the girl she had hit, her red book open in her hand and borrowed glasses sliding down her nose. Satisfied that Storm was subdued and attentive she began to read from the book.

When Dan found her kneeling on the ground his impulse was not to interfere but to stand and watch. No one seemed to notice him, so he remained where he was on the fringe of the crowd, telling himself he would intervene later.

Like a pig in a slaughterhouse, she thought. All round her were faces. A few were gleeful, contemptuous, sanctimonious, but most had the impersonal look of medical students on a ward visit. She tried to move her arms, but someone had her wrists and shoulder. Her camera dangled below her chin. It was not true that all the Chinese looked alike. If only she could speak to one of them. She could see no sign of police or journalists. She wished she was with Gaston and Panni, sitting in a hotel somewhere hearing how disobedient she had been to come out against their advice.

A fly began to dig about in the corner of her mouth. She shook her head but it crawled onto her lower lip. When she tried to brush her face against her shoulder someone bent over from behind and rapped her head gently with his knuckles.

'I can't speak Chinese,' she said. 'I'm sorry.' She caught the eye of a young man standing beside her pigtailed mentor, but he put a finger to his lip as if silencing a child. The girl reader raised the pitch of her voice indignantly, only to be drowned out by another Chinese voice shouting through a loudspeaker. The girl shut her red book and whoever was holding Sally's wrists released them. The crowd of students began to move away from her. No one looked back and soon she was alone in a widening circle of roadway. A few feet away from her she saw the dog. It was lying on its side with its legs stretched stiffly out. Beyond it a fire truck had begun to jet water at the students. Dan Fenwick, his clothes wringing wet, ran towards her out of the retreating crowd.

'Come on,' he said. He was standing over her, extending his hand.

'No, you come down here,' she said. He squatted beside her. 'If it's good enough for that poor dog it's all right for us.'

'The dog is better dead.'

'Don't dare say that!' She was on her feet, camera swinging. He wondered if she was going to have hysterics.

'Take a look at it,' he said.

It lay among broken glass and dropped flags, its nose bedded into the dust, its neck hunched and stiff. Its body, scarred from other battles, showed no sign of a last, fatal blow.

'It just gave up,' he said.

'Poor lamb.'

'Do you still think it's not better dead?'

'Certainly I do. You're like my father. He used to pick up stray cats and have them put to sleep because the idea of their being hungry and cold upset him. That's sick! No one is better off dead. While there's life there's hope.'

'Were you afraid?'

'Of course. Then I got bored.'

'You didn't look bored.'

'You saw? Well, thank you very much. You made notes, I suppose. You might have tried to help me!'

'I did,' he lied. 'I couldn't get through. Anyway you said last night you wanted to find out what fear was like.'

'I thought you were a man.'

'I thought you were the kind of woman who wouldn't say "I thought you were a man".'

'But actually to stand there and watch me reacting! It's so mean . . . and vulgar!'

'I wasn't just standing there. I had only just located you. I was trying to get through to you when they all ran away.'

'How can you say that dog is better off dead?'

'I take it back.'

'Were you really trying to locate me?'

'Really. Otherwise who could I have dinner with to-night?'

It was a moment of self-indulgence in which they both savoured the delicious anticlimax that precedes the next, the inevitable forward thrust.

'Ah,' she said, 'here come the rest of the heroes.'

'Hey, that was real movie stuff,' Koltz said.

'I was knocked over that fence there,' Andy chimed in.

117

'Some bastard hit me with a lump of wood.'

'They kicked his ass.' Andy smiled.

'I kicked one of them in the groin. I would have kicked his face if there had been time.' The German cameraman was squatting beside the dead dog taking a close-up. 'Can someone please shield my lens for me?' Koltz obliged, leaning over the dog's body. 'All in the day's work,' he said to Sally. 'I don't suppose they told you to expect this back home.'

'Hey, you look a bit shook up,' Andy told her. 'Can I take you to your hotel?'

'I'll do that,' Dan said.

'My car is nearer than yours.'

'Mine's behind that mound,' Dan said. He took her arm and tried to steer her away, but she hung back.

'I had an idea to cover that dog with something.'

'Sure.' Andy looked puzzled.

'Let me.' Dan picked up one of the communist flags left by a demonstrator and placed it over the dog.

'Can I take a shot of you by the dog?' Koltz asked her.

'No.' Koltz shrugged. 'Can't we have a drink somewhere?' she asked Dan.

'Yes, let's,' Andy answered.

By the time they were seated in the Pagoda Andy's euphoria had worn off and he was feeling like a third person in an untriangular situation.

'Let's have another drink,' he said.

'We still have one.'

'Come on, what's the matter with you guys? You want me to drink alone?'

'We're still drinking. You have one.'

'That's not the point. Anyway, this is some dump to bring a young lady.'

'It's my local,' Dan said.

'Well, it's not the place I'd bring someone.'

'You want a palm court orchestra?' she asked, looking at Dan.

'He wants a soda fountain and a nice, motherly blonde with big breasts.'

'Speak for yourself,' Andy said. 'I want an occasion, goddamit.'

'You speak for yourself.'

'Oh I do, my friend, I do.'

His second drink restored Andy's good temper for a while. As he tilted his head and felt the ice clinking against his teeth and the cool, slim glass in his hand, he wished such moments could last for ever, but an ice-cube slopped over the rim and skidded across the floor.

'Hey, I show you something,' he said loudly. He retrieved the cube and, standing up, held it to his fly and ejected it through his finger and thumb. The cube bounced across the bar.

'What am I?' he asked Sally. 'I'm an eskimo having a pee. Get it?'

One of the girls at the bar laughed. A waiter picked up the ice-cube and threw it into an ashtray. The Pagoda was empty but for the staff. The gold paper had been stuck back on the walls and a pale rectangle marked the place where a broken mirror had been taken down. The street door was open and a fist of white light thrust through it, splitting the room.

'Music,' Andy announced. 'Let's get this show on the road.'

'He doesn't usually drink. He usually eats polo mints,' Dan said. 'I suppose he's excited by you.'

'He seemed depressed to me,' she said. 'He's like you a bit to look at, did you know? Only he's less dissipated-looking.'

'He's all right.'

'You're tight with your compliments, aren't you?'

'I mean he's a good chap.'

'He admires you very much, he told me.'

'I'll put on a Beatles for you,' Andy said. 'Do you care for the Beatles?'

'Not much,' Sally said. 'I prefer the Animals.'

'They don't have any.'

'Yes, Animals,' a bar girl said. She came listlessly to Andy's side and ran her lacquered fingernail up and down the list of song titles on the jukebox. 'Number forty,' she said. 'Sky Pilot.'

The selector arm prowled sideways and plucked a disc off the rack. 'You buy me a drink?' The girl's face was green in the dim light coming from the jukebox. Andy shook his head. A guitar thumped before a rising electronic storm, beating out an ominous rhythm. A voice of hoarse, insistent authority began to sing.

Andy mooned at the door of the men's room, then flopped onto a stool at the bar. He hoped that Sally and Dan would wonder why he was sitting apart from then, but neither seemed to be giving him a thought. Their heads were close together. She was telling him about her part in the goddam picture. How dared they be so engrossed with one another when he was there two tables away, dying? He wanted to shout at them to look at him, to hear his blood roaring inside him, to help him. It was unfair. Dan knew nothing. What right had he?

The chorus climbed higher and higher, exulting, accusing. Andy clenched his fists and the frenzy passed.

A Chinese boy of about six was hanging around outside the door. When Andy caught his eye he stuck his fingers into his mouth and began to swing to and fro, using the door as a pivot. Andy beckoned him, but the boy walked away backwards, looking serious. Andy fumbled a coin from his pocket and the boy crept towards him among the tables, along the beam of sunlight, coming to rest with his bare stomach pressing against the arm of Andy's chair. His fist closed over the coin. Andy tried to tousle his black hair, but he dodged away. One of the bar girls released a belt of rapid Chinese which sent the boy hopping back into the street, after which she slid into the chair beside Andy and put her hand on his knee. Andy took the hand and placed it on the table. The boy's eyes had darkened with thoughts.

'Nice kid,' Andy said.

'My son.'

'You're kidding.'

'No kidding.' They both looked at the doorway. The boy ducked out of sight, rematerialising as an eye and a tuft of hair.

'No school today,' the girl said. 'Plenty trouble.'

'Where's his dad?'

The girl laughed as if Andy had made a joke. 'Man comes one night, I make mistake.'

'What kind of man? Chinese man?'

'No, no, no.'

'American man?' It pleased him to think that the boy might be half American. Poor little bastard. For a moment, taking in the bar, the jukebox, the silhouettes of Dan and Sally, who were leaning towards one another smiling, he saw himself as the boy's father, paying him through school, teaching him baseball, rehabilitating the mother. Better to be a sick step-father than a sick nobody and anyway she would bear him a child of his own.

'He Polish man.' The girl slapped the table softly with her hand.

'Good?'

'Very good. Very, very good.'

The music ended. The taste of whisky in his mouth had already gone stale.

'Buy me drink,' the girl murmured.

'O.K., O.K., you name it.' Dan was passing his table on the way to the men's room. He did not even look in Andy's direction. When he returned he found Andy sitting in his place. He had picked up the flint Dan had found that morning and was holding it out to Sally in his open palm.

'Stroke it.'

She touched it with her finger. 'It's hard.'

'They made churches out of flint that never fell down,' Dan said. He dragged up a third chair.

'They made arrowheads, I don't know about churches.' Andy's voice was surly.

'It's so cold,' Sally said.

'Sure. You could stroke it for ever and it wouldn't hot up.' Sally removed her finger.

'It needs another flint to spark it off against,' Dan said.

'Isn't that sweet?' said Andy.

'No.'

'People die because they haven't any friends. There was an old guy in Milton once who did just that.' Andy was aware that they wanted him to go and this made him more angry than ever. 'No one cared about him, they were all so goddam busy with one another, so he didn't speak to anyone for months and then he killed himself.'

'If I hadn't got any friends I'd go out and find one,' Sally said.

'I'm not short of friends,' Andy replied.

'No one said you were,' Dan said.

'He lived in a rooming-house.'

'Andy's romantic,' Dan said. 'He thinks old people have the right to be cosy and that women are whiter than white and that men are dirty seducers, except him, that is.'

'Women are nearer the muck than any man,' Sally said.

'I'm not about to listen to that stuff.'

'But it's true. From the moment they begin to menstruate

they see how close life is to muck. It makes them more down-to-earth than men.'

'I won't have this!' Andy jumped to his feet and thumped the table with his fists.

'Why are you being so aggressive?' Dan asked him softly.

'I won't have you living at my expense!'

'What in hell's name is that supposed to mean?'

'You're so clever, work it out. You messed Jean up, you let her kill her baby. You drove her into a nut-house. Sure he did. He drove his wife nuts, or has he already told you that?'

Even as he was speaking Andy saw what he must do and his anger changed course and became more calculating. He would have a child and he would have it by Jean.

'Why don't you sit down if you want to talk?' Dan said.

'Jesus! This guy never loses his cool. He oughta hit me for the things I been saying and all he does is say "you oughta sit". He's like that goddam stone there. He's hard and cold, that's what he is!'

'You're being hysterical.'

'Just you wait!' This was to Sally.

'What's wrong?' she said. She was more put out by one angry man than any mob.

'You really want to know?'

'Of course.'

'Then give me a baby.' This was muttered at the back of Andy's throat.

'I don't get it.'

'O.K., forget it. I'm leaving.'

'You put my flint in your pocket,' Sally said.

'Let him,' Dan told her.

'You gave it to me!'

'Well, now I'm giving it to Andy.'

'Why don't you two can it? Just can it!' Andy tossed the flint back onto the table.

'I was going to explain about Jean,' Dan said when Andy had gone.

'It doesn't matter.'

'It does to me.'

'Is he always like that?'

'Far from it.' Dan felt powerful and at ease.

'What did he mean about killing a baby?'

'That's what I wanted to explain.'

10

At the Press Club, where he met a Chief Inspector of Police who had looked in to answer questions and down a few Scotches, Andy typed out two stories, one each for his American and English customers.

'What I would like to make perfectly clear,' said the Chief Inspector, 'and I speak frankly, is that the majority, one might even say the large majority, of the inhabitants of Hong Kong are law-abiding citizens who are doing very nicely thank you under the existing administration and want nothing to do with communism or any other kind of ism.'

As he issued this dictum sirens were wailing twenty stories below and smoke from a burning garage hazed over Kowloon.

'How far is Peking mixed up in these riots?' someone asked.

'Sir, I'm not a mind-reader, just a simple policeman.'

'There must be data about this. Observers from Canton are out there in the streets now. The point is, are they there to restrain the local Red Guards or stir them up? And where does the local central committee of the Communist Party stand in this context?'

'No comment.'

'Will British troops be called out to assist the police?'

'The short answer to that is no.'

Listening to several journalists debating as to whether the problem was economic, political, ideological, or racial, or politico-economic, politico-racial-economic, or racial-ideological-politico-economic, Andy decided that the theme for his British readers would consist of the sterling behaviour of the island's police force under provocation, while for the Americans he would stress the acute poverty in which most inhabitants of the British colony lived. The machinations of Peking would provide the accompaniment to both. Pounding at his Olivetti portable with two fingers, his tongue protruding from the corner of his mouth, Andy suspended all other thoughts from his mind. The result, more descriptive than analytical, was in a style both genial and direct.

In the elevator afterwards an old man with cataracted eyes asked Andy if it was true that riots were happening in Singapore, too.

'It's our next stopover,' he said.

'So what?' his wife interjected. 'They're rioting in the States as well. Where you from, son?'

'Milton, Kansas.'

'Oh really? Isn't that nice! We're from Oberon.'

'I'm John D. Ruskin and this is my wife, Betty.'

'Andy Burns. Glad to know you.'

They all shook hands, sinking earthwards.

'There's no place like Kansas,' the man said.

'We think so,' his wife added. 'I suppose you do also.'

'I haven't been there for nine years.'

'Well, I doubt if things will have changed much, though it wouldn't surprise me if the population in a small place like that wasn't smaller now than it would have been nine years ago. Young folks up and leave just as soon as they can. John says there'll only be the old people left soon. Are you married?'

'No, ma'm, but I plan on being just as soon as I can.'

'Why, isn't that nice! Is she an American girl?' The woman lowered her voice despite the fact that there were only the three of them in the elevator, reflected a thousand times in rose-pink mirrors.

'I haven't met anyone definite yet.'

'Don't go marrying one of those Asian women, son,' the man said. 'Some of the boys did that in Japan and not one of those marriages worked, not one.'

'You marry a nice American girl.'

'Thank you.'

'Mr Ruskin and I were intending to go shopping for silk, but the management said we should have to have an armed escort so we decided that it would not be a relaxing thing to do.'

'Nor very dignified.'

'So we're just going to have an early supper and read.'

'Well, it sure was nice talking to you. Good luck. Take it easy now.'

'Thanks. Same to you.'

Loudspeakers poking through the upper windows of the Bank of China shook with the volume of communist songs. From an opposite building the British were broadcasting modern Chinese dance tunes. Below this electronic battle crowds of people surged about in the cool evening air.

Earlier, a communist Chinese border guard had been shot by his own comrades as he tried to dash across the mud and concrete which separated the New Territories from the People's Republic, and on a balcony in Kowloon a child, caught in crossfire between snipers and police, had been cut to pieces. Now everything was bathed in a bright, tranquil light and a mild sun, declining over the water, seemed to neutralise the loudspeakers and made the police look out of place as they shunted about the city in their riot trucks, in which they sat facing one another in neat rows, their clubs and rifles upright between their knees. Equally pointless seemed the swinging snakes of demonstrators who wound in and out among the already broken glass of the smart shops.

By the same benign light British soldiers, concealed discreetly in their barracks, checked their equipment. On the quiet hills crowning the island European businessmen sipped their sundowners and tuned in to the BBC.

By the time Andy had got to the clinic darkness had fallen and the old mansion was scarcely visible in its black garden. He wished he had not behaved so badly at the Pagoda. If he lost control like that out of envy or whatever it was he would end up like a jellyfish; the harbour was full of them, as big as hub-caps and poisonous to the touch.

As he drove between the entrance gates two green eyes blinked at him and were gone. The front door was locked and there was no sign of a bell.

At the back of the house, where there was a smell of rotting vegetables, a light showed through an imperfectly drawn blind. Andy knocked gently on a louvered door before turning the handle. A conversation was going on deeper inside the house. He walked down a darkened corridor and the voices grew louder. They were coming from behind a second door, under which bright light streamed.

When Andy knocked the conversation stopped as if a tape machine had been switched off. The door opened inwards.

'What do you want?' Schreiber's voice was as bleak as the naked bulb above his head. He was standing over a young Chinese who was lying on a couch. The boy was bare to the waist, his upper ribs covered with strips of plaster. Five more youths were sitting or standing in various states of undress. All had cuts and bruises, some worse than others. Schreiber's Chinese assistant, who had been packing medical supplies into cardboard boxes, dropped a bottle, which smashed, spreading violet-coloured liquid.

'I wanted to speak to you.'

'The clinic is closed.'

'I won't take a moment.'

'It is still closed. I am very busy.'

Andy pulled the door to behind him.

'You don't even know what it's about,' he said.

'That is immaterial, the principle is the same.'

'Principle, hell. Can't you talk human?'

'Principles are not inhuman, Mr Burns. They are a way in which human beings articulate their higher purposes.'

'We were talking about me wanting a two-minute conversation and wanting it now. Go ahead with your salvage job on the Communist Party here, it won't bother me.'

'There may be a transport strike tomorrow,' Schreiber said. 'I'm packing up some simple things and these boys are taking them out to the first-aid posts in the housing estates for me.'

'You don't have to explain. I don't care whose side you're on.'

'No, I don't believe you do. That's the objectionable feature of western journalism. It has no real convictions. What did you want to ask me?'

'If I can have a child.'

'Why?'

'I want to know.'

'Why not?'

The boy on the couch winced as Schreiber pulled off a strip of plaster.

'You sure have a sweet bedside manner,' Andy said.

'I did not ask you to be my patient. I advised you to seek treatment in your own country, so don't expect me to hold your hand.'

'Your hands are full with the People's Republic, is that it?'

'I thought you did not take sides.'

'That's right, but neither do I get my satisfaction from an interpretation of history. I guess I'm too modest.'

'Ach, *mein Gott*! Too conceited, you mean. You Americans are all alike under the skin. Scratch it and out pours the same mock humility.'

From a cupboard Schreiber reached down a large, bell-shaped jar filled with pale, tea-coloured liquid in which a human foetus was suspended. The baby's perfectly formed mouth and eyes were shut.

'Now, take a look, my friend. That is what you want for your very own, right? Only you do not want it to perpetuate the race so that it might one day fulfil its great purposes. You want it so that it might take upon its shoulders the weight of your rapacious individualism. And you tell me you are modest!'

'You wake up one day with leukaemia and try to care about dialectical materialism. Just try!'

The foetus swayed gently as Schreiber tilted the jar back onto its shelf. 'You must try not to be sentimental,' he said. 'I know it is hard.'

'Charity begins at home in my book, Schreiber.'

'You don't understand.'

'I don't have to. I came here for a straight answer and I'm still waiting.'

The Chinese watched the two men's mouths, turning their heads this way and that as if at a tennis match.

'Very well. You can have your child, have several in the time you may have left, assuming you're normally healthy in that department. No trace of *your* disease will pass to the child.'

'Are you certain?'

'Do you doubt me?'

'No. Do I have to find another doctor now?'

'I would prefer it.'

'You're the only one here who's any good.'

'Go home, then.'

'I have no home.'

'So be it. I have already, as it happens, sent for your drugs. They should be here from Tokyo in a day or so and then we can begin.'

'Well, why are we arguing?'

'Because we're enemies.'

'I said I didn't care whose side you were on. I only want a doctor-patient relationship, don't I?'

'You only want this, you only want that. Has it never occurred to you that human experience does not admit in the end the credibility of these divisions and sub-divisions? If you are really a man you cannot in the end shirk the challenge of the all-or-nothing.'

'At least I don't want to prove my manhood by branding the whole human race. Look at Mao Tse-Tung, your hero. Look at all the people he's wiped out to prove his point.'

'Do you care?'

'No. Not really. But I would if I was there.'

'I want people to live with justice and dignity,' Schreiber said. 'To attain that state many must perish because many will obstruct.'

'You can't change human nature.'

'That is the kind of pap pessimism of conservatism. Tell me, were there any road-blocks on the way here?'

'Nope.'

'Perhaps you would be good enough to lift some of these people into town. Also these parcels of things. It would be safer for the boys than walking and you did say you weren't taking sides.'

'Sure.' Andy and the students looked at one another dubiously.

'Then you and I will meet the day after tomorrow. I will explain to you in detail the nature of the organisms involved and how, in your case, they malfunction. You can follow the course of treatment better that way and it should help you live with it, yes? As I said the other day. So, shall we all go home?'

Once Andy had gone, taking with him four Chinese students, each carrying several parcels of medical supplies, Schreiber walked with his assistant to a small bungalow in the grounds of the clinic, which had once housed a gardener or a cook. They entered the living-room, which was empty, and Schreiber invited his assistant to sit down.

'I will see about food,' he said.

His Javanese wife was not in the kitchen, so he walked through to their only bedroom. She was standing by the window, arranging flowers around a photograph frame, which contained a picture of a small boy. She turned and faced her husband defensively, her dark eyes flashing with suppressed emotion.

'Pala!' He spoke with gentle reproach. 'What is this nonsense? I have told you it is bad for you.' He took the flowers away from the picture, before which there was also a bowl of oil in which there floated a burning wick.

'He is mine,' she said.

'He is dead.'

She shook her head, watching him dismantle her little shrine.

'Now,' he said. 'Chong is outside waiting for dinner. Are we to turn him out hungry?'

He put out his hands to her, but she shrank away.

'What's this? You're not afraid of me?'

'No.'

'What then?'

'I will get the food.'

11

That night rain washed away the chalk marks that Panni's cameraman had made on the pavement. Dan Fenwick took Sally back to his flat and read her some of the unfinished play he had begun to write in the first year of his marriage. The pages of the manuscript were already yellowing round the edges.

When he had done she hesitated to comment, fearing he would find her facile. He waited for her to speak, to bite on the hook, but she was overawed by him. Truthfully she had been less concerned with what he had read than with the situation of his reading to her. This contained man had been trying to offer her a secret. She was grateful and now she wanted him to acknowledge that she was a rare one for having got it out of him.

Watching his nervous, absorbed face, his irritation when he missed a word or misread one, she had been thrilled by his striving, a feeling unspoiled by the intrusion of a rapidly suppressed vision, cinematic in origin, of Chopin and George Sand.

If she enjoyed the sudden advent of a salon, she was more fascinated by the distance, unconcealed by Dan, which lay between them, to which she responded by getting up and strolling about his flat, making him lounge after her.

'I wrote a play once,' she said, 'a ten-minuter for television, but no one took it up. Joe Orton read it, though, and said I should do another.'

'Who's Joe Orton?'

'Don't you know? He wrote some super plays and then he was murdered by his boy-friend with a hammer, you must have read about it. The friend got hung up about having less talent and being left behind by Joe or something and couldn't stand it.'

They were like two ships edging ever closer, boarding parties concealed. She snapped on the kitchen light, extinguished it, opened Kim's door, heard the soft bustle of his half waking and withdrew with a little gasp to settle in a window seat from which she could see the people in the flats opposite, busy as ants.

'Just look at them,' she said. 'They're like a hundred different plays all happening at once.'

'I used to think what fun it would be if they all leaned out of their windows one time and shook hands or something.'

'Oh, that's silly. It's far better as it is.'

'You can see better with the lights out. You can be a real voyeur.' He flicked up the switch and she melted away, a rim of light from outside burning round her head and the back of her neck and shoulders. Her face suggested itself by a movement of shadows as she craned this way and that. The hard rectangle of the window seemed to Dan to have been nothing until she had sat in it.

He came and sat beside her. Their shoulders touched.

'Do you watch them a lot?' she asked.

'No. They repeat themselves too much, you lose interest.'

'There'll come a day when you'll miss something really fantastic, a murder or something.'

'Oh, there's been one of those. I told you, people repeat themselves.'

'That's very cynical.'

'Well, what about Joe Orton, was that his name?'

They sighed simultaneously, she more noisily than he, at

the difficulty of communicating with one another enough even to leap the now incredibly narrow passage which lay between them. Someone had to be the attacker. Neither seemed sure enough.

'I have a friend,' she said, 'who lives in a flat like one of those, all exposed. A terrible thing happened to her just before I came away on this picture. The man she was living with walked out on her. Well, it wasn't the first time. He'd done it before, but this time it really broke her up and she took a lot of pills and someone in a flat opposite saw her on the floor or something. It was all as gruesome and sordid as possible and I visited her in hospital and she was in a terrible state, depressed and her mind wandering, but that might have been because they'd given her more drugs, I don't know. Anyway, I went to take her home the day they let her out and when we got back to her flat, which isn't too far from mine, something really macabre happened. There was this jacket and trousers of Robin's thrown over the back of a chair and she thought it was him, the way it was crumpled it looked like a figure. She didn't actually go and have a close look but she kind of looked sideways and went mad! It was horrid, she sort of shied like a horse and began raving. I got her into the bedroom and kept saying, "There's no one there, there's no one there," but she kept saying where was he, where was he, until I began to wonder myself. She never actually went and checked and it occurred to me later that she knew it was a coat and trousers all the time and just wanted an excuse to really let go.'

'What happened?'

'She went to sleep, having been given the umpteenth pill by me, and I went and folded up the dreaded jacket and trousers and put them away. That was the day before I came out here, so God knows how she is now. I'll find out when I get back.'

'Are you going back?'

135

'I told you earlier. The shooting is nearly over. Just a day or two after that Panni will go to London and look at rushes, he takes ages over that, then we'll do some studio in England, but not till autumn, I guess.'

'I hadn't realised.'

'What?'

'That you were going back so soon.'

'Well, the work is over. I have no reason to hang on.'

'Maybe one will present itself.'

'I like to know what I'm doing and why.'

'Do you like Panni?'

'I respect him. I don't know him enough to say about liking, he's so reserved. He won't explain things properly. I spend most of the time in a state of near panic about the part.'

'Does that other one, Gaston?'

'No! Gaston sails along, thinking he's a great interpretative actor, but really Panni feeds him every gesture; but me he just leaves to myself, except this morning after we were told to stop filming by the police he gave me a Coca-cola and we talked for half an hour and it was really wonderful, like he was explaining things between equals and I was the one person he had visualised for the part. It was great. He really is, he's terrific.'

He wanted to unbutton her blouse and get at her. The thought brought his hand into an upright position along the window ledge.

'What did you . . . Did you like my play?'

'Very much. Do you think you'll finish it?'

'Well, yes. I know how it ends. It's all in my head.'

She looked dubiously at the head, which was large, like a boulder with signs carved on it. She wanted to feel its weight on her chest. She touched it with the fingers of her right hand.

He touched the back of the hand, then took a finger and stroked the inside of it, watching her face, which was glowing with shadows. Her body shivered agreeably inside its loose clothes.

The gap between her front teeth was wide enough, he was thinking, just wide enough to get the tip of his tongue into.

She searched his eyes, but the light from the street was putting a shuttered shine on them. She wanted to make him tell her he was grateful to her. She wanted him to be made grateful.

'Well,' she murmured. He stroked the nape of her neck.

'Well?'

'Yes.'

'Um?'

'Oh, yes!'

The last, half-impatient utterance was swallowed up in their kiss along with the foreboding that suddenly raked her mind like a headlight and as suddenly went out. Later she was to recall that this unbidden warning had shown a truer insight than the ensuing shower of sparks as Dan laid his head on her breasts and made a path with his tongue up her neck and round the intricacies of her ear and ended back at the gap between her front teeth, arched by its puffy little tuck of gum. Her tongue had a sweetish, hot fruit-flavour, mingled with the subtler taste of youth.

It had been a long time since Dan had undressed with a woman without finding the removal of socks and underpants so many trip-wires to his desire, so that the disposal of the impedimenta often got more attention than the performance itself. But tonight they undressed together, exploring as they went, their clothes falling where they might, until she stood there in the window light, naked, her firm nipples demanding attention.

They swayed together, momentarily at a loss, before falling sideways onto the bed, each believing that the other had initiated the move. Horizontal, Dan began biting her mouth.

She liked his smell and the feel of his firm buttocks in her hands. He was in good shape, she found herself thinking, for his age, though too tense. The weight of his body made her profligate and she began to relax him.

He, too, was aware of his age, though marvelling at his luck and, since he was not a modest man, at hers too. But he had even feared failure, wishing he had drunk less. He had almost been daunted.

Sweat made rills between shifting gullies as she furiously offered.

Slowly and thoroughly his dry fingers took possession of her body. It seemed to her that he must have known in advance her wildest places and had she thought, which she was now almost quite beyond, she might have quailed at the sheer competence of those fingers, which seemed to speak a language independent of their owner.

Under the softly slithering, deliberately poking and pinching, sharply tender fingers, the rhythmic flow interrupted by the violent apostrophe, she began to urge and groan until with astonished recklessness and unconcealed delight she came to an expanding explosion whose vibrations melted the insides of her arms and throat and breasts.

'Ah, please,' she said. 'Come on!'

Now he knelt before her like a child begging to be let in. She hesitated, shivering, at the intrusion, but only for a moment. Then it was done. The child had become a sacker of cities, for a curious nervous violence overcame him, as if he had lost his equilibrium. Again she saved him, this time from an early, abject spill, and as she slowed him down she had a magnificently sure premonition of tenderness later.

'Open your eyes.'

Her last articulate words.

He was used to ploughing in the dark. Now their eyes made love as well, glistened, went away, came back into focus.

Sometimes, rising from her body, all he would see would be a shining pupil, or lashes which quivered against his own for moments on end.

At first he worried about the next time, for ever anticipating. But in the end he didn't.

12

Alone in his apartment, Andy Burns booked a call to Jean Fenwick in Lacking, England, then wandered around his three rooms like an excited lover before a rendezvous. What would he say to her? He had no idea and did not try to formulate one. The prospect of hearing her voice was enough. It even enabled him to attend to his neglected collection of timepieces and he hummed to himself as he prowled from one silent face to the other.

When there was nothing left to tap or adjust he lay on his bed and waited. It was hot and he began to doze.

He dreamed that he was standing between beds ranked three or four deep in a hospital ward. The beds were heaped with dirty sheets and blankets and the floor was covered with pools of liquid and little mounds of some sort of fluff. A nurse was telling him to get into one of the beds.

'Why should I?' he was saying, as if to himself, aware of the fact that he was really in his apartment and that the light was on.

'Doctor said.'

'What's the doctor's name?'

'It's not for me to say. Be a good boy or you'll get me into trouble. Why, you haven't even shaved! You *know* you have to shave your whole, entire body, and you wouldn't want one of the boys to do it for you, would you now?'

'I want to go home.'

'You can't. That's your bed.'

'What's wrong with me?'

'Nothing to be proud of.'

'Why do you look so mad at me? Have I got a social disease?'

'Kinda.'

'Did I behave badly?'

'I'll say you did! Don't you remember? My lord, you made a terrible fuss. You broke instruments and they had to carry you in. Don't you remember anything?'

'I'm being dried out, isn't that it?'

'Yes.'

The nurse put her hand between his legs and he discovered that he was wearing pyjamas. They were in a different ward now. It was gloomy, almost dark, and in beds which stood about at odd angles men were lying twisted under tossed clothes.

'They're dying,' he said.

The nurse's face revolved like a searchlight, illuminating sections of bed and wall, on which misty rain was falling, until it came at last to his own bed. He knew it was his because he was lying in it, white-lipped.

And then Andy was on the sidewalk back home. Automobiles and buses were running vertically up and down the sides of the buildings on special rails. A large black limousine such as Presidents used pulled up beside him. Andy saw himself sitting inside on one of the back seats. He was on his way to the hospital.

'We have to give that old man a lift to the hospital,' the driver said, looking over his shoulder into Andy's face.

The old man was wiry and bent. He wore a thick, blue reefer jacket and a jockstrap. Andy got out to make way for him and the old man hopped into the car and shut the door behind him. The car sped away, covering Andy with fumes from its exhaust.

'I have to get to the hospital,' he said to the man standing beside him.

'There,' said Dr Schreiber, pointing to the window of Blaine's Furniture Store, which was the largest store in Milton, or had been last time Andy had been back.

In the window a woman made out of wax was lying in a beautiful four-poster bed hung with white muslin drapes. A man with glittering china eyes was bending over her. As Andy pressed his face against the glass the wax faces began to melt and run down the sheets, down the muslin drapes and out along the gutters of the street.

The ringing of the telephone plucked him from his nightmare.

'Jean,' he said.

It was almost a cry.

'Is that you, Dan?'

Jean Fenwick's voice sounded to him like a little girl's.

'I thought you were Dan,' she said breathlessly.

He knew then that he was not going to tell her about his illness.

'You never wrote,' she said.

'I did so, but they sent it back. I guess they'd discharged you, or whatever they call it.'

'I discharged myself.'

'I mailed another one this morning. I enclosed the pictures we took that day on the beach, remember?'

'That's nice,' she said.

She must be wondering why he was ringing.

'What time have you there?' he asked.

'It's about five, I think.'

'I have a clock here that shows world times and I make London a quarter after.'

'I'm just having tea, anyway.'

'Sure. Well, I just wanted to hear how things were.'

'That was sweet of you, Andy. Things are O.K. Not wonderful, but O.K.'

There was another pause.

'It's rather alarming to be a middle-aged woman starting from scratch,' she said.

'You ought to get married,' he said, crossing his fingers.

'Someone else said that today. The fact is, I already am. But what about you?'

'I'm fine.'

'You should eat more.'

'No, I'm just fine.'

'Dan used to say you were the ideal extrovert. Stable but not hearty. Remember?'

'Big deal.'

'He used to tell me that you kept his feet on the ground and looked after him.'

'Oh, hell, Jean, Dan don't need looking after.'

'Everyone does.'

'You're wasting your solicitude.'

'Yes, I know.'

Her voice seemed to him small and empty.

'I wanted to hear your voice, Jean.'

'Well.'

Sweat was trickling between his shoulder-blades. Words mashed the edges of meaning.

'Listen, Dan's O.K. He's got other fish to fry.'

'What does that mean?'

'It means he's fallen for a young movie star.'

'There were always a few Chinese film dollies around.'

'This one's English, or Irish, I don't know which, and she's reciprocating. I guess she's intrigued by a guy who's supposed to have quote seen life unquote. Maybe it's the first time she's met anyone except actors.'

'What did you say her name was?'

'Sally Maine.'

'Is that what you rang to tell me?'

'I guess it is.'

Having said it, he told himself it was true.

'It's his business.'

'What's that?'

'I said it's his affair.'

'It sure is.'

'Is she . . . how long will she be staying out there?'

'She's shooting a movie, then she says she'll stay on or come back. Anyway she wants to be with him, she told him so this afternoon.'

'You know I'm working for the paper again?'

'That's great.'

'I have my own column, like I used to do before I got married.'

'Why not get them to send you out here?'

'He never writes now. I hear nothing.'

'There's a whole heap of women's stories you could pick up in Hong Kong.'

'He sends me money, of course.'

'Sure.'

'I don't know what to do.'

'Don't let him walk over you.'

'No.'

'I could find you an apartment in my block. They're cheap.'

'We'd only hurt each other.'

'You couldn't hurt me if you tried.'

'I mean Dan.'

'He told me he wished you'd get fixed up with someone else.'

'I expect he's afraid I'll go potty again.'

'He doesn't give a damn. You know what he said to me? He said you were a dry and angry lover.'

'That wasn't very chivalrous of you.'

'I wanted to make you see, that's all. I'm sorry.'

'Isn't he your friend any more? I always thought you were so close.'

'Not necessarily.'

'You're so confusing, Andy. One minute you say come out to Hong Kong and the next you tell me how little he cares.'

'You'll only get the guy out of your system if you see how things really are, instead of staying in England and nursing some memory or other.'

'How long has he been going round with her?'

'About three weeks.' It sounded worse than twenty-four hours.

'What's she like?'

'I haven't really noticed, she's not my type. She's pretty, I guess. Blonde, blue eyes, big ones. She had a wide mouth and a kinda gap between her two front teeth, you know? She's well stacked and above average height and she has a short nose. Things like that.'

'You hardly seem to have noticed her at all.' Jean laughed.

'Do you remember that day on the beach?' he asked. She had laughed a lot that day. 'We ate fish off the stall and then you came back to my place, where I am now, and we drank a bottle of wine and I explained how my clocks and things worked, remember?'

'I do indeed. I stayed late and when I got back to my place Dan was there and we had a row.'

'Do you still have the barometer I gave you with the mother-of-pearl case?'

'Of course. I had it at the hospital and I have it now. I love it.'

'I got to thinking recently that it's stupid keeping all this junk in the house. I mean, it's nothing to do with anything, is it? I mean, who the hell cares?' Pips began to sound with slow regularity.

'You're wasting your money,' Jean said.

'No, no, no. Not at all. Say, what do you do in the evenings? This evening, for example.'

'I'm having supper with a woman friend who lives in the village. She's nice.' Jean sounded defensive. 'And you, what about you?'

'I'm going to bed and wait until tomorrow,' he said.

'Does she know about me?'

'Who?'

'This Sally Maine. Has he told her about me?'

'I guess so.'

'How old is she?'

'Twenty-three about.'

'I suppose it's someone to keep him warm at night.'

'Oh no. They talk about the meaning of love, things like that. And he's even getting his novel out, the one he never finished.'

'It was a play.'

'It wouldn't surprise me if he didn't try to finish it.'

'I don't know. I wish I knew what to do.'

'Marry me, for a start.'

Her laugh came a fraction ahead of his. 'You must go to bed,' she said.

'If ever you need anything, Jean, you only have to let me know.'

'I know, Andy, and I'm grateful.'

'I wouldn't let you down.'

'I wonder if she's found out what he's like?'

'Who knows? All I know is he's goofy about her and she seems to like it.'

'Well, thanks for ringing.'

He flopped back on his pillow as if he had been punched

there. His hands, reaching for a glass of water, trembled with what he had tried to do.

He lay on his side and pulled his legs up against his stomach, pressing his chin against his kneecaps. The pain inside him was beyond reach. He tried lying flat on his back and letting his body go limp, limb by limb.

He tried to imagine her now, sipping tea and staring with her big, black eyes. She would be suffering because of what he had told her. He was not sorry. Maybe she would spare him a thought as well. Poor old reliable Andy!

Then he thought of Dan, but he was too distraught to feel ashamed, though he did feel disgust, not at what he had attempted but because he seemed to have made a botch of it.

13

'What I mean' – they were lying supporting one another like complacent orphans in a self-created storm, their backs against the wall behind the bed – 'is you have to say yes to life'.

Of this she seemed quite sure, judging by the decision with which her blonde hair shook on his shoulder.

'But you might say Genghis Khan and the Nazis had said yes to life.'

'No they didn't. At least, I'm not so hot on Genghis Khan, but my music teacher was a Jew from Warsaw and the Nazis gassed his wife and child. He hid and watched them being put in a van and that was the last he saw of them.'

'Was he saying yes to life?'

'He was scared. He's lovely. Don't be snide about him.'

'How did you get into acting?'

'Oh, because I wanted to do the thing that would most annoy Mother Superior at my convent school and in those days, like six years ago, they still regarded the stage as wicked.'

'I can't believe it.'

'In Ireland, they did. We had to walk out in a kind of crocodile along the street and there was a sister at the top and a sister at the tail and one day some boys in a factory threw some blown-up french letters at us, they must have been practically the only specimens at large in Ireland, I should think, and the sisters thought they were balloons and gave the boys terrific looks of goodwill. It was fantastic!'

'Tell me about where you live.'

'I live in a two-roomed flat in Glebe Place, which is off the King's Road, but for your information I don't turn on or take acid and I work hard and I shop in the supermarket on the corner, where you can buy sanitary towels as well as Canadian processed cheese, and, what else? I'm too pooped, absolutely flattened, to do anything, so I listen to music. I'm crazy about Mahler, I think he's terrific. Or I read. I like Graham Greene, though I don't think he knows much about sex. He makes it so furtive. Nabokov I can't stand. Or else I study my own script.'

'I suppose you have a lot of friends?'

'Oh, herds. They're always coming to the door uninvited. That's the only snag about Glebe Place.'

'Do you sleep with your friends when they happen to knock?'

'It depends.'

'It's easy come, easy go.'

'Honestly, you've got extraordinary ideas about the young.'

'Old grandpa.'

'I sleep with a boy if I want to, of course I do. But to tell you the truth, I'd rather talk.'

'What, after the last two hours?'

'I mean with boys, silly. They're boring in bed, most boys. I'm sure you'd agree.'

'I don't fancy them.'

'Well, I don't fancy girls either, though I had a tumble once with a chum. She was a big, jolly girl from the convent and we spent a rainy afternoon in bed together. That was decades ago.'

'I never had a boy; except at school, we used to play around, of course.'

149

'So we gather.'

'Do you really like acting?'

'Yes. I mean, I wouldn't die if I gave it up, but it is something I think I can do well and make my own thing. That gives you a sort of freedom.'

Her voice was thick from the angle of her neck. She cleared her throat, on which he placed his dry, open lips. He could feel her voice travelling up to her mouth.

'Like you and your journalism.'

'What do you mean?'

'Golly, you are brusque sometimes!'

'As long as you know what you're looking at it's a freedom, but you mustn't be taken by surprise. You must know what it is almost before you see it, then you're all right.'

'Yes.'

'I didn't mean to be snappy, was I?'

'No. Then, you mustn't feel too sorry for people either, must you?'

'I don't.'

'Are you so hard-boiled?'

'Not that, but feeling sorry for people's an impertinence while they've still got breath in them.'

'Like Daddy and cats, you mean. It demeans them.'

'It gasses them to death, in his case!'

'What about your play? That's all about being sorry for someone.'

'The play's all wrong. I'll have to rework it. You showed me that.'

'Me? How?'

'By letting me read it to you. I realised it was far too intellectual. I was telling myself that such and such a character represented such and such an emotion, it's all too schematic and it's so damned smug. Written under the influence of early marriage.'

'Is that what early marriage does, makes you smug?'

'Definitely. I think the time had come for me to tell you about my wife.'

'Why?'

'Because I want to. This is not a misunderstood husband story. If anything, she's the one who was misunderstood, but I can tell you, if she hadn't left I'd have done some injury to her.'

'What did she do?'

'She went home and had a breakdown, about two years ago. I saw her in the place and she accused me of being the author of her miseries. She said I'd allowed her to abort our child, "her" child she called it, and so delivered her over to guilt and despair. She said I did so in order to destroy the marriage because I wasn't man enough to make it work without being destroyed by it myself.'

'It sounds complicated.'

'I forget why I'm telling you all this.'

'Golly, you people seem to enjoy tangles.'

'Really I was just bored by her relentless home-making.'

'I thought babies were home-making.'

'Well, she thought we weren't ready. We married quite late enough as it was, but she thought we had to mature in the wood for a while, in this case eighteenth-century mahogany, with which she gradually filled every room in the house.'

'It sounds morbid.'

'I still haven't forgotten the smell of furniture polish. It even got in the food.'

'Why did you marry her?'

'I loved her.'

'Come on!'

'I did. I told her so in a drive-in movie in Tuscany. We had known each other for about four months and I told her in the movie place that I loved her and asked her to marry me.'

'She said yes with alacrity.'

'You're wrong. She said no. She said she wanted to be a writer and that marriage would interfere with her ambitions.'

'So?'

'Well, instead of gratefully accepting her free pardon, I pushed on. We were driving about Italy. It was very hot and in one place we ate some shellfish and she got poisoned. I woke up in the middle of the night and she wasn't in bed and I heard a moaning sound from the bathroom, so I went in and there she was, lying on the floor being sick and everything, too weak to get up. So I mopped her up and got her some pills and asked her to marry me again and she said yes. She should have married a nice rich farmer or a music-loving stockbroker.'

'I guess she should,' Sally said. She was leaning over him, propped on her elbow, her left breast resting softly and warmly against the arch of his armpit. He pulled her over on top of him. Afterwards they dozed until he roused himself to fetch a drink.

'You drink a lot, don't you?'

'Does it worry you?'

'It's a bit boring. You drink like Daddy used to do at the end, as if you were communing with a third person. Daddy used to swallow in a rather special way, as if he was receiving the host.' Dan was silent. 'Are you telling me to keep off?' she asked. No reply. 'He's telling me to get back in my box.'

'Oh, for Christ's sake!'

'I don't mind, my sweet. I can look after myself.'

She had called him her sweet. She twined her leg around his so that their feet were interlocked.

'I have prehensile toes,' she said.

'I have slightly flat feet.'

'I have little toes that shoot off sideways and cling to chairlegs and things.'
'I have . . .'
'You have a beautiful big . . .'
They giggled.

14

A month passed and the inner harbour was like the face of a great clock on which the ships came and went like hours.

For Franco Panni time meant money. He completed his shooting and returned to Europe, taking with him his leading man, for whom time had grown horns. Sally Maine stayed behind and neither she nor Dan observed time at all. They knew it was still there but they ignored it, to the annoyance of Dan's paper and Maslyn Martin.

For Andy Burns time frequently meant the intervals between the arrival of discomfort and its departure. Since Schreiber had started treating him, the swellings had subsided under his arms and his bowels were back under control. He felt almost at ease inside his body, an improvement which had reconciled him to mingling with the sick people at Schreiber's clinic when he went there for check-ups, although he still made distinctions between them and would have nothing to do with the really far-gone specimens whom he had noticed crawling in and out of the surgery, holding bloody cloths to their mouths. He felt alien to them, his interest in the treatment of his own disease having already obscured from him the deeper reality, which was that it had no cure. It was not that Schreiber, by inviting him to take a pseudo-scientific interest in his condition, had made him forget this fact, but that he had made him believe that it was something that would happen, not tomorrow, not next week, but some day.

Andy's dependence on the doctor had become so important that he felt like a slapped child when, going into the clinic one afternoon, the Chinese assistant told him that Schreiber was away and would he wait his turn in the garden?

'But I made an appointment. Where's he gone?'

'To Macao. I will treat you today.'

'But I don't want that.' How could Schreiber possibly have more urgent things to do? 'I have to go to Vietnam soon and I wanted to discuss it with him.'

'Then you had better call him. Now please go and wait your turn. You are not the only one here who is seriously ill.'

'I'm sorry.' He found a place for himself on a brick wall on which several Chinese were already sitting. The man nearest to him heaved himself sideways to make room and offered Andy a sweetmeat, which he refused, then accepted. When another patient came up, Andy was the one who squeezed sideways to make room on the wall. He did so without thinking.

Another form that time had taken for Andy had been the writing of letters to Jean Fenwick and the reading of her replies. Andy wrote to her several times a week and although she replied less often he believed that he could detect in what she wrote a definite warming up of feeling. He had persuaded himself that if he could only coax her to come out to Hong Hong her fixation on Dan could be broken, if not by his efforts alone, then by the spectacle of Sally and Dan, whose happiness was, Andy thought, of a ruthless nature that would brook no interference.

Before he had got sick Andy would have denied that he was a man to intrigue behind a friend's back, but now he made a point of seeing Sally and Dan as often as he could in order to gather titbits of conversation with which to feed Jean's jealousy. Sometimes, as he sat with them in bars or restaurants, he would finger Jean's letters, which he always kept in his jacket pocket.

He re-read her latest now, and tried to picture her life as he waited for a nurse to call his name.

15

When the train stopped at Lacking it seemed to do so as an afterthought, most of its carriages having overrun the short, uncovered platform before the brakes were made to work.

The more knowing passengers, who included Jean Fenwick, had already walked down the corridor to the last few compartments and were able to get out in the normal way, but further up the train a door was seen to open and three suitcases to fly out and land on the gravel beside the track. They were followed by a large, grey-haired man with a shop-bright sun-tan who turned and raised his arms towards a woman in a green pyjama-suit. She responded by leaping on top of the man and sending him reeling backwards into a gorse bush.

The woman's uninhibited laughter would have told Jean who she was if the pyjama-suit had not already done so. She waited, pleasurably excited.

'You'd think they'd see that the first-class passengers stopped at the right spot,' Maslyn said. Her energy was almost tangible.

'I travel second,' Jean said.

'I'd rather die! The only reason I don't travel super-first is because there isn't one. Gaston, this is Mrs Fenwick. Gaston Gaillard. Give me a case, darling. I do hate seeing men loaded like donkeys.'

'I've seen you in several marvellous old French movies,' Jean said.

'Not so much of the old if I were you,' Maslyn said.

'I think I have twisted my ankle,' Gaston said.

'What a shame. Tell me, Jean, you've been in London doing that column of yours? I read the one you did about me. I thought you did it rather well. You made me sound rather a megalomaniac, but perhaps that's how I affect you.'

'You make me feel a bit dazed always. I don't know if that's megalomania.'

'Probably my cigarettes. I'd like to write an autobiography one day for the press,' Maslyn said. 'I'd show those bloody women journalists, saving your presence.'

'Don't talk about journalists to me,' Gaston said with an attempt to look wry.

'He's upset because one of that tribe has walked off with the girl he's been devoted to for two years. So am I, only I'm not just upset. I'm hopping mad!'

'He will ruin her life,' Gaston said.

'Not he. I won't allow it. You'll see.'

'No, you will see. When Sally Maine makes up her mind she is a rock.'

'Who did you say?' Jean asked.

They were standing in the station yard where people in tweed clothes were greeting friends and relatives from town and putting their luggage into cars and taxis.

'Sally Maine,' said Maslyn. 'I showed you her picture, didn't I? She's my best girl. She's talented, authentic and emancipated. The lot! And now she refuses to come home, though the filming is over, because she's got mixed up with some expatriated deadbeat who scribbles for a living. You were out there. You may even know the man.'

'Yes I do.'

'You mean . . . ?'

Maslyn turned on Gaston like an angry cat.

'You never told me his name was Fenwick,' she said.

'What does it matter?'

'A great deal, *chéri*. Meet his wife!'

That evening Jean had dinner with Maslyn and Gaston at Maslyn's mill-house. Maslyn put herself out to charm and dazzle her guest and Gaston, whom by this time she had primed, was smooth and amusing. After dinner they finished their wine in the high old store-room of the mill and watched the darkness coming down through the trees.

'Now then,' said Maslyn, when the trees had become shadows on shadows. 'It's joint time.'

After pulling close-fitting silk blinds over the windows she squatted beside a low table and began to scrape at a lump of marijuana with a penknife. Then she mixed the brown powder with tobacco, rolled it in cigarette paper, lit it and handed it to Jean.

'Inhale,' she said, rightly assuming that Jean was a novice. 'Right down, that's it. Now you hand it on to Gaston.'

'Why?'

'Because that's the way.'

'Can't we have one each?'

'We can have lots, but it's still better to hand them round, it doesn't waste any.'

They expelled smoke luxuriously through their mouths and nostrils. It coiled heavily above their heads and the room began to smell mildly herbal. Maslyn and Gaston appeared to be finding immediate pleasure in the drug. They lay back and shut their eyes appreciatively, opening them occasionally to look warmly about. At first Jean was unable to share their warmth. The smoke rushed into the recesses of her lungs like surf, only to recede and leave her shivering.

She wondered if the others were pretending to enjoy themselves like children behind the coal-shed. She felt alien from them.

'How do you feel?' Maslyn asked.

'I feel as if I had lost my legs somewhere.'

'What have you lost?'

'Repeat to him what you just said,' Maslyn told her.

'I c ... I can't. I've forgotten. I nearly can but ...'

'That's one of the signs it's working nicely,' Maslyn said. 'Take another pull, then you won't mind forgetting things. It'll all be lovely and we'll talk about Sally and your Daniel.'

Again Jean inhaled and again the surf rushed into her, but this time it did not recede and it did not feel so cold. The nausea that had threatened was now engulfed. She began to giggle. They all sat and giggled at one another until they were weak.

Shutting her eyes, Jean rose gently off the sofa and flew gracefully round the room, only opening her eyes again when she had returned to her seat.

'Poor Jean,' she murmured to herself.

'She mustn't be sorry for herself unless she's going to do something about it,' Maslyn said. 'Now take a look at these.'

She held out a fan of shiny photographs.

'Pick a card,' she said.

The photographs were of Sally Maine. Jean glanced through them, then selected a big close-up of the girl's face and examined it carefully. It told her nothing. The pouting mouth and perfectly shaped eyes seemed to be saying 'Find me if you can'.

'This is a better one,' Maslyn said.

The girl was standing inside some sort of shop and had turned hurriedly to face the camera with a look of amused surprise on her face. Jean saw that Andy's description of her was accurate except that Andy had omitted to say how young her beauty was.

'Do you want my advice?' Maslyn's voice said. 'Tell me if you don't and I'll shut up.'

160

Jean laid the photograph beside her on the sofa.

'Do you believe that your relationship with your husband could be an authentic one?' said Maslyn.

'I thought so, once.'

'You don't think those sort of things, you know. You say yes or no, authentic or unauthentic, otherwise it's not worth discussing.'

'It sounds like some sort of truth game.'

'It is. Did he want you?'

'Yes.'

'Would he still?'

'I don't know.'

'Well, go and find out.'

'It's unworkable.'

'Then you must make it work, darling. Mustn't she, Gaston?'

'She must. She is well equipped to do so.'

'Yes she is. She wants this role of wife to this man, why is her business, so what she has to do is to go to Hong Kong and help herself. She must get off her knees and she must hustle! He'll respect her for it. Why do you think he's so impressed by Sally?'

'My Sally,' Gaston said.

'We'll see.' Maslyn gave him a look in which Jean read an almost wild contempt and wondered if this woman, pacing her vast sitting-room, which she had floored with paving stones from the streets of London, whose declivities had been worn into them by a million feet, was not suffering from megalomania after all.

'Sally is free,' Maslyn said. 'She is marvellous and your Daniel is, let's face it, used to women being cowed by him.'

Was it true? Jean wondered. Her mind seemed to be cleaned out and the thoughts were floating about inside it just out of reach of her full comprehension.

'It's too late,' she said, tapping the photograph. 'Look at her!'

'It's not too late! Look at *you*! Go on, go and look in the mirror. Take a good look at yourself. What do you see? I'll tell you what you see. You see a sensitive, interesting-looking, desirable woman. Don't take any notice of the way her mouth droops at the corners, she picked that up waiting to see the psychiatrist! Smile, darling! You don't know how good you looked when you were laughing just now. You ought to smoke hash all the time. You looked great! Go on, smile at me. That's better. Now look back in the mirror, no, keep on smiling. There. What did I tell you?'

Jean laughed with pleasure, shaking her head.

'Don't say no like that. I know your trouble. You have decided to yourself that the only way you can survive is by nursing a grievance, because you're scared as hell that if your arms are empty you'll have to start figuring out who you really are. So you love a grievance rather than risk loving a living person. It's so much easier to love the dead.'

'I love Dan.'

'Then trust me. I will take that godawful, squawking grievance out of your arms and give you the chance to be yourself. There's only one way of doing it. Go back to Hong Kong and take your husband back from Sally Maine.'

'You don't know him. Nor does she.'

'I don't have to know him. I am talking about you.'

'I couldn't afford it.'

'You could if you really decided to break with this deception you're indulging in. Do you know what you're heading for? You will end up in such a blind alley that there'll be only two things left to you – either lie to yourself for the rest of your dried-up life or else have another breakdown, because that would be the only way you could achieve authenticity. And it'd be a lot more serious than the last one. You'd fall apart at the seams.'

Jean sat in silence.

'Do you want that to happen?' Maslyn said.

'No.'

'But you agree it's a possibility? Then stop talking rot about not being able to afford the trip. Can you afford to live? Then live, for God's sake! I will go with you to Hong Kong, if you like. How would that be? What about it, Gaston? I will even go tourist with you and sit beside you and keep you on the ball and I swear that if you trust me you will succeed.'

'I don't know.'

'Trust me!'

'Do you really think we could?'

'Believe me, darling, we couldn't fail. I may not know your husband, but I know Sally.'

16

'That still doesn't explain why you won't take me along!'

'You'd only be hanging about in Saigon.'

'I'd hang about here, wouldn't I?'

'Anything might happen in Vietnam.'

'That's why I want to go, for heaven's sake. We're supposed to be together, remember?'

'We might lose each other over there. It happens all the time to people. Like the two lovers who went to a carnival in France and got separated by the crowd and although they tried to find one another they did so with less and less conviction as they got more and more distracted by the things around them. Life just dragged them apart, though they kept on telling themselves they were still looking.'

'Where did you hear that?'

'It's well known.'

'You liar! You just made it up! I always know when you're inventing, the way you purse up your mouth.'

Her pleasure in her own body continued to delight him. Jean had never been easy like that, nor he, whereas Sally's nakedness was proud and inevitable. Dan watched her as she came towards him, her bare feet treading into the thick white carpet. She sat with him on the bed they had so recently left and tucked her right leg up under her. With a movement that sketched a whole remembered embrace, he stroked her arm above the elbow.

'Don't you ever think of anyone but yourself?' she said.

She had a habit, unnoticed by Dan until recently, of picking at her lower lip with her finger and thumb.

'Don't,' he said, pulling her hand away from her face.

'Do you?'

'I think of you.'

'Yes, but not really you don't. You use people, Dan. I'm not a hausfrau, you know.'

They had gone far in understanding each other's use of words since the morning she had moved in, but they found their relationship too tense, too uncertain perhaps, to endure much silence and they seldom sat in quiet celebration as Dan and Jean had in the first years of their marriage, when they lived in rented rooms in London. 'You people are always arguing,' Andy told them one evening when he was eating with them. 'Who are you trying to convince?' And Andy had rubbed his gaunt face and looked at them with his gentle, shrewd eyes.

'No, Dan, leave me,' she said now, pushing away his fingers.

'I think of you when I'm not with you,' he said.

'Not enough to stop you going off to Vietnam and leaving me behind.'

'That's not the point.'

'It is the point, very much the point! Or do you just see me as someone fulfilling a particular need for you and other things and people fulfilling other particular needs? Like you wanting to go to the same bar every evening and sit in the same seat, that's a small need I'm not included in, not that I care, I'd be bored to death, but just so long as I know that the really important things we do together.'

'This is what's important.' He brushed her shoulder with his lips.

'You remind me of Gaston when you're facetious like that.'

Although she accepted his thankfulness without vanity and

was thankful in return, on the inside of her pleasure there was a doubt. It had been there from the beginning.

Let her move again, he was thinking, surrendering himself to the memory of her walking across the carpet moments before. The pleasure he took in her was like a torrent over the dry stones of his life before. He had been getting lonely and peculiar and although he did not try to dismiss the experiences he had had as unimportant, he saw them as enemies to be kept at bay. She had helped him to do so. They were still about, somewhere in the world, but he felt that he now could control them again.

'Leave me,' she said. 'I'm angry!'

He went to the window as if sulking at the balconies opposite. They were empty, all but one, on which a Chinese servant girl was scrubbing the tiles, watched by her mistress through the glass. He wondered if the girl realised that the other woman was there.

'You have to be an accredited correspondent to go to Vietnam.'

'That's the feeblest excuse yet.'

She had made him feel young again. He had grown his hair longer under her guidance and bought new clothes. In its indifference to ordinary routine and its aura of impermanence, their life resembled a honeymoon. Dan cabled his editor and told him that he had been bitten by a poisonous spider. 'Lie properly,' he told her, showing her the cable, 'and they have to believe you.'

The editor let sleeping dogs lie for a week or two and then cabled Dan ordering him to proceed to Vietnam at once to cover a fresh campaign which was carrying American troops into new areas.

'Tarzan goes off to war and Jane stays in the tree-house. No thanks!' she told his back. 'It's all that cricketing stuff you revere so much.' There had been a time of confidences when

166

they had believed that to talk of their respective pasts would somehow validate the present. It had been short-lived and they had made a tacit pact not to look back. That she was breaking it unilaterally was a sign of her determination. 'You stroll out to the wicket and smash the ball around and then you come strolling back and Mum's waiting to give you cake and lemonade. That's where it's at for you in Vietnam. Well, I'm not Mum and I won't put up with it.'

It was true that he wanted her to wait for him, pensive and preferably naked, and that he would come back from the world's great snare uncaught and take up where they had left off. And yet why could she not wait in Saigon? It could easily be arranged. Because, he told himself, it would be the end of their affair if she did. The magic could only work for them in Hong Kong, where it had manifested itself and where it belonged. In Vietnam it would be swallowed up by the greater magic of death.

'It's a graveyard out there,' he said. The girl on the balcony was bracing herself on her left hand and scouring with her right.

Every time he gets out of bed, she was thinking, he puts on his shorts as if he was wrapping up something perishable. Gaston used to do the same, though not the Irish boy, who had stood behind the door with his erection and his knobbly Irish walking-stick. She giggled maliciously, surprised that she had coupled the two older men in the same thought. If he would not take her she would find someone who would.

'It's so unfair,' she said aloud.

As she spoke the girl on the balcony sat back on her haunches to wipe a hair from her eyes and Dan saw that there was a ragged, liver-coloured birth-mark covering half her face. At the same time he realised with revulsion why it was that he had wanted to see Sally walking across the carpet. It was the same reason that had prevented him from helping her when he had found her kneeling in the dust being mocked by the students. It was because he had thrilled at the helplessness of her. He had wanted her as an object.

'You remind me of a stranger I read about,' Sally said, playing the story game he had taught her. 'He came to live with some ordinary people and he transfigured them, but one day he left them, telling them that he had to keep an appointment with a god or a star or something like that, but before saying goodbye he gave them gifts. And he said, "I never stay long anywhere. I'm the travelling type." And it was only after he had gone that they took a close look at the gifts and found that they were just little bits of broken tin and used cinema tickets, little worthless things, just nothing.'

The girl on the balcony got up off her knees, stooped and picked up the bucket and mop, and went inside the flat. Her mistress shut the window behind her.

'If you leave me behind I won't be here when you come back,' Sally said. 'I mean it.'

'You're the best thing that ever happened to me,' he said. He came and touched her and she brushed his hands with her hair.

'Then don't let me go,' she said.

'I'll get you accredited as a photographer in the morning.' He sat heavily and she stroked his hair, unsure as to why he had let her win.

'Was I asking so much?' she said.

'I was a fool to think this could last.'

'I can't hear you, darling, you're muttering.'

'I feel ashamed. I could have helped you that day when the students made you kneel, but I just watched you over the shoulders of the crowd.'

'Why?'

'Then I thought if I could keep you here I could stop time somehow. I must have been crazy. You must have bewitched me.' He pressed his face against her breasts, which felt both yielding and hard.

'Do you have to make life so difficult for yourself?'

'Ask life.'

'I'm too busy living it,' she said. 'I'm so excited to be going to Vietnam. Thank you very, very much.'

'You don't understand.'

'No I don't! Nobody does. So why should you be the exception when so many others have to manage without?'

17

The land was blackened as far as the eye could see. It looked like a frying pan that had been left on the flame. Lumps of porous black rind had erupted everywhere, making huts and tree-stumps indistinguishable from one another.

From the mild sky a helicopter descended and hovered above the bombed village. An American NCO, legs dangling through the hatch, threw out fistfuls of leaflets.

Three Vietcong soldiers, who had been hiding in a foxhole, crawled out and stood in the open. The leaflets fell on their bare shoulders like snow. They told them that if they surrendered they would receive a reward. The men raised their arms as if they wanted to touch the helicopter.

The officer examined them through his binoculars, then selected a grenade from the box in which they were packed like expensive chocolates and tossed it through the hatch.

On a mountainside where light broke like surf on grey trees, a communist commissar murdered an old man before an assembled village. The old man's wife was forced to watch her husband, who was the village headman, being dragged by his beard into the centre of the square. Two boys who might have been his grandsons held his arms while the commissar took a sword and hacked off his head. It thumped into the dust where the old man had played as a child.

In a prison camp beside a mangrove swamp a South Vietnamese colonel drowned a communist lieutenant in a bucket of water.

From paddy fields, villages, hillsides, the smoke of burning aircraft, burning homes, burning bodies rose like an unheeded sacrifice.

On an airfield, where American soldiers slept, pinioned to their equipment like butterflies to cards, a Marine general with a Dutch name told his staff that a hill called Forty had to be recaptured at whatever cost. It had been overrun during the night and the field commander had reported that American dead could still be seen lying about its flanks.

The general talked about dishonour and the anger of superiors.

In the forest of thorn trees which surrounded Hill Forty, the American soldiers who had been driven from the summit dug shallow holes for themselves in which they lay and waited for reinforcements. When these began to arrive, crawling through the bushes which dragged at their equipment as if reluctant to let them pass, the survivors stared at them with the faces of old men. The newcomers asked questions about Hill Forty and about the Cong, but the others spoke little and their silence was accentuated by the clink of buckles and the cackle of birds and insects.

In a declivity in the red earth beside a poisonous stream, Dan Fenwick was opening a can of sliced pineapple, watched gravely by an eighteen-year-old conscript from Kentucky. The boy's face was pale under its streaks of mud and his lips were drawn back from his teeth. Dan passed him a slice of pineapple, which he swallowed in one gulp, letting the juice trickle down his face into his open collar.

'Man, I sure wish I had your job,' he said to Dan.

'Why?'

'So I could get the hell outa here when I wanted to, which is right now, 'stead of waitin' for the sergeant to tell me to git my ass back up that hill.'

'I'll be going, too.'

'But you don't have to and that's the big difference.'

'The air force will be putting down the napalm soon.'

'Shit, there's always some of 'em left. They come up outa the ground. They got my buddy las' night and he's still up there.'

Weary as he was, a noise in the bush brought the boy up onto his knees.

'It's only my friend,' Dan said.

He spiked a piece of pineapple on his penknife and held it out to Andy, who had appeared from behind a tree, buckling his belt. Andy waved it aside and pulled out a flask.

'Any offers?'

The soldier took the pineapple and ate it.

'You've a leech on yer arm,' he told Andy.

'Oh God!'

Andy brushed wildly at the leech, which hung from him like a ripe grape.

'Hold it,' the soldier said. 'You'll git poisoned for sure if you break its head off inside of you.'

He fumbled in his numerous pockets until he found a small plastic bottle, which he offered to Andy.

'You do it. I'm pooped.'

'The soldier uncorked the bottle with trembling, gnawed fingers, and stroked the leech with the milky liquid. The leech lashed about before dropping off Andy's arm, where it left a purple mark.

'I seen 'em blown up like golf-balls,' the soldier said.

'That leech didn't do very well,' Andy said.

He caught Dan's eye and the two men smiled. Since leaving Saigon, where Sally had found a room in a hotel, they had indulged in a spurious intimacy, which in Andy's case was spoiled only by the intrusion of his illness. In Hong Kong he could trick it but here it weighed on him like a pack. Schreiber had warned him not to make this journey. He had been right.

Dan had sensed Andy's distress and helped him without asking questions.

'Jesus, I wish they'd let us smoke,' the boy said softly.

'Care for some Scotch?'

The boy took a pull at Andy's flask, gagged and wiped his mouth with the back of his hand. His eyes watered.

'I don't drink usually,' he said. 'I wish my buddy was here. He used to drink. Man, I never saw anyone drink so much. But he's dead now.'

'When?' asked Andy.

'Last night on that son of a bitch up there.'

The hill was visible from where they were. Its sides were covered to about half-way up with thick thorn bushes, after which there was no cover to speak of except a kind of reddish heather. This gave whoever held the summit a clear field of fire for two hundred yards. The sun, which was directly overhead now, shot darts of light off the bits of equipment which lay scattered about on the hillside. Nothing moved.

'I sure would like to be in your job,' the soldier said again, this time to Andy. 'How d'you get a job like that?'

'I bummed around.'

'I went to college,' Dan added.

'I guess I'll go to college when I git back. I have the chance. Then maybe I'd major in what you guys are doing.'

'Would you like to come back here as a journalist?' Dan asked.

'Sure I would. I'd come and look at all the other guys, just like you do, an' I'd say, "What do you suckers think about er, you know, Mao Tse-Tung?" 'cause we got lectures before we came here about communism and stuff. Oh, it'd be great!'

The flask went round again.

'Hey, this is my sister.'

The boy held out a plastic wallet containing a concertina of photographs.

They examined his sister and her two babies.

'I'm an uncle.' He spread out the concertina. 'That's my girl.' A studio portrait, backed by a Japanese screen.

'She's cute,' Andy said.

'And that's my buddy, the one who's at college right now. He's exempt from the draft. Don't you guys have any pictures?'

To Andy's surprise Dan produced a picture of Sally. She was wearing riding breeches and a sun-helmet and was standing outside some kind of mud hut with a gang of armed African tribesmen. A dead tiger lay at her feet.

'Wow!' said the boy.

'It was a film she was making,' Dan said apologetically. 'She doesn't usually look like that.'

'She's great.'

They both looked at Andy, who shook his head. He had a photograph in his pocket, but it was of Jean Fenwick.

At that moment the first wave of dive bombers came in from the coast, sowing explosions across the hill. The boy scrambled closer to the older men.

Black plumes nodded on the brow of the hill. The blast sent a skyful of fluff balls spinning through the air. They descended on the hidden soldiers and stuck on their arms and faces.

All afternoon aircraft bombed the already blackened hill, but at the end of the day the summit looked much the same as before. A sergeant came round with rations.

'I'd rather have you two stay behind when we get the order to go in,' he told Andy and Dan.

'I have to go,' Dan said.

'We can't be fully responsible for you. We can't have you endanger the lives of the men by detailing any of them to look after you.'

'We'll get by.'

The sergeant gave Dan a steady look. 'O.K.,' he said. He beckoned the young soldier to follow him and, reluctantly, the boy picked up his things.

'You left some food,' Andy said.

'That ain't no food. That's a firelighter.' The boy gave a tired, frightened grin. 'Take it easy, now,' he added.

'I'm scared,' Andy said.

'So am I.'

'Then why not let's do as the sergeant said?'

'You do as you want. I have to go.'

'What for, for God's sake?'

'It's my job.'

'Look, you get more information in half an hour at base HQ than you could in a week being a hero in this place.'

'Who's being a hero?'

'I'm sure as hell not.'

'Let's leave it, then.' Dan wanted the hill in the same way that he had wanted Sally, because it would give him definition. He did not put it to himself in these terms, although he did confuse the hill and Sally in the same thought drift. Up there, he was telling himself, there will be no doubt what is expected. It would not be like the last time he was in Vietnam, when he had entered that quiet glade and death had caught him unprepared. Going up the hill, he would anticipate things, as he had always done, in just sufficient time to know what to do with them. He was not like Andy, who carried inside him some built in lode-star all his own.

'You won't be much joy to Sally if you're dead,' Andy said, and it occurred to him for the first time that perhaps Dan would not come back from the hill. The thought made his stomach contract. He wondered if that was why he had insisted on coming with Dan this far – to see him off? He gave him a look of wistful appraisal, almost as if he was willing himself to be seeing him for the last time. It was

175

almost dark and although they could hear the whispers of the soldiers nearest to them, they could no longer see them.

'Listen,' Andy said, his heart pumping under his ribs at what he was being impelled to say. 'I must tell you something. It's been hell keeping it to myself. I've got . . . I'm sick . . . That business last time I was here, when you got me shipped out, that was part of it. I've got leukaemia.' Saying the word was like having an orgasm. 'Oh Jesus!'

'When did you find out?'

'Just then, that's when it hit me.'

'How long, how serious is it?'

'How long have I got, do you mean? Three years, maybe four. Maybe more, you never know, but I sure as hell have something better to do than go up that hill. Man, I have some living to do. I'm going to get married, have a child.'

'Keep the Burnses on the map?'

'Right.'

'Have you anybody in mind?'

'Well, maybe.' Andy thought he could see Dan smiling, but he might have been mistaken. 'So you see, I have a reason to keep away from that bloody hilltop.'

'You'd be a fool to take risks.' Dan spoke without conscious irony, thinking of the young soldiers who went out in Saigon to find women because they did not wish to die virgins.

'Don't you ever wish you had kids?'

'You know as much about that as I do. Jean told you.'

'That was only once. What about with a girl like Sally.'

'Sally's like you. She has a lot of living to do. I meant to send her a message, goddammit, to tell her I'd be two days late back to Saigon. Will you take care of it for me? Say we'll both be back the day after tomorrow. She might get worried.'

'Sure,' Andy said. 'Let's get some sleep.'

The moon had crept into the forest burrows, turning the hands and faces of the soldiers to white stone. Andy propped his head on his pack and slept like a man who has done a good day's work, but Dan was unable to sleep. He sat with his back against a tree, watching the progress of the moon across the sky and waiting for the order to go.

It came just before dawn. All over the forest there were the muted sounds of buckles being fastened and packs fitted to shoulders. There followed one of those dangerous pauses during which the notion began to take hold that something had gone wrong. The forest twittered with speculation. Then, just in time, as it seemed, the officers arrived from a briefing and moved from group to group, quelling thought. The platoon sergeants rejoined their men and held lesser briefings of their own.

Birds chattered, disturbed from their sleep. On top of the hill, North Vietnamese lookouts heard them and sounded the alarm.

'We're ready.' It was the sergeant of Dog Platoon, to which Dan and Andy had been attached.

'Burns stays here,' Dan said.

'He'd better move back to command, then. This area might come under fire.'

'O.K.,' Andy said. 'Take it easy now.' He touched Dan's arm. If Dan got a bullet it would be his own fault. He did not have to go. And if he never came back it would be a kind of miracle. Andy appealed to the trees to witness his innocence before squatting behind one to ease his tormented bowels.

Command H.Q. was a camouflaged tent stretched over a rectangular hole in the ground. Inside, duck boards, tables, maps and pin-ups gave Andy the strongest smell of home he had had in years.

'Mind if I come in?' he asked.

The battalion commander, a greying, clipped colonel with 'Yarmolinsky' written over his heart, gave him a look of granite indifference.

The crash of mortars and the cough of heavy machine-guns told them that the battle had been joined. There had been no element of surprise.

'Sit over there, man. You look sick.'

A Negro lieutenant indicated a camp-bed covered with grey blankets on which a padre was already seated. He did not look up when Andy joined him.

'Were you up on the hill last night?' Andy asked him.

The padre nodded. He had a pot belly over which the trousers of his fatigues stretched tightly. His bare arms were covered with ginger hair and freckles.

'Our boys will get it back,' he said.

No one spoke after that. Yarmolinsky stood like a rock beside his field telephone operator. The noises of the battle began to spread.

'Try again.'

The field telephone squawked.

'It's Major Luke, sir,' said the operator.

Yarmolinsky jammed the phone to a hairy ear.

'What's going on, Lukie?'

The staff officers watched their colonel's face.

'Hell no! Hold on while I get you air cover, do you hear me? Hold on and we'll soften 'em up. Over.'

'Roger,' said the voice. 'Over.'

'The bastards tried to counter-attack. They've pushed Charlie back round the side of the hill and they're pinning down Dog. They're really giving Dog a hard time. Get me air.'

When air command came on the line, Yarmolinsky gave them a shopping order that began with napalm and ended with high explosive. Prompt delivery was assured.

'Where you goin', Al?' a major said.

'I'm goin' up there to see for myself.'

The command post emptied, the other officers being sucked

through the door in Yarmolinsky's wake. Andy took one of the vacant chairs and the chaplain stretched out on the bed and locked his hands under his head. Both men waited. Andy looked at the field telephone. Dog was having a hard time. It might already have been cut to ribbons. Andy took Jean's letters out of his pocket and began re-reading them.

★   ★   ★

By the look of him the boy had been hit in the stomach. He lay doubled up on the hillside, holding himself below his belt and moaning. Dan had stumbled over him in his rush to hide from the communist mortars. As he lay alongside him he recognised the young conscript from Kentucky who wanted to be a journalist. The boy's eyes were shut.

'Easy does it,' Dan said.

The boy stopped moaning and his eyes opened. He gave Dan a gluey, faraway look. The effort must have been painful, for he began crying loudly, great, strident cries, too big for one human being to live with.

'Stop it!' Dan said.

He searched the boy's pockets, found a phial of morphine, snapped off the cap and stuck the open needle into the boy's arm. The terrible animal bellowing abated.

'Come,' said Dan. 'Let's have a look at you.'

He placed the boy on his back and cut away his clothes, exposing a hole which spread wider than the two locked hands could cover. Dan eased the fingers upwards and pressed a field dressing into the wound.

'Hold onto that,' he said.

He bent the boy's legs and placed a knapsack under his head. Then he lay on his side and looked about him. Mortar shells were still coming over the top of the hill, though less

179

frequently. There was heavy firing to left and right and a sharp, barking crash like a field gun, but from the hollow where they were he could see no one.

'Help me.'

The boy spoke quietly and clearly. His eyes were open and he was staring at the sky, in which hawks wheeled beyond the reach of the battle.

'Yes.'

'Oh, please.'

'It's O.K.'

'Oh, Jesus, help me.'

'Tell me.'

The boy whispered something. Dan put his ear close to the open mouth.

'Say it again.'

'I want a name.'

'What?'

'Name.'

'What name?'

'I never got one.'

'You must have.'

'Church name. They were goin' to give it me.'

'What do your folks call you?'

'It's not the same. Help me.'

The boy took Dan's wrist, then stopped, as if he had forgotten how he had wanted to complete the movement.

'What shall I call you?'

'I don't know.'

'What were they going to call you?'

'I don't know.'

'Think of a name.'

'No, you think.'

'O.K.'

'You have to hurry, the sergeant will come.'

'What's your family name?'

'Stukes.'

'All right, Stukes. From now on you're called John.'

'You ain't done it right.'

'It's a good name.'

'What about the words and the sign?'

'O.K. then. In the name of the Father, the Son and the Holy Ghost, I name you John.'

He spat with difficulty on the end of his index finger, but the boy was already dead. One of his hands had opened, palm upwards, as if he wanted someone to tell his fortune. A winged beetle had landed on his leg and sat there quivering in its black and gold shell. Dan wanted to envy the boy, not feel so unbearably sad for him. In the stillness that had been Stukes he felt exiled. He longed for someone to talk to. The summit of the hill was quite near. It looked grey and meaningless. Wearily he got to his feet.

The fighting had moved away and the other members of Dog were nowhere to be seen. Dan made his way back down the hill almost absentmindedly, although when the aircraft came in to release their napalm he was down quickly enough, pressing his face to the earth.

When Andy saw him walking out of the trees he had to turn away to hide his disappointment.

'Let's get out of here,' Dan said. Medical orderlies were filling the clearing with wounded and the padre was kneeling beside one of the stretchers, talking to a boy with a rubber tube coming out of his mouth. 'Did you get that message sent off for Sally?'

'I tried, but they wouldn't make promises. Hey, you have blood on your hand, are you O.K.?'

'Sure.'

'Listen, I must have been in pretty bad shape last night to shoot off my mouth about the leukaemia thing. I wouldn't

181

want to become an object of pity around here. You won't tell anyone, Dan?'

'Not if you say so.'

'Not even Sally, see? Or even Jean, if you were writing, I mean. O.K.?'

'O.K. I get the message.'

18

The crewman of the helicopter that lifted them out of the jungle offered them gum and comic books. He was pink-faced and wore horn-rimmed glasses, through which he looked intently at the ground for signs of an enemy. When he saw a puff of rifle fire he swung his machine-gun and fired back. He did so without comment. Hot cartridge cases piled up at his feet. Dan reckoned he was about the same age as Sally.

At their hotel in Saigon the desk clerk said that Miss Maine had gone to a press briefing. Dan left a message for her. He was relieved to be able to meet her on neutral ground and not in their bedroom.

He chose an ice-cream parlour near by. The place was unusually clean, for which reason it was favoured by GIs, who sat quietly in pairs drinking sodas and malts. A few rather raddled American civilians were there, contemplating their soft forearms while their young Vietnamese mistresses chattered to one another from table to table about Vietnamese things.

Through the wire bomb-screen that covered the window beggars tried to attract attention to their wounds by keeping up a soft tapping on the glass. No one looked at them, although everyone looked at Sally when she dashed in and stood there impatiently. She saw Dan and flew to him. Their knees banged together under the flimsy table and slopped his beer.

She was harder-looking. There were small lines at the corners of her mouth that he had not noticed before.

'I was worried,' she said. Her voice told of eight days of experiences unshared by him. He resented her for allowing him to confirm so totally his expectations about their reunion. He had been unwise to meet in public, after all. He saw the GIs watching them. He put his hand on her arm. He wanted to say something that would bring alive the so recent past but he was silenced.

'Are you all right?' She gave him a speculative smile, ill at ease. 'Just look at those poor cripples at the window! Isn't it grim how quickly one gets used to them.'

'Khaki suits you.' He had not meant it to sound ironic but it did.

'How's Andy?' she said.

'All right.' He rallied, smiling. 'Andy will always fall on his feet. He's full of secrets. They serve as ballast.'

'Now, what about me?'

'What do you mean?' His hands on her body, that he could recall.

'That's what you're supposed to say. Now I'm going to answer.'

She told him about the monk. She told it well.

What had happened was that on the evening after Dan and Andy had reported to the military airport for their mission she had met a group of journalists and American political people at the hotel bar and had agreed to go with them to see a refugee camp, which was about sixteen miles from Saigon inside a nominally safe area. An escort was provided by the American Army which was anxious to show the world press that the refugees were being properly cared for.

They had set off in three jeeps at eight in the morning. The air was keen and the thought that the fields and rivers they passed might conceal communist guerrillas thrilled her and she could not help hoping for an incident. In the villages they passed through she thought that people's faces were like careful masks and that only the children showed any vitality. They laughed and pointed and one threw a stone and then ran to its mother, shrieking at its own audacity.

The people in the camp looked as miserable and humiliated as Sally had expected. They were preparing their morning meal when the press party drove in through the barbed wire gates. Few of them bothered to look up from their cooking pots.

An American official explained that they intended to build communal kitchens but that just now the families preferred to make their own fires, which was wasteful and bad for morale.

'What we are trying to cultivate is camp spirit,' he said as they paused before a ragged little group. 'We are trying to show them that only through co-operating together will they be able to beat this thing.' Sally laughed now, in the telling, imitating the man's accent.

The American went on to explain that there was to be a school run by Buddhists.

'They're rather radical,' he said in a lower voice. 'But we believe that they have to work this thing out for themselves, so we try to give them enough rope.'

It was an unhappy image, but no one minded. The tour was proving a success. Cameras clicked and notebooks were being filled with statistics. Sally felt sad and involved, and when a child with sores took her hand she gave it a bar of chocolate.

At noon there was a break to enable the press to meet the Buddhist abbot and take refreshments, and she had to admit it was a relief to get away from the smell of the camp for a while.

They drove to a newish temple about half a mile down a

road along which Vietnamese soldiers were trudging behind a line of engineers who were making passes over the broken surface with mine-detectors.

The temple's corrugated-iron roof was blistered with heat, but inside the cloister it was cool and quiet. They sat at small iron tables arranged for four and novices served them with iced tea and plates of dried peppers and rice balls. After welcoming them, the abbot withdrew.

'He's quite a guy,' their guide told them, looking at his watch.

'Now there's no call for your people to bolt your food, none at all. Take your time and take it easy. Your next scheduled item isn't until two-thirty, when we have a concert party. We wanted to surprise you, so we didn't tell you about it. It's Mother's Day back home and a Marine unit that helped build the camp has improvised what you might call a musical tea. There'll be a jazz band and individual numbers and some extra rations for the oldest mothers. The guys have been really great.'

It was then that it began to happen, or that part of it to which they were privy, for she presumed that the germination had taken longer. From the shadows obscuring one end of the cloister a young monk carrying a tin can walked into the centre of the courtyard and sat down on the pavement facing them. Sally said she had just had time to take in the scar over his left eye and the moulded, sensual mouth, before the monk upended the can above his head. Shimmering liquid ran over his ears and shoulders and down the front of his face. It darkened his robe and she heard him gasp as it touched his lips. Then he took a cigarette-lighter from an inside pocket and held it to his chest.

It all happened, she said, much too quickly.

At the first flick the lighter failed to work. The monk's face was glistening. At the second, a tiny flame appeared which quickly spread over his chest and shoulders, kind of cupping his face. He made no sound.

People got to their feet, shouting. Cameramen fumbled for their exposure metres. There was a whirring noise, like wind on a bonfire. Someone threw a jacket which landed like a carpet at the monk's feet. The body began to move in the flames. It began to slip sideways. A gong was being beaten inside the monastery, but neither the abbot nor his novices were to be seen.

Before the monk collapsed Sally saw his face once more. His mouth was open and his eyes, black-rimmed, stared at her with horror. And then it was over. The corpse lay on its side like a piece of burned mutton in a widening stain from which there protruded a single, unblemished foot.

Ever since, the smell of meat burning on braziers at the street corners had sickened her. She had been unable to eat. But that was nothing. What had really upset her had been the look in the monk's eyes. She had caught it because he had looked straight at her. He had kind of begged murderously. It was hard to explain, but the look had shocked her by its cruelty. It was like the cruelty of glaciers, that was what it was like.

'You ought it write it all down,' Dan said savagely. 'You don't want to waste it.'

'I have. At least, I've spoken it into a tape machine.'

'Let's go,' he said.

They returned to the hotel and as they crossed the lobby, which was crowded with correspondents, Sally was greeted by people Dan had never seen before.

They found Andy in a cramped doze.

'Hi, Sally, I went to sleep with my mouth open. That goddam ceiling fan has dried out the insides of my mouth, did you ever hear of that happening to anyone? It feels like a paper bag!'

Sally fetched him a glass of water from the basin and while Dan showered in the adjacent room she sat on the end of his bed and told him an abbreviated version of her story about the monk. He was a more rewarding audience than Dan had been and she told him so.

'He's tired, I guess.'

'He's getting old,' she said. 'Perhaps he ought not to come to places like this any more if they make him so surly and depressed. You seem to be O.K.'

'I'm all right,' Andy said. 'I even wrote my copy. Look!'

She read his story with a now professional eye. 'Very good,' she said, thinking it rather perfunctory. 'Has Dan written his?'

'I guess not. Dan moves in mysterious ways. You seldom see him actually working, but the stuff turns up in London right enough.'

'I wish I understood him,' she said. 'He's so remote half the time. One minute he's warm and just lovely and the next he's all uptight and somewhere else and there's a big No Admittance sign on the door.'

'People,' said Andy, swapping cliché for cliché, 'are hard to figure out.'

They sighed and shook their heads, congratulating themselves for being able to manage notwithstanding.

'Saigon is rotten,' she was saying. When Dan returned from his shower. 'It's so rotten you can smell it.'

'That's the garbage,' Dan said. 'Come. Let's go out.'

They left Andy preparing to have another doze.

'He looks awful,' she said, taking his arm.

'He'll manage.' He disengaged his arm. Her tense familiarity jarred on him.

'Where are we going?' She sounded forlorn.

'Where would you like?'

'I wouldn't mind a bit to eat,' she said.

'A lump of barbecued monk?'

'Very witty.'

'Let's go to a bar first anyhow. I need people.'

'Aren't we people?'

'I need a conversation. I haven't had a conversation for months.'

They skirted a hill of uncollected refuse. A large rat walked across the pavement in front of them, taking its time. She recoiled and he put his arm round her shoulder.

'There'll be plague soon, they say.'

'There is already,' he said.

Refuse dumps filled the middle of the streets like road works.

'I didn't just see the monk thing as a good story,' she said. 'The others did, they all took pictures, but I saw it as a human experience that would help me to see myself more clearly.'

'I'm a bit drunk,' he said.

'Yes.'

'But not quite enough.'

'I see.'

'You never get drunk, do you?'

'I get high sometimes.'

How trite of her. He forced the thought until it bloomed inside him. He did not want to live. That had been made clear to him as he watched the silver cords of Stukes's life running up through his body and out through his face. That he did not want to die either had been made clear for the umpteenth time when the planes had rushed down at him and he had grovelled.

'This is it,' he said.

The bar was almost dark and the air felt like warm cobwebs on her face. Dim lights picked out coppery tabletops on which hands lay like starfish. The room's centre was a cloudy sea on whose floor American giants slithered, holding exquisite, miniature girls in their arms.

A grimacing Halloween face swayed towards her, belched and passed on. She gave an exclamation of surprise, hoping that Dan would register her displeasure, but he propelled her on with the flat of his hand.

'Here,' he said. 'You sit and I'll get a drink.'

'Dan, I don't want a drink!'

'Well, I do.'

She lost him. Rags of music boiled in the cobweb soup. She got to her feet, piqued with herself for sitting down in the first place, and tried to follow him, but instead of finding the bar she entered some kind of alcove, where she barked her shins against an empty chair and sat again, telling herself it was only for a minute. She was bewildered by his behaviour. It was almost as if he was jealous of her. She had been thrilled when they gave her the note in his brusque scrawl and had run to him with her story and he had put her down. He had virtually dismissed her. She began to get angry. He had no right, sitting there looking like a weatherbeaten warhorse. She had not recognised him at first glance, the café had been so full of older-looking men. She wished he would come back. She felt as if he was ridiculing her. Suppose he just never came back? Her pride burned at the thought. Come on Dan, she thought, imagining his dry finger on her lips. Her heart flip-flapped inside her. He must have been drinking too much and not getting enough sleep. They were the only explanations acceptable to her.

'Damn!' she said aloud. This was all she needed. She was aware of noises close to her. Someone was sighing and snorting to the accompaniment of other sounds denoting carnal relief. She followed them furiously as they jerked to a climax. There was a scuffling of feet and a cigarette-lighter flared. She saw a small brown face which was enlivened by a pair of bright black eyes. A mouth, in which there were no front teeth, gave her a knowing snigger.

'Exit!' she said ferociously, grinding the boy's shoulder with her knuckles. 'Show me the exit!'

Sticky fingers took hers and the boy pummelled his way through the hot throng until they were out on the pavement, where they stood for a moment still holding hands before the boy pranced into the bar again, pausing only to turn and run his forefinger in and out of his mouth at her. The door of the bar slammed shut and she regretted having left.

She pointed to a battery lamp hanging on the front of a waiting pedicab and offered the driver a dollar bill. 'Ten minutes,' she said. The man eased the lamp off its hook.

Back in the bar mole-like faces blinked at the light.

'Hey, baby, not so fast!'

'I'm looking for a friend.'

'You sure came to the right place!' A hand ravished her waist. Other customers held up lighters in imitation of her and soon there were a dozen tiny flames. Everyone laughed until someone said to quit fooling. The cry was taken up.

And then she found Dan. He was sitting by himself at the far end of the bar.

'Have a drink,' he said.

'Why didn't you come back for me?'

'I got tired.'

'Very funny. It's time we had a talk.'

'Not a chance.'

'You really burn me up, Dan! You just leave me marooned in this filthy place while some slob gets pleasured by a little kid right next to me. It's not funny!'

'You sound ridiculous.'

'That's what you'd like. I can see. You're pathetic.'

'You sound like a maiden aunt in a brothel. You're making a scene, people are listening.'

'Let them listen! You must be mad, talking about scenes in a place like this. Let's go, Dan. Let's go back to the hotel where we can be together. Please.'

'I need conversation.'

'You just said we couldn't. What's wrong with you?'

'I said you and I couldn't have a conversation. I didn't say I was incapable of one.'

'You make everything as confused as you can, don't you? You really love to stir up confusion and then you think that you'll get your own way and that no one will notice how selfish you are because they'll be so confused all the time. Well, I'm not and I'm not going to let you make me.'

'All right, see you around.'

'Don't you want to be with me any more?'

'Stop picking on everything I say, you're always picking.'

'I won't stay here.'

'Well, don't.'

'What's the matter, Dan? Please tell me.'

For answer he put his hand behind her neck and, pulling her face towards him, he stuck his tongue into her mouth. She felt his beard scraping her lips. She had to take a fistful of his hair to get him away from her.

'You're digusting! You're like a dirty old man. I'm leaving.'

'O.K. I shan't be back tonight, I don't expect.'

'I mean I'm leaving Saigon. You were right, I should never have come here with you. The whole time here you've been cold and different and cruel. You've been a different person.'

'You've had your kicks.'

'You resent everything I do that doesn't emanate from you, don't you? You're like Maslyn Martin and the rest of them. You're disgusting!'

'Why don't you go? Just leave.'

'I am.'

'See you in Hong Kong, then.'

'Don't bank on it.'

'Be patient.'

'Patient! You must be out of your mind!'

She went back into the street, half hoping that he would follow her, but he did not. 'Stupid old bar,' she sobbed.

19

Next morning, while they were taking her luggage down-stairs, she went to Andy's room to say goodbye. She was leaving, she said, because she refused to be taken for granted. It was as simple as that. She put her surplus Vietnamese currency into an envelope and told the man at the desk to give it to Mr Fenwick.

The steward on the aircraft was sweet to her. He gave her a seat with extra leg-room and chatted to her rather more than the other passengers might have wished. 'We're crossing the coast now,' he said, bringing her a vodka and tonic.

She saw wooded hills and dark stone mountains marching towards a watery plain where rivers glinted, ending at the sea, which washed whitish against the shore, shading into its own blue as the land shelf fell away. At this remove Vietnam reminded her of one of the relief maps the nuns at her convent school had helped them to make out of plasticine and bits of mirror.

'It's terrible to think what's going on down there,' the steward said.

At Hong Kong airport Chinese customs men and red-faced Europeans gave her a sense of more than physical security. She suddenly felt homesick.

In the lobby of Dan's apartment block she encountered his houseboy Lim, who fled at the sight of her. She looked at herself in the elevator mirror as she rode to the fifth floor but she could see no explanation in her appearance for Lim's behaviour. She thought she looked just as she had done when she left.

As she unlocked the door of Dan's apartment she heard a noise inside and it occurred to her that Lim might be entertaining a girl-friend; but it was not a Chinese who was standing in the sitting-room, but a tall woman with dark hair and dark, rather startled eyes. The woman was wearing a well-cut linen frock and leather shoes with thick, modish heels, details which Sally took in before her suitcase had reached the ground.

'You're Dan's wife,' she said.

'Your pictures don't do you justice,' Jean replied.

She sat down as she spoke and Sally was disagreeably aware of standing before her.

'How long have you been here?'

'Five days. I came with your friend, Maslyn Martin. She's at the Grand. They're hoping to see you there. She's reserved you a room.'

'What made her do that?'

'I suppose because she thought that's where you belong.'

'She's got it wrong.'

'Can you see yourself staying here?'

'That's up to Dan.'

She walked through into the bedroom with her bag.

'What have you done with my things?' she called through the open door.

'You'll find them in the laundry basket.'

'Well, thanks a lot. Did you have to crumple them like this?'

'I didn't crumple them. I had to make a place for my own.'

'Dan always said you might turn up.' Sally began to lay her clothes on the bed, smoothing them to keep busy.

'I think you ought to leave before he comes back,' Jean said. 'He's still there, isn't he?'

'Why should I?' They were facing one another across the bed, in which Jean's night things made a small hillock.

'We can't both stay here and I am his wife.'

'That's no reason, especially after what you two have done to one another.'

'I suppose he told you a version.'

'You can hardly expect to come back just because you're jealous or something, and shake your marriage vows at me.'

'That's what I am doing. What will you do about it?'

'What's Dan going to do, you mean?'

'It's for us to decide.'

'Well, really! I detect Maslyn Martin's reasoning in that remark. Of course it's to do with Dan.' She sat down with a bump on top of her crumpled clothes, the thought coming to her that Dan might not want either of them.

'You probably know more about his thoughts than I do,' Jean said.

'I don't know.'

'It wasn't just me, you know. He nearly drove me out of my mind.'

'Well, why come back? So he can finish off the job?'

'I didn't think you'd be so hard. In your picture you look different.'

'Who's being hard? You talk like a novelette! Let Dan make up his own mind.'

'Then you don't love him, that's all I can say.'

'If only it was.'

'I didn't mean us to quarrel.'

'What else can we do?'

'Talk sensibly.'

'No! I'm fed up with all this beating about the bush. Dan's just the same, he refuses to say what he means straight out. I wonder sometimes if any of you have proper thoughts at all or whether it isn't all a brew of emotion and self-pity.'

'Has he started drinking yet? Have you seen that side of him?'

'I don't care if he does drink. Anyway, he doesn't with me. You walk out on him and have your half-baked breakdown, and then the moment the man who is so relieved, let me tell you, to get you out of his hair finds a bit of happiness, you pack your bag and try to smash it up.'

'I haven't come to smash anything up.'

'What, then?'

'I want to complete it.'

'Complete what?'

'You needn't raise your voice. Complete whatever it is with Dan, one way or other.'

'I don't believe it and I don't care anyway, but I just know you're trying to be a dog in the manger.'

'Do you expect him to marry you?'

'Oh, for heaven's sake, one was enough, I should think.'

'Supposing he wants a child.'

'He might.'

'You have no right!'

'Who's raising their voice now? Why don't you forget rights for once? All right, I will leave. The flat's a detail. Make the most of it. We'll see what Dan has to say.'

'What about your things?'

'I don't fancy them.' Sally picked up her suitcase and left, but Jean ran after her down the corridor.

'Don't brush me off,' she said. 'Please, just listen for a minute, you won't listen. You are young, you don't understand, just do as I say.'

'What now?'

'Just get out and leave. For God's sake!'

The elevator door slid open and Sally got in and stood with her back to the corridor. Jean tried to hold the door but it bucked against her hand and she let it go, watching the indicator light flick down to the lobby and rest there. She did not regret begging. It could have been a lot worse.

She went back to the flat and began packing Sally's things carefully into a suitcase. Some of the dresses were so light you hardly knew you were holding them. She held up a trouser-suit made of shimmery gold material. It had been made in Paris. The girl knew what she wanted. She was hard, but only in the way the young often were. Jean wished she had never come. What would it avail if Sally were to leave Dan? Why should he take her back?

The possibility made her flush.

20

'Darling! Let me look at you. Come to the light. There!'
Maslyn peered at Sally through her darkest sun-glasses.
'There,' she repeated, as if to say things were already more as
they should be. 'How clever of you to come back all by yourself, unencumbered, as it were. How sensible, but not more
than I should have expected.

'He had to stay on for a while,' Sally said. 'He'll be back
soon. I got the wind up over there. He said I would. So I did
a bunk.' She still had the tendency to fall into baby-talk with
Maslyn, but the older woman no longer impressed her as she
once had. The magic cave that Maslyn used to make for
herself by the power of her presence and the disposition of her
possessions on tables and chairs and hooks remained for
Sally an ordinary bedroom into whose windows there stared a
white, ungenerous light.

'Never mind. We'll all have to think and decide how to
cope with him. He sounds a formidable gentleman.'

'Nobody has to cope with him. I want him back. I mean,
he's never gone, we just got a bit upset and kind of lost one
another. He knows I'm here and he'll come when he can.'

'Of course he will. I don't suppose you had a row, did you,
because if you did, that's nothing to get upset about, is it?'

'We did, Mas. We had a corker. He was late back to Saigon
and we'd agreed to meet and he was two days late, and, well,
they have to rely on the charity of the Air Force out there,
it's very difficult.'

'Naturally, dear.'

'So they can't always be punctual.'

'Nor are they, I'll be bound. I can just see them romping about some leech-infested spot feeling sixteen again, can't you? Men are always willing to plunge backwards at the drop of a bomb.'

'I wish you'd take your glasses off. I can't see you.'

'Later, dear. I'm just being Mrs Sphinx at the moment, if you don't mind. I'm taking stock. I'm so glad to see you. I was terribly worried and really got into a stupid state because I thought you were throwing yourself down on your knees and begging for the fetters to be hammered onto you.'

'I want him,' Sally said with a touch of petulance.

'Well, you have him, don't you?'

'I don't have to justify myself all the time.'

'Of course not, or we might think the lady doth protest too much.'

'He treats me seriously.'

'Like a real person.'

'Yes.' Yet it sounded thin and the horizon she and Dan had pushed out seemed now to contract again. Maslyn removed her glasses and Sally prepared for battle, but the older woman seemed suddenly tired.

'Human kind cannot bear very much reality,' she said. 'T. S. Eliot.'

'Dan and I managed all right.'

'I'm sure *you* did, I wonder a bit about *him*. People who have fantasies instead of proper reactions to life can often be very convincing when they're coaxing other people into their parlour, because they need other people in there, naturally, they can't live all on their own. Who can?'

'He's a creative sort of person and he needs help and no one's ever given it to him.'

'Oh, you're a helper now. I thought it was a partnership of

equals, but you're midwifing a talent now. I hope it won't be stillborn, marinated with too much brandy and water.'

'He's writing a play.'

'Every schoolboy starts one of those. Has he put pen to paper since you've known him?'

'Oh, Maslyn!'

'Well, has he?'

'I don't know, I don't sit and count the lines.'

'I only asked because I'm told there's been a long interval between the acts.'

'You've been talking to his wife.'

'Of course! I take it you've met?'

'Just now. Dreadful!'

'All hot and clammy inside.'

'She's put my clothes in a beastly old basket!'

'Really?'

'I told her to keep them. I didn't want them, after that.'

'I don't blame you, dear.'

'But Mas, I blame you for egging her on to come out here and coming yourself and trying to interfere. I'm not having it. Not any more. Where's Gaston? Hiding in the cupboard, I suppose?'

'Gaston wanted to come but I told him better not. To be frank with you, I think you've outgrown him, don't you?'

'I could have told you that.'

'Jean Fenwick reminds me of Gaston a bit, they're both like those fish, what do you call 'em, that swim after sharks in the hope of picking up scraps.'

'And who is the shark?'

'Me of course. I am the avenging shark because I see you in danger of wasting yourself on a folly. He is using you just as he used her, only she wants it now, she's prepared to put up with it, so she says.'

'But everyone uses each other. What's the matter with that?'

'Don't be thick, dear. You know exactly what I mean.'

'Dan's not like that with me. You haven't done your homework, shame on you.'

'I'm not suggesting he's been like that with you yet, I'm saying it's his essential character. Drink is a mainstay, though I dare say the novelty of your presence may have enabled him to lay off for a while, if only to ensure a more romantic performance in bed.'

The two women paced about the room as they talked, Maslyn's fatigue having curiously diminished. They looked at themselves in the mirror when they chanced on it and an observer would have been excused for thinking that they were really quite enjoying themselves.

'I bet you've begun to lead him in lovemaking.'

There was no reply.

'I bet he really wants to sleep in the end and you listen to his breathing and wonder whether to wake him up. I bet you do.'

Still no reply.

'I will tell you what kind of man he is,' Maslyn said. 'Then tell me honestly if I am wrong. He is a brave man who sees himself as a kind of hero. He's living in a kind of Byronic fantasy world where he is alone, preferably wounded daily by invisible darts of evil, on some bleak shoreline littered with droppings of civilisation. There is no one in sight, no one real, that is. He craves love, so he thinks, but does not know how to find it. Then along comes you and he invites you to join him on the shoreline. He is a kind of male siren. He makes you think you have been offered an experience which is unique, that you have awakened his love at last. You are therefore unique. You ignore the other human shapes you see lying around among the empty brandy bottles because they don't square with the fantasy you have now embraced, which is that he and you together are real and everyone else is unreal. Am I right? Has there not been talk of love and shore-lines and reality and evil?'

Memorising Andy's letters to Jean, in which he had reported Dan's conversations with Sally at length, had occupied Maslyn from London to Bangkok.

'It's easy to sneer.'

'Not to do it properly, it isn't.'

'Wait till you meet him.'

'You can't mean it? Anyway, I've no intention of.'

'Why did you come, then?'

'To see you, of course, and to tell you, incidentally, if you'll let me get a word in edgeways, some rather splendid news.'

'What news?'

'I'm telling you! You know that Panni plans to make a picture about Maxim Gorki after this one, starting shooting next summer? Well, he wants you in it. How does that grab you?'

'What's the part?'

'Oh, what's the part, she says. Very good, my darling. One of two women, his lovers. You're the younger one, who superseded the older lady, so I believe. In other words, you'd be *it*, isn't that good?'

'I suppose it is.'

'Suppose? You must be mad! After the trouble getting you into this picture and all Panni's doubts and all your complaints to me on the telephone that he didn't like you! There's no suppose about it! It's what we've been waiting for!'

21

At Saigon airport the booking hall was always so crowded that influential people preferred not to go near it, driving straight onto the runway instead. It was like a blocked drain, its floor covered with old food and other refuse. Dan and Andy had to place their feet carefully to avoid treading on babies.

American servicemen, waiting in slow-moving lines for planes which would take them away for weeks or for ever, divided the hundreds of Vietnamese civilians into random squares and triangles.

To Andy the place was an obstacle course in which every kitbag seemed to grow in size as he tried to work his way past it. He felt so shattered with fatigue that he could barely recognise Dan, who was carrying the luggage. He was oppressed by the close atmosphere and the dim electric lights which yet hurt his eyes.

The air was less used in the underfurnished office behind the reception desks, where an official crossed out two names from a passenger list and substituted their own. He counted Dan's bribe with a cashier's fingers.

The plane flew high over a countryside which seemed to be very largely in flames. Andy had rapidly doped himself to sleep. Dan drank brandy and by the time he next thought to look out of the window Vietnam had vanished into the sea.

A ship was scratching a delicate line across the waves, leaving behind it a wake that seemed of no concern to it.

Dan thought of all the used-up, empty things under the sea, bottles and old tins and the shells of ships and indestructible things such as false teeth and rings.

He looked at Andy and saw that he was dribbling. He wondered how he would be if his own white corpuscles were to go wrong or if, like Stukes, he had a hole in him the size of a pudding plate? Stukes should have been given a Viking send-off into the sea, there to meet with the woman he had seen in Hong Kong harbour. Stukes would have wiped his eyes in her long, black hair, instead of which they would put him in an aluminium box and fly him back on one of the mail planes and he would be covered with a flag and lowered into the ground of some cemetery in Kentucky, after which his mother would be given the flag to take home with her.

He wondered what Sally would have said if he had tried to explain to her about Stukes. She had asked him about the graduation ring once and when he told her that he had taken it from a dead man she had made some funny remark about looting or grave-robbing. She had not understood. The money she had left for him in the hotel envelope had been touching and had smelt of her perfume, but it was not money he had needed. He half hoped that she would have moved out of his flat, yet when he arrived there early next morning and found it occupied by his wife instead he changed his mind violently.

Jean had heard him coming and had taken up her station by the mantelpiece. He took in none of the details about her that Sally had and although he thought almost as soon as he had left her how much larger her eyes seemed to be than he remembered, all he could do at the time was to stand and frown at her while the red anger rose and boiled inside him. Her presence seemed to invalidate his time with Sally and drag him into a shared failure with her which made him hate her. He had never realised before how much he could hate a single human being. It was all he could do to prevent himself from striking her face. He picked up an earthenware bowl and dashed it to the ground.

'Where is she?' He could hardly speak to her.

'At the Grand.' She wanted to say more, but he shouted her down.

'You're mad,' he said and rushed out, leaving the flat door swinging open.

A newspaper had been pushed half-way under the door of Sally's bedroom. A notice hanging on the handle said she did not wish to be disturbed. He opened the door, which she had forgotten to lock. She stirred under the bedclothes. He pulled back the curtains. Light flowed over her and she started up with a violent movement of her arms as if pushing someone away, then hid her face in her hands.

'Don't,' she said.

'Too late. I already have.' He sat on the bed. 'Did I frighten you?'

'No, it's the light.'

'Look at me, then.'

'I am.'

'No you're not.'

'I'm looking through my fingers. Your wife is here, I suppose you know that. And Maslyn.'

'Give me a kiss.'

'All right.'

'Properly.' The kiss was deep but unsatisfactory.

'I never knew you wore pyjamas.'

'When I'm alone.'

They kissed again and she buried her face in his neck and clung to his head with her two hands.

'I left my clothes at your flat,' she said. 'Your wife ruined them.'

'You must get up,' he said. 'Before people start to arrive.'

'What for?'

'Come on, we can get the ferry to Macao and then we can decide.'

'Decide what?'

'What to do. Get dressed, Sally. I'm sorry about Saigon. I did warn you. I meant to behave properly but there seemed no way. Come on, show a leg.'

'I was planning to leave your flat whether she'd been there or not, do you know that?'

'I went back, I could hardly wait, expecting to see you, Sally, and you weren't there.'

'Don't, Dan. Your breath smells awful. Have you been to bed at all since we saw each other last? You don't look like it.'

'Listen, let's go to Macao and then we can talk.'

'You said conversation was out for you and me.'

'I said a lot of things. I'm sorry. I knew when I went in and you weren't there and she was standing looking so bloody hopeless at me that we had to give it another go, Sally. Just once more, so's we can decide.'

'You know, I've thought a lot since the bar, Dan, and neither of us has ever used the word love since we met each other, do you realise that?'

'Get up now, Sally, I'm going to pull the bedclothes off you.'

'It's no good, Dan, you can't dive away like that. It's you who never have the conversations, did you know that? You just want an audience, not a conversation.'

There was a knock on the door.

'It'll be Maslyn,' Sally whispered. 'Don't let her in till I'm in the shower.'

Maslyn came in to find Dan alone, draining the last drops of brandy from his flask with a faint guzzling noise.

'Ah,' she said. 'I see you're on the hard stuff. Let me send for some more.' She rang for service. 'What was it?'

'Brandy.'

'Right.'

'With ice and water.'

'Of course. Brandy with ice and water, please.'

'Large or small?' a voice asked.

'I should think so.'

'Large?'

'Yes.'

She sat on the end of Sally's bed and smoothed the sheets. 'Been here long?'

'No.'

'I'm Maslyn Martin.'

'Yes.'

'How was Vietnam?'

'Hasn't Sally told you?'

'People's versions of things vary so wildly, I always find. How long do you plan to stay here, now you're back?'

'I live here.'

'I know. I travelled out with your wife. I had no idea we both lived in the same village, and for all those years!'

The woman's brittle manner repelled him. He disliked the small, pallid face, with its huge, catlike eyes. He wondered if she was a lesbian.

'I suppose it was you gave Jean the notion to return here?'

'I suppose it was. At least, I encouraged her.'

'I can imagine. Well, you don't know what you're doing. She's been very unwell.'

'She's stronger than you perhaps like to think.'

'What does that mean?'

'You want labels, pigeon-holes, so much easier, of course.'

'I suppose you'll tell me you're doing her good?'

'In a way, certainly. At least she doesn't have that psycho-somatic hay fever any more, does she?'

'As if you cared! She served your purpose and now she might not exist for you.'

'That's quite untrue. You know nothing about me.'

'You've used her.'

'Oh, used! used! What about you and Sally? What about that?'

'I don't want to suck the life out of her the way you do.'

'What I care about is her talent.'

'Balls!'

'You mean guts, don't you?'

'I suppose you think she's impressed by that jargon about freedom and authenticity you use all the time. Well, she's not. She told me she thought you were ridiculous.'

'She told me she thought you were a selfish failure. She did.'

'She said you were a comic little kind of thwarted man in a woman's body.'

'Ah, ah, now come on . . . that doesn't ring true. Sorry, but she knows me too well to make a mistake like that.'

'She doesn't trust you.'

'She certainly doesn't trust you.'

'I never asked her to!'

'You didn't have to, which helped you salve your intellectual conscience, I suppose. Men always like to have their cake and eat it. You didn't have to because she was hooked. Well, I'm here to tell you she isn't any longer, and it isn't even me who's unhooked her. She's got down all by herself. She's coming home with me.'

'I don't believe you.'

'Wait and see. Anyway, surely you aren't so surprised, Mr Fenwick? You can't really have expected it to last beyond a certain point. Sally is young. She's learning all the time.'

'You have an incredible nerve to think you can narrate

other people's lives for them. Have you lived in this fantasy for long?'

'Strange, that was just what I was telling Sally about you. She agreed. She said that in Vietnam the scales fell from her eyes, as they say.'

The bathroom door opened and Sally emerged. She was wearing an embroidered Chinese dress, its side seams open to her thighs.

'It's all I have,' she said.

'It's lovely, dear. Isn't it, Mr Fenwick? Poor Mr Fenwick, he's been waiting so long for his drink. I wonder if he'll hold out?'

'Are you coming with me or staying with this . . . with her?' Dan said.

The waiter chose that moment to bring in the brandy. He looked quickly at the three faces before handing it unerringly to Dan.

'What are we all waiting for?' Sally said.

'For me to drink this.' Dan downed it in a couple of swallows and got to his feet.

'Well, I'm waiting to see poor Sally smile,' Maslyn said. 'She used to be so gay, Mr Fenwick. What have you done to her?'

They both looked at Sally, who avoided their eyes and walked out into the corridor. Dan followed, closing the bedroom door behind them.

Maslyn sat down again on Sally's bed to have what she would have described as a think, and what she thought was that on the whole she had little to worry about.

After a while she rang Jean, but there was no answer.

22

When Dan had gone Jean's first reaction was to start closing things, the door to the common passage, a window, her own hands, which she made into tight fists. Only when she had closed everything did she allow her mind to look out from its inmost chamber and contemplate what had taken place.

When he had come in just now she had been made crudely aware of the gulf between their two beings, so big that their joint past was lost in it, yet at the same time the springs of the past had gushed up in her and it was as if he had been trying to reach across the preposterous gulf and restore to her some piece of herself that he had been carrying about inside him. Standing there in the doorway, he had lifted with a look the boredom of her years away from him.

Wait, she had meant to say. Don't walk out. Let me explain. It'll be different now, I've changed. I'm not who you think I am.

But it was too late because before she had found the first words he had flown off and left her, and now he was somewhere else.

As she thought about Dan and Sally she felt heavy and empty. A telephone began ringing, but she ignored it. It stopped, then rang again.

'Jean? My God, I can't believe it! This is Andy. I'm coming over right away, O.K.?'

'How did you know I was here?'

'Dan just came by and asked me to pick up some of his things from the flat.'

'Where is he?'

'He's going to Macao on the ferry. He reckons he'll stay over there for a while. He told me not to tell anyone, but that couldn't include you.'

'Did he say that?'

'I mean I couldn't include you.'

'Yes. Is he with her?'

'Sure. Listen, Jeanie, are you O.K.? Jean? Is there anything I can bring?'

'I wish I'd never come, Andy.'

'You won't be sorry, honey.'

'I am already.'

'Not in the end.'

'He just won't listen.'

'I guess that's true.'

'Do you think he'd listen?'

'Not the way he was just now.'

'I know.'

'Don't cry about it.'

'Will you help me find him, Andy?'

'What's the use?'

'Will you?'

'If that's what you want. I'll be over in twenty minutes, make it fifteen, O.K.?'

He hurried, humming, back to his kitchen, where he had been eating a plate of gooseberries he had found in the ice-box. Excitement made his movements erratic.

The gooseberries, which came from China, were fat and crisp and had cold insides. Their tart flavour subdued the cloying aftermath of the drug he had taken on the long flight from Vietnam. He ate them greedily, standing up. He did not really want any more but, seeing them grow less on the plate, he finished them off, thinking that Jean's cheeks would probably be wet and that he would kiss them, as he always did, but that this time it would be different.

*   *   *

The ferry was broad-beamed and smelly and the hectic cadences of Chinese dance music crackled through its loudspeakers. Jean and Andy sat on a wide side-deck next to a Chinese family, which bowed to them courteously. The father had large puffs of cotton-wool coming out of his ears. He was reading a book of poems. Andy saw Jean looking at the old man and gave her a wink.

The sea was skittish. White waves tickled the little, empty islands which lay unstrung along their way. A north-east wind flung the following birds slap against the sky and junks with creaking black sails flew across their bows. Fish with gaping mouths rose from the sea, dripping sapphires, but neither of them noticed.

On the quayside in Macao touts lay in wait and from among the disembarking passengers they selected single women and old men whom they bullied into handing over their luggage. If a family was waiting to greet an aged grandparent or unmarried sister the touts would be driven away with shouts and even fists, but many were greeted by no one and it was they who could be seen, as they tucked away their identification papers, hobbling anxiously after some hard-looking stranger who had seized their bags and was carrying them off to lodgings of his own choosing.

'What we have to do is to tour the hotels,' Jean said. 'They're bound to be in a hotel. They could be nowhere else.'

She waited for confirmation of this view. Andy was sitting on a sea-wall breathing heavily through his nose. His car, searched inside and out by the Portuguese customs men, looked violated. An old woman was resting her bundles on the outside bumper. She was railing to herself in a high, childish voice.

'Let's get going,' Jean said.

They climbed into the car. Andy's brain felt as if it was loose inside his skull. He took out a plastic phial and teased a pill into the palm of his hand.

'Shall I drive?' Jean asked. Desperation at the sheer vulgarity of her situation was giving her a new energy. Her voice was edged with command. Andy shook his head.

As the engine began to turn over the old woman lifted her bundles off the bumper and a tout grabbed them and made off with them. The old woman had to trot to keep up with him.

'Where to first?'

'It doesn't much matter. There can't be that many hotels.'

'Do you really have to go through with this?'

'Oh, Andy!'

'You stand to be awful hurt.'

'Aren't you well, Andy? Am I being very selfish?'

'I am perfectly well and no, you're not being selfish.'

The first hotel was closed. They went to the annexe of the sailing club. No one answering to Dan's description was staying there. Had they tried the Empress? The Empress was all broken bottles and burned paper. A mob of Red Guards had daubed slogans on the outside walls and the reception desk was stuck over with portraits of Chairman Mao. A ripe-looking woman, whose breath came in unpredictable gusts from beneath her silk blouse, told them to please leave because her premises were being watched by communists and she did not want more trouble.

'Well, that's it,' said Andy.

'They must be somewhere.'

They drove without aim past dusty, tranced gardens

where monuments to Portuguese travellers bleached and crumbled until Andy thought of returning to the harbour and asking the immigration officers to check their arrivals lists.

A ferry was coming in. They could see a group of white men among the hundreds of Chinese.

'It's Koltz and the agency people.'

Koltz spotted them as they waited with upturned faces among the touts. He waved, pushing people out of the way with his other hand.

'You're ahead of us,' he said, when his neat feet were on dry land. 'How did you get to hear? They only released the story ten minutes before this ferry left.'

'What story?'

'Some high-up has defected from China and Peking is putting the heat on the Portuguese to hand him over. Some intelligence colonel. The Portuguese are holding a press conference so the guy can be seen in public. Why, I can't imagine, because there's likely to be a riot when the commies try to grab him back.'

'There's Dan!' Jean pointed to the ferry, her heart turning over.

'Sure,' Koltz said, smiling at Andy.

Dan was coming down the gangway. He was followed by Sally. He carried a suitcase in one hand and a typewriter in the other.

'Get in the car,' Andy said.

She obeyed but started to get out again.

'I'm not the one who's hiding,' she said.

'Can you guys give me a lift?' Koltz cocked a leg into the back of the car, getting in Jean's way.

Neither Dan nor Sally showed that they had seen her. Their eyes stared unsmilingly from their tanned faces. Inside her the insulted woman surged up. The yearning she felt as she peered over Koltz's shoulder at the two figures, who kept appearing and disappearing in the crowd, was for her own half-remembered self.

'Let me get out.' She wanted a new life. She was choking with resentment in the back seat.

'Take it easy,' Andy pleaded.

'They're going to the conference, too,' Koltz said.

'Will nobody help me?' she thought. She saw that Sally's lips were moving, though she and Dan were still standing at stiff angles to one another, like statues in a window.

*　　*　　*

'She's in Andy's car,' Sally was saying.

'Has she seen us?'

'Probably.'

'Hm.'

'What?'

'Nothing.'

If he used his turned-off voice on her that was his bad luck. On the ferry she had found everything so defined, deckhands from stokers, boxes and bundles from the shape and limit of the decks, rails from the discreet bridgehouse. She had always loved ships and the reason, she now decided, was because everything about them except the passengers had a clear and exact purpose.

She no longer felt hurt, she told herself, by Dan's aloofness, which had come out of hiding again as soon as they had got under way. She wondered if it meant anything more than selfishness. She thought that it had to. His mouth as he had leaned over the rail a foot away from her, had been set in such downward lines of self-pity and his eyes when he looked at her had held such a kind of cold accusation that she had decided there must be a real deficiency in him, on whose altar he was prepared to lay her. She had smiled to herself at her choice of words and a Chinese in a blinding white suit had smiled back.

'They think they are birds,' he had said, indicating the flying fish.

Dan had looked up and he also had smiled.

'Poor things,' she had said. 'They don't want to belong to the sea only.'

'They're escaping from enemies,' Dan said.

'Not for long, they fall back so soon.'

'But they're not to know that when they take off.'

'No.' She had decided what to do and would choose her moment.

A black fin had been following the ferry for several miles.

'Good for soup,' the Chinese had said, and Dan and Sally had looked at one another with a kind of grim satisfaction.

'Well?' she said now.

'We'd better go to this press conference.'

'But first to the hotel.'

'Why?'

'Because. To clean up.'

'All right.'

They climbed into a taxi and drove away, Andy following. Jean believed that she saw them kiss.

'Are we being followed by your maudlin wife?' Sally asked.

'She's not maudlin.'

'She seemed so to me.'

'Then you've got the wrong word.'

'You're defending her!'

'No, I'm not, I'm being accurate. Anyway, why shouldn't I?'

'Only that it makes you like everyone else, which you are, of course. You like to think you're different.'

'She had lots of other irritating qualities, but being maudlin's not one of them.'

'Oh, let's leave it.'

'Or a nag. That she never was.'

'She hadn't got the guts probably.'

'She knew how to stop.'

'She was probably afraid of you.'

'Never.'

'Scared stiff, I could see.'

They eyed one another with spite and excitement.

The boarding-house was owned by an emaciated remittance man from Lisbon called Luis, whose bar was hung with minute fairy lights which winked on and off without order. His four bedrooms had outer doors and inner half-doors and during the daytime, when the outer doors were usually open, the place had the appearance of a stable.

'Long time no see.' Luis patted Dan's shoulder. 'You can have the same room as last time, near the toilet.' He gave Sally a look, sucking in air over his ruined teeth. 'Danny and me are old buddies,' he said.

The high walls of their room were mapped with mildew. Luis brought them clean towels and a bottle of brandy and withdrew, shutting the outer door. Dan closed the warped shutters and sat back against the wall. She was overflowing, so it seemed to Dan, with a kind of youth gold.

'Why don't you get undressed?'

She said nothing. The boards creaked comically under his feet as he came over to her. He took her arm and pulled her to her feet.

'Please.'

In the lavatory at the end of the veranda Luis was supervising a Chinese boy who was scraping the insides of the porcelain bowls with a piece of bamboo.

'I'm sick of this garbage heap,' Luis said. 'I think I'll go home this year.'

'Me, too.'

'What? Going home, are you?'

'No, sick of the garbage heap.'

'What will you do, Danny?'

'Sit on it.'

She was in bed now. Her body beneath the sheet made mounds and declivities, taut plains and rippling gullies. He would be losing all that. A desire to be violent swelled.

'Get up.'

'What for?' Her voice had a kind of sullen expectation.

He tore the sheet off, grazing her shoulder with his nails.

'Sorry,' he said, like an actor who had forgotten his lines, then resumed the attack. His mouth worked on her and she bit dutifully back. 'That's not enough,' he said. He was kneeling over her. 'Get up and walk.'

'Dan!' She was sceptical.

'Walk to the door and wait there till I say and then walk to the window and bring my drink.'

'What for?'

'Do it, will you?'

He shoved her off the bed and sent her half running across the boards.

'Now stay there. Now come and get the drink. Slower, that's it. Slower. Why don't you listen? You'll be sorry, I'm telling you! Now, kneel down and offer the drink.'

He took the glass and tossed the dregs of brandy and melted ice-cube into her face. 'Brandy and water,' he laughed. Lean forward and put your hands on the floor. On the floor. Lean forward! No, don't move your hands, I want to . . . I want you to stretch your back.'

Listening to his choked voice she thought how white his kneecaps were and how splendid his two feet, splayed out before her. His toenails needed cutting.

'Now put this where it belongs,' he said, squaring up to her. 'You like that, don't you? Do you like it?'

219

Suddenly he withdrew and was crouching down beside her. 'What's the point?' he said in his normal voice. 'It's all a pretence, anyway.'

She took his face and kissed his mouth, pulling him over on top of her, loin and limb. This was her moment and now it was his habit of pride that forced him to go through the motions. When she felt the coolness of his response she went wild.

'Make me!' she commanded when they were on the bed.

So they ended well enough, if cheaply, if falsely, yet with style enough to subdue the absurd floorboards. And when it was over they had said goodbye.

He took her back to the ferry quay. They were both silent and exhilarated. Neither was looking further forward than the time of the departure.

A priest was embarking blind women whom the communists had allowed to leave the People's Republic. Their eyes seemed to have been plucked inwards by some malignant hand. The lids had puckered into wet triangles. They climbed the gangway, holding each other's elbows. Sally faltered before joining the line of women, whose brown faces turned this way and that, as guileless as sunflowers, but she did not look back. She walked up the gangway straight and golden, trying not to be touched.

When the ferry reached Hong Kong she went to Maslyn, whom she found writing letters in her room.

'Hullo.' Maslyn suppressed surprise. This was quicker than she had expected.

'I want you to help me buy some clothes.'

'What a sensible idea. When in doubt shop, I always say.'

'When can we leave?' Sally spoke almost curtly now. There was no more baby-talk.

'As soon as you're properly dressed.'

'Tomorrow! I don't want to stay after tomorrow.'

'I'm sure it could be arranged.'

'Why don't you ring them? I'll have a shower. I'm filthy. I don't want to go to my own room just yet.'

'Be my guest.'

'I want to hear more about the Gorki picture. I don't even know who he was, really. He is dead, isn't he?'

'As far as I know, dear, though I believe there's a widow lurking about in the steppes somewhere.'

'There's no ash-tray in here,' Sally called from the shower.

'Coming.'

When Maslyn peered round the bathroom door Sally was already under the shower, her cigarette extended in one dry hand.

'You can hold it for me,' she said.

23

In a eucalyptus tree outside the library where they were holding the press conference, tits with pale blue heads were gobbling the bugs that lived in the bark. The weight of the birds' bodies caused the branches to tremble and dip at their extremities.

Someone in the gathering crowd threw a stone at the birds, but it flew wide and hit the window below which the runaway colonel was sitting. He looked upwards over his shoulder, but all he could see was a piece of framed sky.

No one was paying him much attention. He was sitting on a hardbacked chair, passive except for a pulse in his neck which was beating delicately to the roar of his inner fear. The communist Chinese journalists who had come to the conference stared at him from time to time with envy and contempt, but it was his gold-toothed interpreter who got most of the attention. The colonel murmured softly, addressing his remarks to the backs of his own hands.

Few of his replies seemed to interest the Western correspondents, who tended to talk across him other things, other defections, and toss packets of cigarettes to one another, or lighters.

'He hasn't much news value,' Andy said.

Jean had secured Andy a seat at the end of the front row and was leaning against the wall beside him, watching out for Dan.

'He hasn't answered the last question yet,' came Koltz's sceptical voice.

'He says he is not a farmer.' The interpreter was apologetic.

'He doesn't have to be to know when the crops have failed.'

If she comes with him, Jean was thinking, I will humiliate myself. That will drive her away.

There was a tramping of feet outside followed by a confused conversation, then the sing-song slogans began.

'Here we go,' Andy said. He put his arm round Jean's waist for a moment, leaning his head, which was aching, on her firm hip.

What was it she wanted Dan to know, after all? That she was a different person, was it? Someone he had never seen?

The defector was trying surreptitiously to read the Chinese faces around him. The Western ones were indecipherable. He had hoped to reach Hong Kong but had failed. He knew the danger he was in.

I have chosen the wrong place, she was thinking. There is too much to distract him here, he will never be made to look at me.

When Dan entered he saw the colonel's death hanging like a gas around his head. It seemed to set him apart from everyone else. It was green and emanated from the man's inner self, contradicting his blood. Dan pushed roughly through the gossiping journalists until he was standing before the colonel's chair, staring into his unnaturally quiet face.

The colonel returned the stare, then lowered his eyelids. He was still hoping, poor devil. Dan thought of Sally out in the mainstream, getting herself together, as she might have put it, for the next experience that life had to offer. He told himself that if there had been one glance of true recognition between them he would never have let her go.

The colonel was looking at him again and gratitude stirred

in him that this proud man, from whose face he had not yet taken his eyes, was to carry whatever burden the day might bring.

He looked away and saw Jean. She was making her way across the room towards him, giving him nervous, determined glances. He thought she looked very womanly with her untidy hair and her pursed lips and he felt a sudden tenderness for their joint past and might have reminisced with her had the door of the hall not been kicked open by the demonstrators, who began to squeeze in, one by one, spreading through the room like gate-crashers at a party.

They nodded at the journalists and mimicked their talk. 'Ah, yes, o' course,' one kept saying. 'Ah, yes, o' course.'

When there were enough of them they began to pull books from the shelves and tear them down their spines. Some, like the Bible, were too strong for them, so they threw them on the floor and trod on them. A box-file about practical anatomy was flung into the rafters, to return as a shower of shiny diagrams.

Portuguese Marines, picked more for their strapping size and general good looks than their spunk, fought only to get out.

A man who had previously mingled with the journalists now got up on a chair and ordered the demonstrators to stand the Europeans against the walls. Jean found herself pushed against the man's chair and accidentally knocked him over. She had just time to see his sandalled feet where his head should have been before she, too, was thrown down.

Dan heard her call his name, but it was Andy who went for her attackers and landed on top of her for his pains. Dan stayed with the colonel, who, when the first demonstrators had entered, had leapt onto a table and tried to claw his way up the window like a great cat, but had fallen back and was now standing pressed against the wall.

The first thing they did to him was to tie his arms and feet together behind his back with wire, forcing his body into a hoop, then they streaked his face with red paint and hung a placard round his neck on which they had listed his crimes against the people. After that, they ran a rope over one of the rafters which supported the roof, secured one end of it to the mess of wire round the colonel's hands and feet and hauled him off the ground, bumping his stomach and genitals, then raised him in short jerks until he was hanging upside down like a fowl in a poulterer's. A thread of shining spittle spun down from his open mouth.

There was a hush as people observed the unmanning of the colonel, during which time he died. They had not meant to kill him, only to make an example. It was not for them to decide who was beyond social redemption, but they had been ignorant of his heart condition.

Dan went wild. He began to punch and kick the Chinese around him, welcoming their return blows on his face and body. He clutched off a man's glasses and went for his eyes. The man screamed and covered his face with his hands. His fingers went into a mouth and he felt the shocked recoil of a tongue. He wanted to kill someone, but an arm caught his throat from behind and a knee screwed into his groin.

It ended when someone hit him over the head with a piece of wood.

24

When the guards told Jean to stop attending to Dan's cuts, Andy was glad. Dan had groaned and she had got up, but the two students who were spying on them through a hole in the brick wall opened the door and made her squat down again on the earth floor of the latrine. She looked regretfully at Dan's body, spreadeagled between two of the three parallel holes which occupied the centre of the shed. Serve her right, Andy thought. Dan's suffering was self-invited whereas his own lived like a squatter inside him. Let Fenwick groan himself to hell. If only he had died on Hill Forty. Andy could admit it now without a tremor. When Dan had come back into the glade he had hated him for being so unfair.

He rested his face against the wall of the latrine to try to delude the pain, but it had eyes in the back of its head. His pills were in the car. You swallowed one and then waited for the slow spread of comfort.

'Do you think he's all right?' Jean said.

'He's a mess,' Andy murmured.

'Why did he do it?'

'Search me. I used to think he was the real cool Englishman, but not any more.'

Dan groaned again and adjusted his knee so that it straddled one of the rank holes.

'I wish I had a cigarette. Can't you look in his coat, Andy? He might have some.'

Andy began crawling round the wall, expecting the guards

to rush in. 'There's nothing here,' she said, looking at Dan's face while he went through his pockets.

'I wish I'd never come.'

'I sure don't.'

'I don't suppose I ever would have if you hadn't kept sending me those descriptions of what he was telling her about me.'

'Watch it, he's probably coming round.'

'I'm not saying anything I wouldn't say to his face. I didn't come here to patch it up, you know, though Maslyn Martin wouldn't believe me, I'm sure. Nor would the girl, I expect. She hated me, I could see that. He'd given her a pretty one-sided picture and anyway why should she care?'

'You won't regret it,' Andy gasped, contracting his buttocks. It was as if a corkscrew was being turned in his guts. What if he had an attack right in front of her? He had had one before when he was out. It had happened in the elevator of the Reuter building. He had done it right in his pants and had had to beat it back home.

'Let me look,' she said. 'I know where he keeps them.'

The guards had left their peephole. She could hear them talking on the blind side of the shed. She felt for his inside pocket, remembering what it was like to have someone to touch and wait for. She was allowing her hand to rest on the lapel of his jacket when she saw that his eyes were open.

With a rough, backhand gesture, he pushed her away from him.

'Watch it!' Andy said.

'Where are we?'

'In the shit.'

'I can tell that, but where?'

'Behind the library, thanks to you. What got into you?'

'You were upset about the poor man they hung up,' Jean said.

'You sure lost your cool that time.'

'Good old reliable Andy. He turned into a very special correspondent, didn't he?'

'Son of a bitch! You were awake all the time!'

'I wouldn't have needed to be. It was obvious every time you came scampering after us, you were like a human tape machine. Sally even acted up for you sometimes.'

'That's a lie!' Andy began unbuckling his trousers. 'Christ!' he said.

'What's the matter?' Jean asked.

'I'm sorry . . . I can't . . .'

'Poor Andy,' Dan said. 'We should always remember to bring the nappies along.'

'Don't listen to him, Andy. There's one thing: it's happened in a convenient place.' Dan laughed, but stopped when he saw that she was smiling too.

'He's sick,' he said.

'Don't,' Andy murmured.

'Listen, Dan, you must listen.'

'I'm a captive audience.'

'I suppose you think I came here to spoil things for you? It's not true. Of course I feel jealous, is that surprising?'

'Not at all.'

'You would say that. You like to be such a maharaja about women.'

'Why did you come then?'

'Listen. Have you any idea, I wonder, what I went through in that hospital?'

'It must have been very unpleasant.'

'It was hell! It wasn't just unpleasant! I was totally, utterly humiliated. I was carried in like broken furniture to be glued together again. I wasn't the worst off. There were lots worse off than me. There was one woman who used to put her head down the lavatory bowls and drink whatever she found there

228

and they used to draw it all out of her at night with a huge syringe!'

'She ought to be with us now! And you blame me?'

'No, no, why should you immediately say that? I blame us both.'

'So you came to remind me that I share the guilt? You could have put that in another letter.'

'Don't be so bitter. I should be bitter.'

'I'm not bitter. I'm bored.'

'I've nearly finished. I've changed since we last met, that's what I really wanted to tell you. I no longer need you to explain my humiliation to myself. I can do without you. I can't even remember why you were able to make me so unhappy. Isn't that peculiar?'

'It's good.'

'Yes, it's good.'

'Now you can find someone more suitable, I mean it.'

'Yes.'

'I really hope you do. Someone more reliable.'

'Implying that unreliable is more authentic? I used to think you were going to be a great writer. I had quite made up my mind to work off my own creative urge typing out your manuscripts. Just think!'

'I thought you said you'd changed? I don't notice it.'

'You haven't written anything, really. I don't suppose you ever will; it was wrong of me to place such store by it.'

'You should have invested in a painting: you can't lose.'

'You're so unmanly sometimes. Andy would never say mean things like that.'

'Andy's a doer, aren't you, Andy?'

'Let's try to talk rationally.'

'I hated you when I saw you in the flat today. Then, at the press conference, I didn't. Just like that. Not rational at all.'

'I suppose you felt sorry for me?'

'No, I felt good things.'

'Where was she?'

'She's gone back to Hong Kong.'

'Why?'

'Oh, we . . . it was time.'

'You don't mean she's gone for good?'

'It was my idea.'

'Why?'

'Because it was over.'

'Oh, Dan!'

'You ought to be gratified.'

'I didn't mean to interfere.'

'Don't overdo it. Anyway, it had its moments and now, well, that's it.'

'You can't just dismiss people like that. Or relationships. Once they're made, they're made. They exist, even if in the past.'

'I don't know what that's supposed to mean.'

'I mean our relationship still exists in a way.'

'You just told me you couldn't remember how you could have been so hurt by it.'

'Yes, but there is something, a common store we both helped to fill.'

'Somewhere down memory lane? You'd do anything not to face the present, wouldn't you? That was it with you, Jean. Anything! Any plan for the future so's you could postpone real experience. Let's put it off, you said, about the baby. Why? Because the time wasn't right, there was some more appropriate time somewhere ahead when we would all be more real or something. Jesus, I used to . . . You used to really hurt, Jean, the way you planned everything, planned us out of our lives.'

'You let me.'

'Yes. O.K. Guilt. I accept it. So what? Here we are, older,

230

that's all. And there's nothing except this, here and now! There's nothing except you, me and Andy in this shit-house, right? You can't place it in some higher context, Jean. There isn't one. And you can't ignore it because it's all there is at this moment! Look at Andy, oozing his existence at every orifice.'

'For Christ's sake . . .'

'There's nothing to be said, you see, so you wasted your journey.'

'We used to talk to one another.'

'Never!'

'You just say that because you don't want to have any responsibility for the past or anyone in it.'

'Listen, I'll tell you. I'll try. We did talk at the beginning, of course we did. But all the time we meant different things. You were building things, building for the future, trying to stop bloody time, as if you could!'

'And what were you doing?'

'Doing something very different, which you never understood. Did I ever tell you about a tapestry I saw in a museum once in America? Maybe you saw a reproduction of it, it's very famous. It depicts the hunt of the white unicorn. Each panel shows a different stage in the hunt which is both sacred and mythical. In the first one they're all setting off, men, dogs, people watching over battlements, ladies waving. There are men with trumpets and spears, men on horseback, and hounds, of course, lots of grey and brown hounds in and out of everyone's legs. The hunters look radiant with excitement. They gallop under the trees, urging their hounds to flush the undergrowth. Then you see the unicorn resting in the innermost depths of the forest. Gentle, proud and mysterious. Kind of unfeeling. Totally ambiguous. Then there's more crashing about and then the really fabulous moment when the hunters get a glimpse of the great beast in the distance and all the trumpets ring out and the birds in the branches make their cries and the tapestry trembles with what it has done, with what all the stitching has arrived at. Nothing definite, but a kind of amazement in the ripple and flow of the colours, as if the people who made it, crouching over it for years on end, suddenly saw where it might lead. It was a kind of miracle. In the end the unicorn is caught and you see him sitting in an enclosure and a virgin is crowning him, but there are tears running down his face. I didn't get that bit, but the bit I did get, the great, marvellous bit, was when the hunters heard the churning of the hooves and thought they had seen the flash of the white belly and the haunches grinding in flight . . . that was it for me!'

'I should have had a child.'

'But you didn't. I would certainly never have left you if you had.'

'I left you.'

'Well.'

'Why should I take the blame always ?'

'Because you are you. Why shouldn't you ?'

'Because we loved each other.'

'I'm sorry, not enough.'

'Oooh,' Andy groaned.

'Andy is rejoining us,' Dan said. 'I think he needs some paper. Perhaps some of your old letters to him. You'll find them in his pocket.'

'Don't be such a pig,' she said.

'I was trying to be funny.'

'It's nothing, Andy. Don't be upset. There are much worse messes than that.' She handed him a handkerchief.

'You can't expect him to do it for himself! I'm an old hand at this. Come on, Andy, let Jean learn how it's done. Wipe and burnish! There we go!'

'Take your goddam hands off me!'

'Come on! Don't be shy. There. That handkerchief has seen honourable service. Down the hole with it. Brace up, Andy, old man. Kansas expects. They found the trail of the white unicorn because of its droppings, you know.'

'You go stuff your white unicorn.'

'Don't be like that. Remember that English hunter we met in Borneo? The one in the crazy pith-helmet you said didn't realise that world war two was over? He told us about the elephants, remember? He said . . . what was it? . . . in that pompous voice . . . I can hear it now. "Those droppings are warm." Christ, we laughed! I can't think why we did but we did, didn't we, Andy? "Those droppings are warm"!'

Dan was buckling up Andy's pants as he talked and propping him against the wall next to Jean. Andy tried to collect his features into a scowl, but Dan's wild laughter suddenly made him want to cry. He let it catch hold of him and was too weak to shake it off.

'You're both childish,' said Jean, which made them laugh all the harder.

'Oh Jean,' Andy said. 'Oh Jesus!' He put his arm round her waist.

When the guards hurried back to their peephole they were perplexed to find all three of their prisoners roaring their heads off, tears running down their cheeks. They were still laughing when the American consul arrived to negotiate their release.

25

On the evening ferry to Hong Kong they looked like a trio of bums and the other passengers kept away from them, giving them a piece of deck to themselves on which they huddled together as if they were still imprisoned. The night reached over the edges of the sea and joined its hands above their heads.

'You have to tell her,' Dan said when Jean had gone to the washroom.

'In my own good time.'

'She may leave, then it'd be too late.'

'We'll see.' With one of Schreiber's pills inside him he felt the need to assert himself.

'Well, if you won't tell her, I will.'

'Don't you dare!'

'It's what she's waiting for. You could have a child, that's what you want, isn't it?'

'As if you could care.'

'As if you could care whether I care! I do, as it happens. It's so wasteful for the two of you to be blundering along by yourselves when you might be travelling together. It's untidy.'

'I'm not about to ask favours of you.'

'There speak generations of Burnses! Do it as a favour to me, then.'

'Why should you care?'

'Because I'm sorry for her and I don't like being sorry for people.'

'You burn me up.'

'If only you'd told me. You told me about the leukemia thing, why not this?'

'If you can't see the difference you need your head examined.'

'Don't come your male pride over me. You can have her and I will be the broker. It's a pity you can't snatch her out of another's arms, but that's Africa, baby.'

'Jesus, you have contempt. Just who do you think you are?'

'Here she comes. Remember, if you don't tell her, I will.'

In the days that followed Jean began to recognise Andy's secret signs without understanding them. Of Dan she saw little and that always by accident.

She took a room in a Chinese *pension* behind Andy's flat. The walls were so thin and the house so full of lodgers that the noise was like a continuation of life in the street. Jean no longer minded the absence of privacy. There were even certain noises at night that she came to rely on: the bed-squeaks of the couple next door and a hoarsely whispered conversation which took place every evening outside her door.

One night, as she lay smoking in the dark, such an unusual silence fell that she wrapped herself in her sheet and hastened into the corridor, there to come face to face with a middle-aged Chinese in vest and underpants, whose instant misinterpretation of her behaviour comforted her. She shut her door gently in his face and listened to him breathing outside.

When she told Andy about the Chinese, he urged her once more to use his spare room, saying he was only too willing to breathe outside her door every night.

She spent most of her days with Andy, who helped her to gather copy for articles for her paper. He showed her the sights of Hong Kong, hoping she would mark favourably the contrast between his good-natured, leisurely excursions and the stormy ones he knew she had had with Dan. Dan had made her work for her evenings and she could remember every row, every rare revelation, whereas Andy's evenings tended to merge. Even so, he had a way of turning to her for confirmation of a remark with a look that went beyond the rather dull, cosy conversation. Soon his tired eyes and crooked smile and the way he had of bumping against her as they walked were things she had come to look forward to as she did the cheerful noises in her hotel.

Each day Andy would repeat his proposal of marriage, watching her face for signs that she was making up her mind. He did so with open anxiety, fearing that his illness might soon come into the open, tormenting himself with visions of becoming helpless in front of her, yet he could still not bring himself to tell her what was wrong with him. He wanted her to accept him first.

'Please, Andy,' she would say, until whenever he rang her he would tell her that it was 'Please Andy' speaking. It was as if she was waiting for a sign.

It was vouchsafed her on the tenth day after their return from Macao, in a large, glittering restaurant during the course of a noisy cabaret turn.

The restaurant consisted of a single open chamber supported by rows of columns garlanded with red streamers. At one end was a stage on which a rumpled-looking jazz band was trying to compete with the noise from the kitchens behind it. Andy was showing Jean how to use chopsticks when she looked over his shoulder and saw Dan.

'Has he seen us ?' Andy wanted to know.

'I don't know.'

'Shall we ask him over ?'

'Just as you like.'

'Let's then.'

'No.'

'All right.'

'Perhaps we should.'

Andy rose to his feet.

'He'll only make things disagreeable,' she said.

'Well, let's not ask him.'

Their indecision was ended by Dan himself, who saw them and came over.

'I won't stay long,' he said. 'There's a new dancer. She'll be on in a few minutes.'

'Aren't you eating?' Jean asked.

'No.'

They all looked in different directions.

'You're not drinking,' Dan said.

'No. We don't want to.'

'I see. Two minds with but a single thought. Ginger ale.'

'That's the way we like it,' she said.

'You're very defensive. How's the old guts, Andy?'

'Top-hole.'

'Tight-lipped and tight-arsed, is it?' Dan watched them eating for a while. 'You'll never teach her to use chopsticks if you live with her for a lifetime,' he said. 'Especially in your case.'

'I'm not living with anyone. Why do you want to spoil the evening for us?' Jean said.

'I don't know. I suppose because you're such a pair of hypocrites, that's why.'

'Why don't you just go, then?' Andy said.

'Can't I sit with my own wife?'

'What kind of creature are you, Dan?'

'Go on, Andy, give her another lesson with the chopsticks. Time is pressing. Have you told her yet?'

'He's told me he wants to marry me. Dan.'

'Ah, I meant something else.'

'Look, why don't you just piss off?' Andy's eyes beseeched.

'What else?' she said.

237

'Andy?'

'Oh, for Christ's sake!'

'What is this?' she said.

Your would-be husband,' Dan said, getting to his feet and standing over them, swaying somewhat, 'is dying of leukemia. Not much of a catch, really.'

Andy put his hand over his face. Jean kept her eyes on Dan. 'Coward,' she said, her voice drowned by a ragged fanfare which announced the new dancer. 'I'm going.'

She paused at the door and looked back. Dan had taken her seat. Andy was still sitting in his place. He appeared to be staring at the table-cloth through his fingers and did not look up until he felt the pressure of her hand on his shoulder.

'Aren't you coming?' she said.

'I thought you'd gone.'

'I was waiting for you. Let's go to your place.'

26

The new dancer was naked now except for a triangle of stuff between her thighs. She had turned out to be a Eurasian girl with a quite ordinary face and long, rather thin legs. As she reached for her last covering the band stood and brayed its appreciation. At the last moment the lights went out. When they came on again the stage was empty. Dan made his way to the men's room.

If he had not been drunk, he told himself, he would never have acted as if he was jealous of them, for the impulse that had made him go over to them had not been banal jealousy, but a more obscure sensation, which he had experienced too often lately to mistake for anything except itself. When it came it was like a fire, reducing other sensations to ashes. That there had been some jealousy he would admit, but he knew exactly when the other thing had taken over. It had been while he was watching Andy's hand moving over Jean's, as his own had guided Sally's, playing with the cool bone chopsticks, feeling the warm current of life going back and forth. The idea of being alone had suddenly become abhorrent and he had lurched into their evening in flight from his own panic. He had needed to join them, but their eyes had been private, in contrast with the public behaviour of their hands, so he had turned on them and tried to wound them, which was what they had wanted. He had behaved as Andy might have done in the circumstances and they had left in triumph, having been given the last word.

'Look,' he said aloud, finding his forehead pressing against the mirror in the men's room.

A pair of crossed, bloodshot eyes looked back at him. He touched his forehead and felt the blood pumping round inside. With each thing that happened he felt himself losing the initiative, but over what?

'I must,' he said, watching his thumb and forefinger directing the blind jet.

What he had to do was to find some place to be in before the crisis. No! That was Jean's game and Andy's. There was nothing so definite as a crisis, there was only life.

He tried thinking about Sally going up the gangway onto the ferry in a cloud of gold, but already overuse was wearing the memory thin. He was overcome with wretchedness that he no longer knew how to conduct himself.

That morning he had received a letter from his editor complaining about his work. It was written in a fatherly way, but its intention was threatening. It reminded him that, with unemployment as it was, there were plenty of younger men who would jump at the chance to take his place. The editor was new to his post and anxious to promote his own friends.

If they recalled him to London they would try to make him resign because they would be embarrassed to have him around. They would make him do reporting jobs with eager beginners. England was a threat to him.

There was dirt under his fingernails. He began to scrub them viciously on a brush which was attached to a metal chain so short that he was obliged to bend low over the basin to use it. He snapped the chain in petty anger, then tried to get a hold on his situation by asserting his contempt.

He was foiled by the memory of a little girl, no younger than ten, sitting beside her mother in a pedicab, whom he had seen the day before while his car had been held up at a traffic light. Her legs had been straight and brown and, as she had twisted sideways to explore her mother's shopping bag, shadows had stirred under her short, white skirt.

Into the cold silence inside him there floated a thin, dark blade, which became a clay idol, whose features were melting over its flat body in a waterfall of dust. He shivered from the base of his spine up, feeling the sweat running down in the opposite direction.

The water in the basin was cloudy and his nails were now clean. Although his fears were immense, his anxieties were tiny and his evils unremarkable. Jobs and little girls played trite tunes on the stretched wires inside his skull.

'Must,' he said again.

The mirror face looked back theatrically, like that of an actor playing the part of a god.

Laughter spilled out of him. To fail at being a failure was worth a laugh.

He dried his hands on a towel already dark with use. He felt trapped inside his tumultous body, which he could not even hate, from which there was only one, unacceptable, escape.

For a long time he had been unable to admit it. He had known what had to be done, but not how to begin. For how was he to make into everyday experience the realisation that there was nowhere to go and nothing to run from? How, unless with help?

'There must be someone,' he said.

He felt as if he had entered an underground movement whose membership and aims were unknown to him. All he did know was that there would be no more beginnings, middles and ends for him, nor any higher plane of suffering onto which to hoist his pretensions to keep them dry.

He had to learn to keep his mouth shut and to live under the shameless glare of his own inner eye, outsilencing Stukes with a silence of his own making, but to do this he had to learn a true reticence and a true courage.

What his meeting with Sally recalled to him, now that it was over, was that unless he could find someone whom he could love for the woman she really was, who would love him for the man he really was, he would never find the courage to be properly alone. He would go on cringing behind a false reticence and finally crack under the ignominy of existence.

The dancer showed no surprise when he joined her table and she looked away when two Chinese came up and demanded that he pay a dinner bill and leave.

'Not my dinner,' he said. He must have taken hold of some part of her dress because he saw their fingers prying his loose. They twisted one of his arms up behind his back and frog-marched him down the restaurant between rows of glistening eyes which swayed this way and that, as if hung on wires. One of the men holding him had a wart on his face with a long hair coming out of it. This was the man who searched him and held up his gaping wallet before his eyes. When he tried to get back into the restaurant they threw him into a sitting position on one of the dustbins and punched his throat, but only lightly.

'I'm sick,' he told a taxi-driver who was waiting for a fare, but the man waved him off with fanning motions of the hand. Dan leaned against the wall of the restaurant for what seemed like a long time. Later he was seen at the Press Club and later still a police patrol found him lying on the pavement near his flat. They identified him from a letter in his pocket and delivered him to his servant, Lim.

27

Moving as the sea moved, the ceiling beams made a noise like the rubbing together of old, hard hands, while overhead, at the top of masts, pennants spilled lions and roses.

Andy shut his eyes again against the stabbing light. On deck, to the cry of birds, the comic cook was drenching himself in a spray of slops. He had been pressganged into service, knew nothing of winds or cooking. But he could not in any case eat because he was sick. The sea foamed over green reef-teeth and leaning over his bunk, trying to make him swallow some grog, was Clark Gable, wearing white breeches and his blue officer's jacket. He leaned closer and became Sarah, one of whose eyes was smaller than the other, who had the concession for the candy-stall at the moviehouse. She would lean down to the kids to catch their orders. Andy was in a log-jam of kids round Sarah's stall, from which a paperchase of popcorn led back across the lobby and into the hot auditorium.

A full bladder drew him out of sleep, but he lay on, listening to sounds to which he was still unaccustomed.

A train dragging its load across the fields back of the village must mean that it was after nine. Jean had gone to London to work. The house was empty. A clock down a flight of crooked stairs played ping-pong with the minutes. The train's metallic churning mixed the air into fresh folds from which there issued the insinuating laughter of women, whose soft hands moved over his eyelid's inner eye.

The clock began revving its engine and backing down Lacking main street. It began to skid. Snow.

He opened his eyes again, screwing them up in the light. Birds were scraping and fighting in the loft above his pillowed head. They ought to be cleared out, Jean said, but she had not the heart.

Her doctor had told him that the honey-coloured beams in the bedroom ceiling had been taken from the hulls of sailing ships. Andy had been aware of them during his delirium. The two supporting ones were twenty-five feet, three inches long. He had measured them on his first day out of bed. What he liked was the way that these roughly worked trunks sprang across the room, and the delicacy with which they entered the walls. They were like shafts of light. The man who came to discuss their central heating – Andy wanted it hotter – had warned them that the beams would contract because they still contained moisture. They thrust with a kind of inner violence from wall to wall and held up the entire house. That was why Andy liked them. After three hundred years they were still alive.

'Coffee,' he said aloud. He was vaguely aware that Jean had got up in the night and gone to the smaller bedroom, a cupboard, really, with a window no bigger than your hand. He must have been threshing about again. Her pillow, indented still, smelt of lemons and cold cream. He picked a long, black hair off the white linen.

Voiding himself, hand on wall, he smelt his sweat with appreciation, took a long breath and sighed out relief that he could do so again without nausea. His illness had moved to what the gruesome medical book called a new 'plateau'. To Andy the effect felt like a restoration of will.

'Don't thank me, thank her,' Jean's doctor had told him. 'She's a born nurse.'

He checked his water, which was still cloudy but not so

deadly-looking as the bloody mahogany with which for two months he had filled his bed-bottle, found unexpectedly on a shelf at the local chemist's.

'You've married a wreck,' he had blurted in a lucid moment, but she had smiled and emptied his bottle. Her divorce from Dan was still unwinding itself.

He raised his eyes and looked out of the bathroom window. He could see the outline of his own cheekbone and the jut of his nose. He had lost weight and his skin was papered to his bones. He looked out from his thinness and congratulated himself on his recovery.

It had only just stopped snowing and the land was quite blank, without a mark on it. The hedges were draped with white lace. Trees sat in the small fields like melting brides and the black needle of a Saxon tower seemed to pin the sky to this bit of earth, whereas where he came from the skies were always hurrying somewhere else.

Life seemed to have drained from the land and to be concentrated in the crouched farm-houses, which were very black, very red. Birds which were flying low and fast looked unnaturally large. By a trick of light objects seemed to be offering not merely their outwardness but what he took to be the very thing of them itself. They had the luminosity of myth and fairy-tale.

A solitary figure, man, woman, was making an unhurried journey down the side of a field. The figure turned at the angle of a hedge and appeared to stand, half-hidden, watching something. Back home such a sight might have seemed odd, even sinister.

He shaved carefully and bathed. When Jean had brought him to Lacking he had been too sick to lick his lips. Convalescing, he had acquainted himself with the interior of her house, rearranged the attic, mended the clock, sipped glasses of soapy beer at the local pub with other unoccupied men and gone back home to lie down. But today, drying his flat stomach until the flesh tingled under the towel, he needed for the first time to look at a river or a ditch and write his name on the snow and see what went on in that wood about two and a half miles away. He felt homesick but he did not know for what.

He miscalculated about the wood and by the time he reached its frozen outposts he was feeling light-headed. A notice nailed to a tree told him that the wood was strictly private. Two paths led into it, one wide and straight, as if for foresters, the other twisting between touching branches, as if for lovers and thieves. Unhesitatingly Andy took the straight, wide path and found himself walking between rows of young firs, whose reddish scales oozed gum, filling the air with a keen, evocative smell. He looked with satisfaction at his own footsteps marching evenly behind him over the crisp snow.

The wood marched with them and soon it had obliterated all evidence of the unwooded world beyond its perimeter. Sounds became echoes and seeing no end to the path he began to feel weary. He was not a reflective man, yet because he was tired or perhaps because the smell of resin tanged with wood-smoke had fuddled him, he began to wonder, which made him falter in his stride. He saw himself from the outside as some-one without roots or family walking in a wood where the trees had labels on them inscribed by strangers, where the sky bent benignly over a state of affairs which existed without the slightest reference to himself.

'Boy, oh, boy,' he said aloud and for a fleeting moment he had the mad notion that the tracks behind him had been made by the stuffed feet of some scarecrow thing he had been humping along on his own back. He longed suddenly for the messy largeness of the creek bank where he had bathed as a boy, leaping into the fast current, his fingers pegging his nose, crawling out, flashing water-drops, to lie on the warm clay and listen to the portable radios and the sounds of tractors coughing like old giants in their giant fields. If you stood still in the creek fish came and nibbled at you. He could feel the tickling sensation now.

He was almost relieved when he heard the cry. It sounded human, fear and pain stretching it beyond the human, as only humans can. It came again, off to his left, rising dolefully until it cracked into separate strands of sound.

He was led to an older part of the wood, where weedy birch trees and rot-encrusted oaks sucked each other's nutriment. There was no snow here and the cries fell through the branches like hot shrapnel, as they had done when they began bringing the wounded back off Hill Forty and Andy had stood in the glade waiting furiously for one man only.

He was on top of the cries before he recognised their source. A hare was caught in a trap and was trying to rip its hind leg from between the rusted metal teeth, scraping the earth with its front paws for purchase and shrieking as it did so. As he approached it fell silent, watching him with eyes hugely too big.

Andy stooped to loosen the trap but the hare twisted round and tried to bite him, baring its front teeth the way he had seen hares do in cartoons, where they were depicted as silly, vain creatures who came to bad ends. Andy turned away, wiping his hands on his coat. The hare was not his business.

He had an excellent sense of direction and was soon back on the broad path, where he found that his footprints had been broken up by the tracks of some vehicle. The hare's cries had ceased and the twittering of birds sounded subdued, giving an air of expectancy to the wood, as if a hundred traps were stretching their unseen jaws. Andy made for home, his bony knees banging together as he walked. Now that he was so much better they must go back to the States. He would tell

Jean it was time. The decision made him feel clean and exhilarated.

He made coffee and waited for her. When he heard her key in the door he went to meet her in the little hall and kissed her mouth, which rain had made cold.

'I'm soaked.' She dropped her bag on the hall floor and smiled at him with a kind of appraising pleasure.

He guided her hand to the back of his head so that she would stroke the nape of his neck. He wanted her to say something to match his own excitement before telling her.

'You're looking much better' was what she came out with.

The moment over, he followed her into the kitchen.

'Coffee?' he said.

'No thanks,' then, seeing his face, she changed her mind. She knew that look.

'I'm all in,' she said. 'What have you been doing?' Half her mind was still at the office, where she had had a successful argument with her editor and afterwards been taken by her for a drink.

Andy was telling her about the hare in the poacher's trap. 'Jugged hare is jolly good,' she said, unpacking her shopping basket and putting a square, black bottle on the table in front of him. 'Here's your new pills and the evening paper. You read it while I get the dinner. And here's the proofs of that article you helped me with. I didn't use your suggestion for the opening in the end. I thought it better the way it was before.'

'I'll cook dinner,' he said.

'No, you read your paper.'

'It's your paper. I never read it.' He spoke almost rudely, resenting her bossiness.

'Well, talk to me then. It's nothing really.'

'Whether dinner is nothing depends on who cooks it.'

'Thanks a lot!'

'Baby, I am Escoffier, you should know that by now, so you just take a back seat for once and wait for it.'

'You must be feeling better, but I don't like to see men being domestic.'

'That's your problem.'

'I mean for them. It's so horrid for them. Did you go to the pub at lunch-time?'

'No, why?'

'You usually do.'

'I do not.'

'Oh.'

'You know I don't! It really bugs me down there!'

'I only asked.'

'It burns me up the way people are so inaccurate.'

He bustled about the kitchen, waiting for an opportunity to forgive her her imperfections and be forgiven.

'You just went to the wood, than? I haven't been there for years, since Dan . . . since we first came here, I think. It's private, really. Belongs to the Lord of the manor of Lacking, so you were trespassing.'

'You must be kidding!'

'No, truly, though one never meets him. He's an earl, no less, and he keeps to his own kind, though the tradesmen will tell you plenty about the unpaid bills he mounts up.'

'How *shocking*!'

'Well, you can talk. You get terribly het up about owing people money. What about that final notice for the oil? You made me post a cheque in the middle of the night, practically.'

'That poacher must be like a lord, too. Not like these commuting creeps in Lacking.'

'Did the central-heating man come?'

'Lords look out from their castles and think "Screw you, Jack" and that's enough to live by, a kick like that.'

'They usually leave a card if there's no one in.'

'How do I know? Look on the mat.'

'Let's have some wine,' she said.

The gadgets in her kitchen chuntered and buzzed. He looked at her, but she turned her head away.

'I'm sorry,' he said. 'I'm an ungrateful son of a bitch, is that what you're thinking?'

'No,' she said, detecting a note of self-congratulation in his voice. She knew him so little. 'No,' she repeated, pursing her lips with an 'I know about you' kind of look, and fiddling with the kitchen radio.

'What's that?' he asked.

'Music.'

'Ha, ha. Mozart, it sounds like.'

'It's Schubert!'

'I suppose Dan was a music-lover?'

'Yes.'

'He had to love something, I guess.'

They looked at one another warily.

'What are you making?'

'Potato pie.'

'I bought lamb chops.'

'They'll keep.'

'So will the pie. I mean it doesn't exist yet.'

'It does. It exists in my mind. Take it or leave it, lady, it's all there is on the menu.'

He poured himself wine and toasted her brutally.

'Cheers,' he said.

'You should take your pills, Andy.'

'Yes, nurse.'

'What's the matter with you?'

'I'm feeling better, that's all. Why don't you drink? I mean it's O.K. for all these ball-less wonders to rot here and go drink their Scotches at the pub and pose as country gentlemen, but it's not O.K. for me, right? We have to go back home.'

'This is home. I don't mean it can't be exchanged for somewhere else, but I won't just let you write it off as if it was some sort of lay-by or something. This has been a place for me.'

'Well I don't get it.'

'You said we could work together here . . . for a while, I mean.'

'Yeah, I could lick your envelopes.'

'Oh, Andy!'

'A guy has to operate in his own territory.'

'I didn't ask . . .'

'What?'

'Oh, nothing.'

'Ask me to come here, you were about to say, right? But don't tell me you're not glad, because I know you are. Don't tell me you don't tell them at the office that you have a man to look after and warm the bed up for you.'

There was a loud bang on the front door and the flap of the letterbox began to rattle.

'I'll get it,' Andy said.

'No, let me.' Jean knew who it was. Nancy had called twice while Andy was ill in bed, but she had warded her off, telling herself he might not understand but in reality fearing that Nancy's failure might in some way rub off on her.

The light from the snug little hall lit up the swaying, bloated face. It was like opening a door on chaos. From behind Nancy's shoulders, which were improbably draped in a fur stole, the night streamed in.

'Hiaaa . . . Coming in.'

'No, you can't.'

'Only a moment, weeny moment, sit down . . . Nancy's tired . . . Ooh, he's good-looking, he won't be cruel to her.'

She had spotted Andy, who was leaning at the foot of the stairs, summing her up. He knew about drunks.

'Hiii . . .' she said, allowing herself to fall forwards in the hope that Jean would fall back, but Jean pushed her out onto the step and shut the door on her, feeling the weight of her body on the other side.

'Wow,' she said.

'She's not going to go away,' Andy told her.

'She's . . . poor thing.'

'Poor thing! She's putrid.'

'She can't help herself, I suppose.'

'I could smell her from where I was standing. You're too soft-hearted.'

'I know.' Jean felt relieved that Andy was so casual about Nancy. After all, she was only an alcoholic. What had she been getting so upset about?

There came a crash of glass as a bottle hit the side of the house.

'Are you going to let her break up your house?'

'She may go away.'

'Jesus! Just go out and put the fear of God into her.'

'The neighbours will think we're having a drunken brawl. They've complained about her already . . .'

'Well, screw the neighbours!'

'I'm not . . . it's too dark, I'm not going out!'

'Then I'll go, but don't tell me afterwards that I'm nasty and hard-hearted, right?'

He gave her a wicked smile and she smiled back, shaking her head, wishing he would touch her as he passed her in the hall. He shut the front door behind him. She turned out the light and peeped through the little sliver of hall window.

She could see Nancy retreating across the road. She opened the window so that she could hear. Nancy had stationed herself under a street lamp and Andy was standing close in front of her, legs apart. She heard the rumble of his voice, then Nancy's pitiful wail. Andy made a forward move and Nancy threw up an arm. She yelped something about 'telling my brother of you' and something more about 'big bully', as if she was a schoolgirl in a playground instead of a middle-aged wreck with neither family nor friends.

'Don't touch me!' Jean heard her shout suddenly and saw her hoiking up her skirt and pushing herself against Andy's body. Andy slapped her face with the palm of his hand. The blow was light enough, but Nancy thumped onto her knees and stuck up her white elbows.

'Get up,' Jean heard Andy say. 'You're pretending. I'll call the police.'

'I'll kill myself. I'll go to the river!'

'For Christ's sake go, but don't tell me about it!'

'You don't believe me!'

'I don't care!'

He had taken her arm and was trying to pull her away, but she was clinging with her other hand to the rim of a dustbin. She had begun to shout for help. Curtains began to twitch, and a window went up.

'I'll kill myself!'

'I don't care!' Andy had seen the listening neighbours, stuck behind their little Tudor front-doors, disapproving. They were nothing to do with him. Jean had got in a rut here and he was going to take her out of it. His love for her had never seemed more adequate than it did now.

'I don't care,' he shouted, wrenching Nancy away from the dustbin. 'We have no room for you in our lives . . . I'm sorry . . . but that's it . . . so just piss off and don't come back!'

He gave her a shove which sent her dipping and clutching along the side of a blank wall, leaving a snail stain, he had no doubt, of filth. His anger against the village with its excluding windows was extinguished in his loathing for Nancy. He could have killed her. It was lucky for her that she was leaving, he told himself. If he had had a stone he would have thrown it at her. God, he felt contaminated touching her.

He found Jean at the hall window and turned her face towards him with his hands, took her cigarette from between her pursed lips and kissed her mouth.

'I love you, Jean.'

'Thank you,' she said.

'Let's eat.'

'I got a letter from Dan's lawyer today,' she told him when they were back in the bright kitchen. 'Dan has agreed to give me the freehold of this house outright. I can do what I want with it.'

'He took long enough.'

'Not so long. He's been in Vietnam again. You should read the paper sometimes.'

'Poor old Dan. I wonder what he'll do when there's no more wars to go to.'

'There always will be.'

'Or when he's too old? He'll get too old for that stuff.'

'They say he drinks all the time now, yes, more than before. If he's not careful he'll be a kind of buffoon.'

'Or else have a crack up. I pity him, really.'

'Do you?' she said.

'Listen, Jean, let's not talk about Dan. Today was the first day I went out really properly and I made this decision. It suddenly came very clear when I was in the wood of that Lord of yours. We have to go home to the States. I have some money there. I used to send it back from Hong Kong.'

'You told me.'

'Enough to look around on. How do you work this oven?' He was treading flour all over the clean floor. His clumsiness made her feel tender.

'Could I get a job over there?'

'You could get something.'

'I was just getting established again here. They congratulated me on my piece at the editorial conference today.'

'Nobody's congratulating me.'

'Would I get a work permit?'

'When we're married you'd be an American citizen automatically.'

'Shouldn't we wait a bit?'

'No, now! Don't you want to?'

'If that's what you want.'

'That is what I want. You could sell this place if you wanted; they were saying in the pub the demand is terrific.'

He went to bed before her and she finished typing out a story before putting her machine under its plastic cover.

Locking up, she found his jacket lying on the hall floor. It looked alarmingly out of place, like the shoe she had once found in her bed at the mental home. She smoothed it out and took it upstairs with her.

Undressing in the dark, she stood at the bedroom window in her pyjamas. The night was dry now and the street was without Nancy. The stars looked newly washed. She touched the window-pane with her fingers, pretending to imagine, as she had really tried to imagine when she was little, that she was wearing them for a shawl, but since she was pretending, the stars stayed obstinately far away and she began to shiver, the central heating being defective.

On a picnic with her mother once she had thought she heard voices on the other side of a haystack, but when she had gone to look there had been no one. Had she heard voices? Her mother had told her that of course she hadn't, and had made the very idea sound reprehensible, but when she had told Dan about it years later he had seemed to understand.

When she got into bed, Andy pressed himself against her. His breath smelt faintly of medicine. She stroked his side, bony at the hip. Andy sighed contentedly. She had the power to make him happy and she was grateful for a second chance.

If there was ever a time when she might have known another kind of reality, that time was no more. It had been rolled up and was all stuck together inside her. There could be no spreading it out.